# BLACK CROW

# BLACK CROW

## THE RAVEN SERIES, BOOK 2

## J. L. WEIL

Published by J. L. Weil
Copyright 2016 by J. L. Weil
978-1-954915-01-5
http://www.jlweil.com
All rights reserved.
Edited by Kelly Hashway & Allisyn Ma

# ALSO BY J. L. WEIL

**ELITE OF ELMWOOD ACADEMY**

(New Adult Dark High School Romance)

*Turmoil*

*Disorder*

*Revenge*

**DIVISA HUNTRESS**

(New Adult Paranormal Romance)

*Crown of Darkness*

*Inferno of Darkness*

**DRAGON DESCENDANTS SERIES**

(Upper Teen Reverse Harem Fantasy)

*Stealing Tranquility*

*Absorbing Poison*

*Taming Fire*

*Thawing Frost*

**THE DIVISA SERIES**

(Full series completed – Teen Paranormal Romance)

*Losing Emma: A Divisa novella*

*Saving Angel*

*Hunting Angel*

*Breaking Emma: A Divisa novella*

*Chasing Angel*

*Loving Angel*

*Redeeming Angel*

## LUMINESCENCE TRILOGY

(Full series completed – Teen Paranormal Romance)

*Luminescence*

*Amethyst Tears*

*Moondust*

*Darkmist – A Luminescence novella*

## RAVEN SERIES

(Full series completed – Teen Paranormal Romance)

*White Raven*

*Black Crow*

*Soul Symmetry*

## BEAUTY NEVER DIES CHRONICLES

(Teen Dystopian Romance)

*Slumber*

*Entangled*

*Forsaken*

## NINE TAILS SERIES

(Teen Paranormal Romance)

*First Shift*

*Storm Shift*

*Flame Shift*

*Time Shift*

*Void Shift*

*Spirit Shift*

*Tide Shift*

*Wind Shift*

## HAVENWOOD FALLS HIGH

(Teen Paranormal Romance)

*Falling Deep*

*Ascending Darkness*

**SINGLE NOVELS**

*Starbound*

(Teen Paranormal Romance)

*Casting Dreams*

(New Adult Paranormal Romance)

*Ancient Tides*

(New Adult Paranormal Romance)

For an updated list of my books, please visit my website:

www.jlweil.com

Join my VIP email list and I'll personally send you an email reminder as soon
as my next book is out! Click here to sign up: www.jlweil.com

*For my grandma, whose light, sparkle, class, and creativity will never be forgotten. This was a hard year, and I will miss you every day.*

M ists spiraled up from the water like the ocean breathing life into the air. The moon shed pale, cool light as it woke, setting the crickets to their nightly summer chorus. A crow squawked, so arrogant and powerful.

None of it was familiar, not the sounds or the sights, but this was now my home. No matter how beautiful or what ties bound me to Raven Hollow, it would never be the home I wanted or wished for.

Home made me think of Mom and of Parker. An ache started deep in my bones, a longing to see his familiar face. Home was supposed to make you feel safe and secure, not scared out of your wits. Home wasn't about size or quality; it was about the emotion it enticed.

But under the wishing, aching, and longing, fear bubbled inside me, scorching the back of my throat. My life was in danger, putting those around me at risk. TJ was the only family I had left, and it was now my job to make sure he was protected, even if it meant hurting me.

I was no stranger to pain.

It was peculiar how a journey could change you and how much you could learn from it. Coming to Raven Hollow had been a journey I'd been reluctant to take, but the knowledge I'd gained was life-altering. I learned my father was a coward, and my mother wasn't who I thought she was. That my grandmother wasn't even human. I learned I had an ancient power, passed down to me upon my grandmother's death, a power that frightened me and I had yet to control.

I thought it all over and over again. Every choice, every mistake, every sacrifice, wondering if I could do it all again, would things have turned out differently? If my mom had been given a second chance, would she have told me what I was? Would she have let me make my own choice when it came to love?

Some nights I dreamed of home, of my small condo in the city where I knew every building and bend in the roads. But more nights I dreamed of Zane Hunter.

I could hear his voice, the soft lilt of an ancient Celtic. The scent of him so potent and tantalizing, it gave me a sensory-gasm. If there was such a thing, Zane could induce it. These were my favorite nights, because in my dreams, Zane and I were free to do the things I really wanted to do to him. Like play tonsil hockey. A ton.

There were other dreams, dreams that brought sharp fear rather than longing or desire. Nightmares of the dead, of reapers, and the murders of two women who'd been completely different kinds of important to me. It was their deaths that haunted my subconscious mind. Both in their own way had tried to protect me, but in doing so, had left me utterly alone. And clueless.

I stared straight ahead, avoiding sleep. In the distance, the heart of the island shone brightly. The lighthouse, of course. What offshore New England island would be without one? This one was a dazzling pure white, rising above the craggy cliff. Directly above, the crow squawked again, perched on the balcony railing.

Everyone had a ghost in their past, but whether it was Casper or the Blair Witch was what made the difference. I had both.

The ocean, the quietness of the evening, and the call of the crow reminded me who I was destined to be …

The White Raven.

I only hoped I could live up to the task. And survive.

# CHAPTER 1

L ife could be perfect one day and in shambles the next.
I'd had more than my share. And I suspected more to
come, sort of inevitable when you were a banshee.

I was a reaper. It had taken me time to come to terms with this,
and even now it was hard to believe I was anything but human, that I
had powers. I wasn't just any reaper—I was the last White Raven, and
the pressure to fill this role was mounting.

My beloved mother had been murdered in a heartbeat. The grandmother I'd just barely begun to accept and understand had sacrificed
herself to save me. My father was off gallivanting around the globe,
probably drowning his misery in booze and spending the little money
we had left. But I guess money wasn't a problem anymore, now that
I'd inherited a fortune—well, I would on my eighteenth birthday in
two weeks. I'd rather be dirt poor than without the two most vital
females a girl could have.

Wrapping my arms around my middle, I stared out the window,
overlooking the lush grounds. Except, since the passing of Rose, the
atmosphere in Raven Hollow had taken a dip. I got this sense the
island was mourning the loss of their queen along with me. The sun
hadn't shone in days, the exotic flowers stayed closed and withdrawn,

petals withering, and the waters were turbulent, rolling and hissing in a sad song.

The last few days had been a blurry whirlwind. Closed off in Raven Manor, I hadn't left the grounds, avoiding the world. But I'd hardly had five minutes to myself. The rest of the island might not know that the eccentric Rose was gone, but the staff and Zane's family did. They had banded together to make sure my safety wasn't in jeopardy. And that meant more security, including a shadow that more or less followed my every move. I swear, I couldn't even go to the bathroom alone.

All I wanted was five minutes of peace and quiet, and now that I had it, I wanted the noise back. At least then my mind wasn't wandering off in a hundred different directions—and doubting everything.

*Should I stay on the island? Could I be the White Raven? Would I be doomed to a loveless marriage? Did I have it in me to do all of the above?*

Then there was my younger brother. As luck would have it, TJ spent most of his days locked inside his room, burying his pain the only way a fifteen-year-old boy knew how—in video games. I knew he was confused and angry, and how could I blame him? There was so much I couldn't tell him for his own well-being.

Even with a full staff at the manor and people coming and going, I was lonely.

Alone to deal with death, a power I didn't begin to understand, a world I couldn't comprehend, and life-threatening danger.

No sweat.

*Who am I kidding?*

Sometimes it was just me against the world, and there were no easy answers. People were depending on me—three sectors of reapers to be exact—but a huge part of me wanted to run away from it all. Yet another part of me knew that no matter where I ran, death would follow. It was my curse and my gift, depending on my mood.

The price I paid for being a harbinger of death.

Today was the day I'd been dreading. Rose's funeral. Mother Nature must have been dreading it too because the sky opened up in a torrential downpour. Against almost everyone's counsel, I made my first executive decision as the White Raven to have a small funeral for Rose. Family and friends only. Very hush-hush. Not just for me, but for TJ, who had no idea how seriously seven different circles of messed up his family really was.

Zander, my future husband, was propped in my doorway, looking sharp in an all black suit. His blue eyes radiated a slight purplish tint. "You ready for this?"

Each time I thought about marrying Zander, I got green in the face, like now. I sat on the edge of my bed, hands folded neatly in my lap, and sighed. "Does it matter?" These days little did. To say I was in a rut was an understatement. My wants and needs were lower than the scum on Death's boots.

Zander stepped into the room, his expression softened by lamp-light. "It does to me."

I glanced up. He had a quality about him that would make most girls swoon. I'd already proven to be unlike most girls. "I just want this day to be over with."

It had been decided Zander should escort me to Rose's funeral. As with most decisions regarding my life lately, I didn't have much of a say. Zane and Zander's father, Roarke, who also happened to be Death, had sort of stepped in as my guardian, since my father was conveniently absent. Roarke believed we needed to set a precedent among the sectors, effective immediately. Zander and I were to be seen together as much as possible. And not a word about Rose's absence was to be uttered.

I didn't know what I thought about any of this. My brain had taken a vacation, leaving my body to move through the motions with no real thought as to why.

"You don't have to worry, you know," Zander said. "We've secured the area, and I'll be by your side the whole time."

I nibbled on my lower lip. If Zander had been Zane, he would have known my trepidation wasn't only about safety, but also my general dislike for funerals. "I know."

*Plip. Plip. Plop.* Rain pelted against the roof and the windowpanes.

Standing, I walked over to the full-length mirror to take one last glimpse at my appearance. My skin was washed out, emphasized by the flaxen color of my hair and the dark hue of my outfit. Black was becoming my signature color. I straightened the invisible wrinkles on my skirt. My large, sleep-deprived eyes were dry and would stay that way.

I'd shed all the tears I could.

Slipping a headband over my head, I adjusted the black lacy veil. It was a tribute to Rose, and her love for finer things. She'd been classy, and today I tried to have a fraction of her poise. With a stiff chin, I spun around, grabbing my clutch from the polished white dresser. "Let the spectacle begin."

Zander's lips curved in a small, sad smile. "It will surely be the most secretive, elaborate funeral to date."

That was Rose. Elaborate didn't begin to describe the woman. I didn't know another soul who had planned their own funeral down to what color roses. I'm surprised she didn't have a dress picked out for me to wear. With her, everything had been orderly and larger-than-life. She was the kind of person who demanded attention and obedience. There was still so much I'd never gotten the chance to learn about her and her world—the important stuff like how to be a banshee, how to command an entire race of supernaturals, or how to keep the hallows from destroying everything. I couldn't help but feel cheated.

My frown deepened in the mirror.

"Ready?" Zander asked, holding out his hand.

I didn't think anyone was ever ready for death. This was my second funeral in a little over a year. "As ready as I'll ever be," I mumbled, putting my hand in his. He lacked the chill I'd grown to look forward to whenever Zane touched me.

I prayed I wasn't doomed to compare every detail to his brother, for both our sakes.

Zander led us through the long halls and down the winding stairs until we got to the main foyer. "You've done this before," I commented as we rounded the corner. He maneuvered through the grand-scale house like a pro. I'd been here weeks and still couldn't find my way from one end to the other without getting lost.

"Raven Manor used to be the hub for all reapers. Zane and I spent many weekends exploring every inch of this place."

I couldn't help but think how awkward that must have been for Roarke, Ivy, and Rose, knowing that Rose's and Roarke's souls were a perfect match. "Great, maybe you can draw me a map."

He let out a low laugh. "Better yet, I could show you all the hiding spots we found."

This is what we were supposed to be doing, getting to know each other. Then why was I so reluctant to spend time with Zander? "Sure, why not?"

He grabbed a long stem black umbrella propped on the wall before stepping outside and opening it. Such a gentleman, he waited to escort me through the rain. I was sure Zane would have just made a mad dash assuming I would follow, and honestly, I wouldn't have minded getting a little wet.

A town car waited for us on the circular driveway with its engine idling as we traipsed out of the house. I stepped over a puddle and failed, my feet splashing water on my bare legs. *Joy.*

"Where's TJ?" I asked when we were tucked in the back seat.

"He went in the car ahead of ours. My dad thought it would be wise to keep you separated in case …"

In case I was attacked. "Oh." I'd been kind of hoping TJ would be with us, the perfect buffer between Zander and me.

Not going to lie. There was an awkwardness we both tried to pretend wasn't there, making it all that more weird. In the not so distant future, we were going to have to *talk* and about more than just the weather.

I was dreading it almost as much as the funeral.

We didn't say much on the way to the ceremony. I stared out the window, tracing the waterdrops with my fingertips, deep in thought, selfishly thinking about my life. He didn't know what to say, and neither did I. We were still very much strangers.

When the car stopped, I gathered myself by having one of my

famous Piper pep talks in my head. They rarely worked, but it didn't stop me from trying.

*You can do this. You're practically a funeral expert ... mostly because everyone around you dies,* I added sarcastically. *Nice, Piper. Don't think about that now.*

I wanted to thump my head on the car.

The self-pity and psychoanalysis was going to have to wait for later because I needed to be something I wasn't. Dignified. A leader. Resilient.

Miraculously, the rain ceased before we arrived at the memorial, and the first peek of sun in a week snuck out from behind the gloomy clouds. I reached for the handle, but the door opened, and I stopped breathing.

Zane.

Tall. Dark. And annoying. His expression was eerily closed off, eyes so dark they were black orbs. He cleaned up well, I had to admit —too well, uncharacteristically wearing a dark gray shirt and tie.

I drank in the sight of him, forgetting everything. Where I was. Who I was with. None of it mattered for those first few seconds our eyes collided. Time ceased. Then the noises around me came rushing to the surface, like I was swimming and just broke through the water.

Zander was suddenly standing beside Zane, both reapers waiting for me to exit the car. Extending a leg, I pushed out of the seat, glancing forward and seeing TJ unfold his long, lanky legs from the vehicle in front of mine.

I exhaled, taking comfort at seeing my irritating kid brother.

Then I was moving, one foot in front of the other, heels sinking into the mushy ground, but I felt nothing, my body numb. Zane and Zander flanked me on either side, escorting me down the brick path.

"It's going to be okay," a voice murmured in my ear.

Zane's touch, even a simple hand on the small of my back, brought me comfort, easing some of my anxiety. I didn't say anything, couldn't say anything. It was enough he was here.

I took a seat but couldn't take my eyes off his. A thousand unsaid words transpired between us. *How are you doing? When am I going to see you ... alone? Why do you have to be so good-looking?*

We might have stayed spellbound if Ivy hadn't stepped between us, breaking our gaze. Death stood at her side—strong, dependable, and authoritative. Ivy's sable hair fell straight and sleek down her back. She placed a kiss on each of my cheeks before framing my face with her slender hands. "If there is anything I can do for you, Piper, don't hesitate to ask. You're family."

I gave a short nod, a lump of emotion clogging my throat.

After that, I made sure to look anywhere but in the direction where Zane stood. I recognized a few faces among the small group. Zach and Zoe were there. Zach caught my eye, giving me a wink. He looked as he always did, like he was up to no good.

The funeral procedures for the White Raven were supposed to be extravagant. In a sense, she had been their queen, and her ceremony should have been fit for royalty with an abundance of flowers, live music, and a procession a mile long, not this simple, small gathering done in secret.

I glanced down at the inside of my wrist, and there laid the proof of who I was. Glowing softly in white, a raven with his wings spread in flight.

Our small group gathered in a semicircle around Raven Hollow Cemetery. TJ squirmed in the seat beside me, and I understood. Too many eyes. Too many memories. Too many old feelings drudged up.

I surveyed my surroundings, thinking about my life, anything but death. Off to either side of the extensive grounds were two giant statues of an ancient king and queen, reaper monarchs no doubt. The stone statues loomed vigilantly, like they were protecting the dead. It was a comforting thought.

My eyes lingered on the statues for a long time before I turned back to Roarke, who was finishing his final words. The sun had started sinking down over the horizon, but the day's heat still hung in the air. It was a short and sweet tribute and gave both TJ and me a chance to say our good-byes. I stood, legs shaky, clutching a long-stemmed white rose between my fingers.

I approached her casket, decorated with jewels and an inscription, words I didn't understand. I ran a finger over the smooth surface, unsure of myself. "I don't know what I'm doing," I whispered, feeling foolish for talking to her casket, but I knew she was here. Her body might no longer breathe life, but her spirit lived, and knowing Rose, she was probably listening. Or I hoped. "But I'm willing to learn now, I think." I nibbled on my lip for a moment. "I'm just sorry we didn't get more time, Grandma." I dropped the single rose on top of her resting place, my chest heaving as I fought to control the mess of emotions overwhelming me.

I took a step back.

You can imagine my shock when the statues behind me blew up, crumbles of stone flying through the air. My chest halted, filling with shock.

And then, all hell broke loose.

# CHAPTER 2

*reat balls of fire!*
G I couldn't believe my eyes. The statues had literally blown up. Flames and smoke billowed, unfolding into the air. The explosion shook the ground, and I steadied myself on Rose's casket. For a moment, all I could do was stare, too stunned to move. It was like having a front row seat at an action film, except the heat from the flames was very real, crackling and climbing.

Then the banshee in me took over.

"Zane!" I screamed without thinking. His name tore from my lips, knowing danger was soon to follow.

He reached me in two long strides. "You okay?"

I nodded. "TJ?" I asked, concern escalating in my voice.

His eyes moved over my head, and he gave a simple nod. "Zander got him. He'll be taken care of."

"Hallows?" I asked, assuming the statues hadn't spontaneously combusted.

He ripped his tie off, tossing it to the ground. "We need to leave. Now." His fingers laced firmly through mine, but as he spun us around, a flash of white caught my eye.

I jerked against him. Cresting over a hill in the distance was a mob of flickering spirits, their whitish forms moved sporadically and far faster than I could run.

"Shit," Zane muttered. "Time for plan B."

I didn't even know there had been a plan A. Frantic, I searched for TJ, needing to assure myself he was safe. Zander was ushering him into one of the running town cars. TJ's eyes found mine in the pandemonium. "Piper!" he called. The car door was ajar, one of his feet in.

*Good Lord.* Now he unexpectedly decided to worry about me. "I'm fine," I yelled. "I'll be right behind you. Now get in the car."

Indecision crossed his boyish face, and I thought I was going to have to be a jerk, but then his gaze shifted to Zane beside me. Whatever he saw must have given him security, because he folded the rest of his body into the car without another word.

*Thank God.*

Except as the car sped away, chaos broke out as everyone scrambled, trying to get away. It was a disaster. There were maybe ten of us and … too many of them. Things were bound to get out of control quickly, and panic and terror took flight inside me.

Just what the culprits undoubtedly were hoping for.

The fighter in Zane kicked in, and the veins around his perilous eyes darkened, spreading down over his angled cheekbones.

"What's plan B?" I squeaked.

"We fight, Princess. And send as many of these assholes as we can to the other side."

I gave him a dry look. Zane knew taking souls wasn't something I especially enjoyed or was good at. I didn't strive to be a badass like him. I just didn't want to die. Pretty simple. Or so one would think.

Three hallows leaped into our path. Zane surged forward, putting himself in the line of fire. He was all over two of the spirits, as fast and as lethal as I remembered—merging in and out of the shadows, only to reappear and punch one of the ghosts on the side of his jaw. The hallows kept moving. Pain didn't seem to be a problem for the dead. But Zane was superior.

He crashed into the other, smaller spirit, and with one furious motion, Zane wrapped his arms around the ghost and heaved him to the ground. Frigid power spilled through the air as Zane clamped his hand onto the hallow's chest, and I knew what was about to follow. I watched enthralled as a willowy darkness took over, sucking the spirit's soul until the last drop was gone. Next came the blinding light.

I turned my head, shielding my eyes.

One down, a gazillion more to go.

It all happened so fast.

Clenching my fists, I took a few steps back, ready to defend myself. A girl a few years younger than me stalked toward me. She had a lean, strong build, and her whole body braced as if she was ready to tackle me. Good grief.

It was hard to tell what color her hair might have been when she was alive, a dark auburn maybe. I thought I caught hints of coppery tones in the light of the setting sun. And there was something familiar about her. I studied her face before she attempted to scratch my eyeballs out.

"Amber?" I guessed, remembering her from school. She had been in TJ's grade.

Her gaze narrowed, clearly not liking that I'd recognized her. "Not anymore." She fixed me with a glare of disdain, eyes unflinching as she continued to come at me. "So, you're the White Raven." Apparently, she didn't seem to approve of what she'd found.

"Yeah, I get that reaction a lot," I said with sarcasm.

My eyes darted around, looking to see an escape or if anyone was going to save me. No such luck. Zane was duking it out with two other hallows. Those who stayed were engaged with other angry spirits lingering in this realm. We might have been outnumbered, but they picked the wrong funeral to crash. Not a smart move. These particular Crows were the strongest reapers I knew, with powers to send these hostile hallows to the other side.

So I was on my own.

Amber's leg snaked out just enough to hit me in the knee, and my leg buckled, sending me to the ground. Stumbling slightly, I started to stand, but the little bitch grabbed my hair and yanked back. I yelped, twisting out of her hold, and I was pretty sure she took a chunk of my hair with her.

"What's your deal?" I barked, grinding my teeth to push back the tears of pain. Pulling someone's hair was playing nasty.

She angled her head in a way a human's wasn't supposed to move. It creeped me out. "You mussst die," she hissed in a croaky voice.

*So I've been told.* I was about to roll my eyes, but the hooker tackled me, throwing all her weight into the move and hitting me like a brick wall. It rattled my brain cells, and in the meantime, her hand wrapped around the back of my neck and gave a casual twist. My fingers instinctually flew to her arms, but I wasn't able to maintain my grip, and the next thing I knew, the girl had me in a chokehold.

Damn. I wasn't fairing too well.

No surprise really, I wasn't trained in butt kicking.

But I did have an internal need to survive, and my battle instincts took over. Arms flailing, I fought like a hellcat, scratching and clawing at her face to no avail. The air in my lungs was quickly dissipating, especially since I was near a full-blown panic attack. I gasped, and it was my last. If I didn't break free soon, I was going to pass out. Or worse …

But I told myself not to think about "the worse," only how I was going to get my next breath of air. My eyes bulged, and my body tingled. Tiny silver stars danced behind my vision, and my ears began to roar like the sea. Even as I bucked, I could feel my energy depleting. I opened my mouth to scream, but nothing came out, only a silent plea for help. The tingles grew tenfold, and I was sure the white light was next, the one you saw right before you died. But the white light never came. Instead, a few seconds later, a dark and furious face emerged, and Amber's manic look vanished, replaced with wariness.

I couldn't blame her.

Zane was about to annihilate her.

He tangled his fingers around her pale throat and lifted her into the air. I gulped one greedy breath after another, sinking to the ground, the weight of my body too much for my legs. My esophagus burned as fresh oxygen filtered through my lungs.

Zane hadn't been given the nickname Death Scythe by being stupid. "Do you know who I am?" he rumbled, the sound coming from a deep part in his chest.

"Ssshould I?" she mocked.

*Someone had a death wish.*

His brows snapped together. "It doesn't make a difference, because you're going to know who I am."

Her feet dangled in the air. "Let's get acquainted."

For just a moment, I took the opportunity to appreciate the fierce elegance of his profile, the perfection of his body, the iciness of his eyes, and the darkness that seemed to follow him everywhere.

His lips curled with pure male confidence. "I'm the reaper who is going to absorb your soul." With a hiss, he brought her down, and as soon as her feet touched the ground, she curled back a fist and hit Zane with enough force to make him grunt. Sharp claws raked down his shirt, ripping through material and flesh.

He spit blood on the ground. "Piper, take her soul," he roared, keeping a firm grip on Amber's throat even as she continued to cause him pain.

I froze.

The idea of what he was asking sent me into a state of frenzy. I knew I was supposed to be this all-powerful banshee, but that wasn't the case. I mean, yes I had power, lots of power, yet I had no idea how to use it. And I wasn't sure I wanted to use it. This was my world now, but at the same time, it wasn't. I was still adjusting. The concept of taking a soul wasn't pleasant. I'd seen too much death in my almost eighteen years. I'd killed a girl just a few weeks ago, and I wasn't jumping at the chance to reap a soul. Too soon.

I shook my head, clamping my teeth together. "I can't," I whimpered.

An emotion flickered in Zane's piercing eyes, but only for a flash, and it was quickly snuffed by his darkness. My stomach sunk, feeling as if I'd let him down somehow, and I probably had. I'd let down an entire race.

Zane's fist sliced through the air, judo chopping Amber on the forehead, and she fell limply to the ground. A dark, murky shadow appeared in front of Zane, sliding down his arm and spreading to Amber's slender neck. When he spoke, his voice was an insidious murmur among my own thoughts. *You can't run from this, Piper. It's your destiny.*

A strange chill spread over me, tendrils of darkness, thick and cold, wrapped around me. I felt it call to me, whispering a hundred promises. A crackle of light started and grew until it burned my eyelids.

I was on my feet now, barely breathing, and I could feel the power of absorbing her soul through Zane. It was exhilarating and terrifying, causing every cell in my body to come alive. I curved my fingers against the material of my dress. This link Zane and I had was the most intense thing I'd ever felt.

Shoving a hand through his midnight hair, he turned to reveal his eyes glowing with a scalding blue fire.

I shivered.

I'd met my fair share of dangerous predators lately, but nothing like Zane.

"You're glowing," he stated matter-of-factly.

"Huh." I glanced down, and sure as shit, my skin was lit in a network of veins like a constellation. "Just perfect," I grumbled.

He held out his hand. "Come on. Let's get out of here."

I didn't hesitate, slipping my hand into his. "I thought you'd never ask."

Regardless of the fight still raging on around us, we managed to make it to the other black car without being attacked, but the driver was long gone. Zane got behind the wheel, his long legs no match for the cramped seating of the town car, and cranked the engine. His foot hit the gas, leaving a trail of dust and gravel clouding behind us. Time stretched in the warmth of the car as he steered us toward the exit, occasionally hitting a bump in the road I hoped wasn't a body part.

He cleared his throat loudly. "You okay?"

I pressed my cheek to the glass. "If I had a dime for every time someone has asked me that, I'd be—"

"Rich?" he supplied. "You already are."

"Ugh. Thanks for the reminder." I scooted down into the plush leather.

"You're literally the only person I know who would scowl at inheriting an island, a massive house, and a small fortune. Not to mention buckets of power."

What a day. This was going to be the longest damn drive of my life. Zane and I alone, in close quarters nonetheless. He had stayed at the manor the first night after Rose died, but we hadn't been alone since. It wasn't helping that my body was hyper aware of him. Thanks to my banshee abilities, my soul responded to his, magnetized by the power he exuded—among other things.

How very inconvenient.

With the immediate danger behind us, assuming we weren't being trailed by a group of bloodthirsty hallows, the events of the day caught up with me. I was drained. Emotionally and physically. It wasn't just my body. My heart and soul were exhausted.

And hungry.

I placed a hand to my stomach in fear of it making a loud rumbling noise.

Zane's fingers flexed on the wheel as he expertly steered the car out of the cemetery. "You never answered my question."

Demanding as always. My head fell back, and I turned in the seat, eyeing him. "Can't you tell what I'm feeling? Do you really need me to spell it out for you?"

He snorted. "Just because our souls align doesn't mean I begin to understand you, Piper."

"I'm sorry," I blurted. It came out of nowhere, but I realized there was this guilt inside me, along with a clutter of feelings. Everyone wanted me to be someone I wasn't sure I wanted to be or could be, and it was making me a complete mess. Snappy one minute and regretful the next.

An array of emotions went through his eyes, turning them from bright blue to a stormy color. "You don't owe me an apology."

"I screwed up." When he didn't say anything, I added, "Didn't I?"

"Piper, no one expects you to be Rose."

I gave him the look.

His lips tipped. "Okay. Let me rephrase. I don't expect you to be Rose."

And that was kind of more important to me. "What am I doing? I choked back there. In front of everyone."

"You did."

I swatted him on the arm. "So not helping."

"No one said it was going to be easy, Princess, but nothing worth gaining ever is. It might not feel like it now, but finding out what you are might change your life for the better. I know you see it as a hindrance and maybe you're still bitter about the secrets your family kept. Maybe you're trying to protect yourself from getting hurt. Maybe you'll be a better banshee than Rose. You won't know until you open yourself up and give it a shot."

I couldn't help but wonder if he was talking about more than just being a banshee. Regardless, I had a lot to think about and hard decisions to make. They couldn't be put off for much longer. Things were only going to get worse.

The car rolled to a stop in front of Raven Manor. I fumbled with the end of my skirt, not ready to leave. Each time we separated, I didn't know when I would see him again, *if* I would see him again. I wanted to lie to myself and say I wouldn't be devastated, but in all reality, it would shatter something inside of me. We were both deluding ourselves. Things couldn't continue as they had been going. There was going to be a point where I either accosted him with my mouth or he broke my heart. I didn't see any other option.

"You should be safe here," he said, eyes focused straight ahead and jaw locked.

It was impossible to ignore the tension in the air, but he was right about Raven Manor being safe. The perimeter was guarded around the clock by a defense system I definitely didn't understand. I reached for the door handle, glancing over my shoulder for a last glimpse at Zane.

# CHAPTER 3

The manor was veiled by gloom, so I headed to the back of the house, seeking comfort. I had an agenda. Food and bed. Preferably in that order. I found Gracie, the head housekeeper. She was exactly the distraction I needed, because inside I was still reeling from the unsettling events, my stomach in knots. My brain couldn't handle anything strenuous.

These last few days had been difficult and surreal. Sometime during the haze of misery and disbelief, the realization I would be staying here longer than just the summer hit. So I began to notice the people who worked for Rose—what their names were, how long they'd been employed, and what they did around the house. It became apparent that the manor was more work than met the eye.

I wasn't sure I was ready for the responsibility.

I wasn't sure I was ready to be a banshee.

I was most definitely sure I wasn't ready to be anyone's wife.

When I'd first arrived here, I wanted nothing to do with anybody, and I regretted that now. Life was short, and there was no time to leave important things undone.

Gracie had been a godsend, taking care of us and making sure we didn't starve to death. I learned she had two grown daughters and five grandchildren she spoiled rotten. She was also one of the few people on the island that was human, and I had taken an instant liking to her. This house needed a bit of normalcy, and that was exactly what she brought.

"How was it?" Gracie asked. She stood over the sink scrubbing overbaked lasagna from a pan. The kitchen was covered with half-eaten casseroles. Gracie cooked when she was feeling out of sorts and had been shoving food down my throat since the passing of Rose. Death never made me hungry. So much food had gone to waste, but of course now I could eat a five-course meal.

I planted my butt on one of the country style stools, resting my arms on the counter. "Depressing. Eventful. A hot mess."

She was a round woman with friendly eyes and a motherly smile. "Rose wouldn't have wanted it any other way."

Gracie had a point. I angled my head, the soft kitchen lights high-lighting my face. "It was an utter disaster." *Like my life.*

"You're hurt," she gasped, moving fast for someone of her size. Her fingers grasped my chin to get a better look at my battle wound. She clucked her tongue. "I'll get something to clean it."

Since she'd mentioned it, my left cheek was throbbing. I lifted my hand and winced when it came in contact with a gnarly gash. "It's nothing. Just a scratch."

"Mmm-hmm," she said, pressing her lips together. "I've heard that a time or two."

Obviously, working for someone like Rose for more than a decade, a person might get used to the unusual and out of the ordinary. Ultimately, secrets no longer stayed hidden. She was the only person, other than TJ, who didn't pressure me or make me feel like I was a joke. I was still uncertain how much the staff knew, but Gracie knew more than I did.

"It will heal," I said.

She smoothed back my hair with her hand. "You know what will speed up the process?"

I lifted my brows. If she even thought about kissing my boo-boo, I was going to my room without supper.

"A bowl of hearty soup."

My shoulders relaxed. Life was complicated and sticky, but a simple bowl of soup sounded heavenly. "You read my mind."

As Gracie reheated a robust portion of ham and bean soup, I went to the fridge and grabbed a Coke. "Did TJ already eat?"

"Eat? That boy consumes everything in sight." She set the bowl in front of me as I took my seat again. I smiled a little, dipping my spoon in and blowing on it. Pressing her elbows on the counter, she asked, "You want to talk about it?"

I shrugged. "Where to begin? The whole thing was a debacle. Statues blew up. I freaked out. And I don't even know if her casket made it into the ground." Let alone if the secret of her death was spreading like wildfire.

Gracie listened to my ranting without batting an eye, and even though it didn't make a whole lot of sense, she managed to understand my babble. "*They* came for you?"

*They* being the hallows. "It feels like that's all they've being doing since I arrived here. Attacking me."

Her eyes sobered, crow's feet crinkling at the corners. "Things are changing, chica. *I* can feel it. There is strife among the harbingers of death and an alliance between the restless souls. The island is under siege."

I frowned. "You feel it too?" It wasn't just the land, but the people as well. What I thought had been mourning maybe was something more. Fear? Edginess? I'd come to understand Raven Hollow wasn't just an ordinary place. Like the unconventional woman who cared for the island, this land, the surrounding waters, and the people who lived here, were all unique, nothing like where I'd grown up.

Her hip rested against the cabinet. "What I feel isn't important. What do *you* feel?"

A cold chill pierced between my breasts, and it took me almost a minute to recognize what it was. "Death."

She nodded. "Your abilities are expanding. Your mind is opening."

I swallowed, twirling my spoon in circles around the bowl. "What am I to do about it?"

"That's for you to decide and part of your journey."

Cryptic much? I wasn't up for a journey or a lesson in the hard-ships of life. I just wanted a peaceful, quiet life with a white picket fence and 2.5 kids.

Finishing my soup, I mulled over options, unable to think of anything else. Harbinger of death? Was that something I could be or be a part of? Did I have it in me? Tonight I had totally flaked out, embarrassingly so, and I wasn't proud of it. I couldn't freeze up again.

*Banshee.* Couldn't see myself putting that on my college résumé. Not that college was in my future now. I was seriously contemplating giving up everything. My home. My friends. My family.

TJ chose that moment to burst into the kitchen. "What the hell was that?"

I dropped my head onto the table. "I don't know, TJ. I'm extremely tired. Can we talk about this tomorrow?"

"Are you shitting me? Things blew up." There was the teeniest bit of cool factor in his voice.

My head snapped up. "Watch your mouth. I'm in no mood for your crap. We just buried our grandmother. Give it a rest." Now might have been a good time to tell him he was leaving Raven Hollow, but I didn't have it in me to battle with him.

Frustration lined his face. "I would if you would be honest with me."

When I didn't respond, he spun around, slamming both palms on the door. I let my forehead hit the counter again.

"FML," I muttered against the cool granite.

---

IN MY ROOM, I poked around, avoiding the bed and impending twilight. There was this strange throbbing in my chest, and my eyes burned as if I wanted to cry, but the tears wouldn't come. Today was supposed to be about Rose and honoring her life. Instead, it had become a train wreck. I'd met my acceptable supernatural daily limit. It had been maxed out.

Lifting my hand in the air, I watched as it trembled slightly. I wasn't sure how much more my nerves could take. So far life as the White Raven sucked ass.

I needed to quiet my mind. Grabbing a pad of paper, I sat on the window bench and did a quick sketch of a girl wading in the sea, the salty breeze blowing her lilac hair, but my heart wasn't really in it. Putting the pencils and notebook aside, I walked to the bed and flopped on my back. I stared at the ceiling, running a hand through my hair.

It was fruitless trying not to think about all the crap plaguing my mind. Regardless of how conflicted I was feeling, one thing was clear. TJ couldn't stay here. It was too dangerous. Putting my feelings and wants aside, I knew it was what was best for him no matter how much it upset me. Sending him away would crush me. He might be a pain in the butt, but he was my pain-in-the-butt little brother. I'd spent most of my life looking out for him and the last year taking care of him. Whether or not either of us admitted it, we depended on each other.

Telling him to leave was another story.

No doubt TJ had his suspicions about what was happening. Zombie apocalypse. Aliens. Heck, I didn't even know if he could see the hallows, but I wasn't ready to divulge all our family secrets. The less he knew, the better. I had to believe, in his case, ignorance was bliss. The worst of it was I was going to have to get in contact with our father. He probably didn't even know his mother-in-law was gone.

I often wondered if he knew Mom had been a banshee. Had she also lied to him? My gut told me he knew, that he knew it all, which was why he was across the globe, far away from me. What kind of parent left their children to deal with a supernatural world on their own? Coward.

When I saw my father again, I planned on giving him an earful that would make the Pope blush. I was having a crisis here.

When I wasn't worrying about TJ or stressing about being inhuman, I was thinking about Zane. It was stupid to try to pretend I didn't like him—I really, really liked him.

And that was the problem.

I didn't know if I should be fighting these feelings or embracing them. He invaded my mind no matter how hard I tried to suppress him. And I tried … until my eyeballs felt like they were going to pop, but he wasn't the type of guy who was easy to forget.

Except I shouldn't be thinking about Zane at all. There were a million other things I could be contemplating, yet none of them made my stomach flip, my pulse race, or my soul sing.

Rolling over, I shoved my face into the pillow and screamed. At the edge of the bed was his hoodie. I had tossed it there earlier when I'd been searching for something to wear. His scent was there, clinging to the material and teasing my senses.

I groaned. There was no escaping him.

How had my life gotten so tangled up? I was living a bizarre, bad afternoon soap opera.

With nothing else to do, and because I couldn't tell my mind to shut up, I started mentally listing all the pros and cons about my complicated relationship with Zane in my head. And there were many. Pros: He looked incredible in jeans. He made my heart patter. And he'd taken a vow to protect me. Cons: I was promised to his brother by a supernatural treaty. Sometimes he needed an attitude adjustment, but what guy didn't?

Hmm. And that got me thinking. Was there no way out of this arranged marriage? I mean, I was the White Raven. Could I break the contract? I didn't claim to be a supernatural guru, but it seemed to me there had to be a loophole. I just needed to find it. But where to start? With Death? The thought of telling Roarke I didn't want to marry his son gave me chills. I wasn't backing down from my duty as the White Raven, but by God I should. Everyone knew I was going to be the worst banshee in history. However, if I was going to fully commit to this insane job, which I still couldn't believe I was doing, I felt I at least deserved something in return.

Was a chance at love and happiness too much to ask for? A chance to figure it out on my own without it being forced upon me? I couldn't help but feel that Zander, Zane, and I were all just pawns.

The more I dwelled on the contract promising me to Zander, the smaller my room became as the walls in this castle-sized house closed in on me. Every minute that ticked by I felt *my* world slipping farther and farther away and the pressure of stepping into Rose's shoes clamping down on my chest until I was gasping for air.

No matter how much the security at the manor was beefed up, I never felt safe unless I was with Zane. I didn't know whom I could trust, but Zane had proven to be immeasurably significant to my safety countless times. There were still so many questions unanswered.

What did the hallows want from me, other than to annihilate me? Why couldn't I have Zane instead of Zander? What was the big deal? Who had killed Rose?

That particular question spun and spun in my head, and I knew I wasn't the only one who was certain it had been someone close. Someone she'd trusted even. Someone in Raven Manor. Thinking about the possibility left a bitter taste in my mouth.

# CHAPTER 4

Z ane was leaning one shoulder against the wall, his dark shirt stretched over his broad shoulders. His presence took up the entire room. "Have you come to a decision about TJ?"

A cool tingle skated across the nape of my neck. I forced my gaze to his eyes. Arctic blue, like a frozen tundra. "Hey, to you too." He wanted to know if I had decided to send away the only family I had here or tell TJ the truth about everything. What I was. The danger we were in. Why Mom and Rose had been killed. Yada, yada, yada.

Unruly dark hair fell over his forehead as he tilted his head. "You called, remember?"

I swallowed. "Not intentionally," I said drily. Apparently thinking about Zane too keenly sent out a distress call. "I haven't finished reading the instruction manual on being a banshee."

"I guess we need to work on that."

I twirled the pencil in my hand, seriously considering poking him with it. "What? Like training?"

He sauntered into the room. "Exactly like training."

I bit my lip. "You and me?" An unhealthy amount of excitement entered my body at the prospect of seeing him on a daily basis. Zane was a total babe, but at times he could be a douchebag, which canceled out his hotness.

Right now he was looking good. Too good.

His gaze dropped to my lips. "For part of it. You have a lot of catching up to do. There is more to being the White Raven than controlling your new abilities. You need to learn the laws and physics of being a reaper and the inner workings of the different sectors you govern."

"Why does this sound a lot like school?"

He slid me a grin that did funny things to my belly. "Think of it as boot camp, and I'm one of your counselors."

"Can't wait," I mumbled, doing everything in my power not to stare at his lips. "When is this so-called boot camp supposed to begin?"

The bed dipped as he took a seat beside me, careful to leave enough space between us so we weren't touching. "If my father gets his way, now."

My eyes widened. "Now?" I echoed. I got that time was of the essence, but we'd only buried Rose yesterday, and I wanted TJ off the island before things got really crazy. "I thought I would have a few more days to take care of some things."

"So you decided to send TJ home?"

"Do you want me to tell you you're right? Fine. You're right. He needs to be as far away from here as possible."

Thick, sooty lashes fanned the tips of his angular cheeks. "It's for the best."

Yeah, but that didn't mean it didn't suck. I picked at a loose string on the bedspread, keeping my eyes averted before I found myself lost. "I guess."

He turned his body so it was angled toward me, our thighs touching. "Piper, you're doing the right thing. If he was my brother, he'd already be gone."

It was hard to keep my emotions in check around Zane. I blamed our stupid souls. "Then why do I feel so horrible?"

"Because being a banshee doesn't mean you're heartless." He

moved a fraction of an inch closer, brushing his thumb against my chin. A jolt of electricity danced along my skin.

A strangled gasp escaped the back of my throat like one of those silly girls in movies. I swayed toward him. His lips tipped up on one side as he leaned toward me, his mouth inches from mine. *Holy sweet reaper babies ... He's going to kiss me.* My hands dug into the bed, clenching the sides of the covers as my eyes were drawn to his totally kissable lips. They were right there, and I inhaled his outdoorsy scent that was all around him.

My eyes fluttered closed, lips parting, and ...

A soft knock sounded on my bedroom door. Zane and I separated like a submachine Uzi had gone off, and I regrettably broke my gaze from Zane's to see Zander standing in the doorway.

*Oh dear God, this should be interesting.*

I wanted to crawl under the bed and die. Heat swept over my cheeks as the stretch of silence became too heavy. "Is someone going to say something?" I squeaked, feeling like an idiot, but the awkwardness was killing me.

Zander cleared his throat. "I wanted to come by and see how you were ..." His eyes shifted from me to Zane. "But Zane beat me to it. I should have figured." He shook his head. "You just can't stay away." With that said, Zander turned and left.

"Shit," Zane swore under his breath.

For a stunned moment, I didn't know what to do. It wasn't my intention to hurt Zander ... or Zane. I jumped to my feet. "Zander," I called. "Wait."

It was the first time he'd shown any real emotion at seeing Zane and me together. I was bumbling this whole engagement, and as soon as I could think a coherent thought, I was going to find a way to fix this mess.

Zane or Zander?

I didn't know what to do, which one to choose, which one to fight for. My heart? Or my duty?

The struggle was real. And I had never been good at making decisions.

Until I did decide, it was probably best to keep the peace. This island was rocky enough as it was without me causing World War III.

I caught Zander in the hall, placing a hand on his bicep. I tried not to think about the power that was contained in that arm. "Hey." I wasn't sure he was going to turn around and look at me, but I sighed when I glanced up and saw his face.

His blue eyes had a slight purplish tint, and he was clean-shaven, unlike the two-day stubble Zane was sporting. "You don't have to explain. I know this isn't what you want."

My arm slowly fell away. It was sort of uncomfortable touching him. Actually, everything about this was weird. "That might be true. I don't know what I want, but I've had my entire world flipped upside down. I'm trying to work through it."

"We both are," he stated. Shifting his weight to his other foot, he softened his tone. "I just think it might be easier if we work through it together."

I couldn't help but think it shouldn't be this hard. It wasn't with Zane, minus the moments he drove me utterly batty. My feelings for him came naturally, fierce and wild. Part of me wanted to scream this wasn't fair, and the other part was tired and wanted to give in. I forced my expression blank. "Probably," I agreed, unable to keep the aloofness from my voice. It was hard not to take my frustration out on Zander, even though I knew it wasn't his fault I was in this predicament.

His eyes shifted over my head, behind me, and I wondered what he was thinking, knowing Zane was still in my bedroom. "I didn't just come by to see how you were doing."

I lifted a brow.

"I was wondering if you wanted to go out and get dinner some night."

There was something almost too sweet about Zander. It made the guilt I was feeling heavier. *Figures I would fall for the bad brother instead of the nice guy.* "Oh," I managed to clumsily utter.

The corner of his lips curved. "*Oh?* That's all you've got?"

What did he expect? Not only had he caught me off guard, I wasn't really in the "dating" mind frame. "Sure?" I replied.

"Look. We've got to start somewhere. I know this is awkward, but there's no avoiding it."

Touché. "You're right. I'm not normally so flaky. I promise."

"Really? Because I find that hard to believe."

I stared blankly at him.

"I'm joking," he laughed.

"Good, because I was seriously thinking about standing you up."

The smile lines around his lips deepened. "You're going to make a helluva banshee."

I shrugged. "We'll see. One day at a time."

"We have a lot to talk about, but I want you to know I'm here. For whatever you need. A shoulder to cry on, a punching bag to hit, or someone to listen. I don't want things to always be strained between us. It would be easier if we got along."

"You're right. It would be easier. I need a little time to figure things out—"

"Like Zane?" he interjected.

Dead air.

What did I say? No? I was a sucky liar, so what was the point? Denying I had feelings for Zane would make me look like a fool.

Zander frowned. "If you want things to be easier, try spending less time with my brother."

*Ouch.*

Just when I thought he was a softy at heart, he goes and zeros it out with a comment like that. Made my kitty claws want to come out. It could be he was testing me to see if I would automatically jump to Zane's defense. Truth be told, it was exactly what I wanted to do, but I bit my tongue, which took effort. "I'll take it under consideration," I said.

He nodded, and with one last glance down the hall toward my open bedroom door, Zander left. If every confrontation with him was going to end like this, we were doomed. Even in the ground, Rose was causing me strife. I slumped against the wall as a pang hit me in the temples. These migraines recently plaguing me were only getting worse.

Shoulders heavy with responsibility, I kicked off the wall and headed back into my room. Zane was sprawled out on my bed with his hands linked behind his head, staring at the ceiling. Wisps of dark curls laid over the lines of thought creasing his forehead.

"You lied," he said as I plopped down on the window seat.

I glared at him, tucking my legs underneath me. Don't tell me he was going to start harping on me too. "What about?" Not that I really cared all that much.

He turned on his side, propping his head on his hand. "You're not okay. I can feel the tangle of emotions you're trying to hide."

Uncertainty. Fear. Sadness. Anger. Lots of anger.

Yep. They were all there inside me.

I hugged my legs to my chest, resting my chin on my knees. "So, what if I did? Things are already messy." My emotions wouldn't be a jumble if I didn't want to attack him with my mouth every time I saw him.

"And about to get messier." The words came out of Zane's mouth like ice.

"What do you mean?"

"We're going to have to be more careful, especially now that you're expected to hone your powers. There's no one to guide you. Many of the elders have the basic knowledge of your skills, but not the full extent. Your training will test the symmetry of our souls, which is a problem. A big problem."

"Do I even want to know why?" I mumbled.

Sitting up, he swung his long legs over the side of the bed, which he made look all too inviting. The seriousness of his expression told me I should get my head out of the gutter and stop thinking about him on my sheets.

"With the upheaval of rogue reapers and the increase of hallows, the last thing we need is for the monarchy to crumble," he said. "There is an order that needs to be followed, one that's been in place for centuries. Your marriage to Zander, Death's firstborn, solidifies the

monarchy's lineage." Death was the sector overlord for the Black
Crows. That much I understood, but there were so many rules I didn't
begin to comprehend. "If anyone outside of my family found out what
you were to me …" His voice smoothly trailed off.

Most days I didn't know what I was to him, but I got what he was
implying—mostly. There were still a million questions. "It would be
bad," I supplied.

"Bad doesn't begin to cover it, Princess. If you thought your life
was in danger before, it would be Hell on Earth if the other sectors
found out our souls resonate. They would take advantage of what
they saw as a chance for new management. We need to be careful. No
accidently merging souls."

Duly noted.

The thing was, I didn't know how to do it, so not doing it should
be pretty simple. Excellent logic. But what I really wanted to know
was where did we stand? I wanted him to give me a sign of hope,
something worthy of risking everything for. I fiddled with the mark
on my wrist, tracing it with my fingernail. "Can I ask you something?"

"Depends," he replied coolly.

"Do you feel any … different when you're around me?"

A half smile played across his lips. "You mean, do I still want to
lock you up in a tower for all eternity?"

"Zane." I sighed. "You know what I mean."

He ran his hands through his hair. "It doesn't matter if we're
together or apart. Since the day you came to Raven Hollow, I've felt
different. A cool tingle starts at the base of my neck, and the shadows
I manipulate quiver. The closer you are to me, the more intense it
becomes. Is that what you mean?"

Gulp.

Yeah. And then some. "Glad it's not just me. Does your mark
ever—?"

"Feel like it is going to come alive and fly off my wrist?" he
finished. "Whenever you're near."

Heat swamped my cheeks, and I totally blamed Zane. It was hard
to stick to my resolve of duty first when he was actually nice … and

charming … and so good-looking. "Is there no other way? Is my only option really to marry Zander?"

One second he was sitting on my bed and the next he was beside me, eyes frosted. "What you want and what I want doesn't matter. You're no good to me or to any of us if you're dead. So yes, your only option is to marry my brother."

Hope shattered.

There was anger in his expression, but was it directed at me or the injustice of our bleak situation?

It didn't matter, because he'd ruffled my feathers. "I take it back. You're a complete asshat!" I yelled, but it was a waste of breath.

He was gone.

I gave the shadow where he had stood a big fat middle finger. *Suck on that, Zane Hunter.*

# CHAPTER 5

I was having one of those days where I wanted to break crap, hoping it would make me feel better. I stared at the lavender vase on my dresser thinking it would do nicely, and that was when I knew I had to get out of there.

I was going stir-crazy.

Rolling off the bed, I quickly changed into a pair of spandex shorts and a sports bra. Running was not my favorite thing to do, but there was all this excess energy buzzing inside me that I didn't know what else to do with. Calling Zane was out of the question.

So I laced on my Nikes, strapped my phone to my armband, and trotted down the balcony stairs. The heat of the sun hit me in a wave, guaranteeing I was going to work up a sweat. Perfect. Maybe I could ooze this outlandish need to scream Zane's name right out of my pores.

Looping around the gardens, I headed for the gates leading to the beach access. I punched in the five digit code, and as the doors slid open, two of the security details appeared behind me. I stopped and turned around. "What are you doing?"

Backs rigid, their eyes were hidden by the dark sunglasses. "We were instructed to discreetly follow you," the taller of the two informed me, though they were both over six feet.

"Uh, okay." I let the idea simmer for a minute. "By who?" I asked.

Neither of them appeared dressed for a run in business type suits. They looked at each other before the one on the left said, "Zane."

Shocker. "Aren't you supposed to take orders from me?"

"Yes, ma'am."

Problem solved. "Well then, let's get one thing straight. Don't ever call me 'ma'am.' I'm not even eighteen yet," I said without flinching, making sure to catch each of them in the eye. "And I don't need an escort. I'm just going for a run on the beach. Capisce?"

The *Men in Black* doofuses didn't object. They stood with their hands looped in front of them, feet slightly apart. Satisfied we were finally on the same page, I took a little band off my wrist, bound my hair back with a couple twists, and kicked off into a brisk jog.

The air was sizzling for the end of July and the sun was bright. I never tired of watching the way the light, sun or moon, played over the water. Forgoing music, I liked listening to the subtle and lulling sounds of the ocean. I paced myself, the sand kicking up off my heels. Five minutes in, I heard a squawking overhead. Cranking my neck, I blocked the sun with my hands, only to see two hawks circling in the sky above.

I frowned. *So much for ditching my security detail.* Apparently Zane's word held more weight than mine. Could be he'd scared the piss out of them. I didn't precisely have the threatening tactic at five two with sunny blonde hair.

They had underestimated me. Another time, I might have shown how much, but not today. I had an overwhelming amount of information to absorb about reapers, but I did know that Red Hawks could morph into … pretty much anything—any *living* thing that is. I guess that explained why neither Agent Tightass nor Agent Stick-Up-His-Butt had put up much resistance about me leaving the manor. How very sneaky and annoying of Zane to stick me with two reapers who could virtually follow me everywhere—even into the bathroom.

What a horrifying thought.

But now that I was thinking about Zane—good or bad thoughts—there was no stopping my brain.

I was as confused as ever on where Zane and I stood. Was I being completely foolish thinking there could ever be something between us? Probably. Did it stop me from hoping? Not a chance. Underneath all this sarcastic, broken, tragic exterior was a girl who believed in love, who desperately wanted to be in love. But I was slowly coming to terms with the fact that it might not be in the cards for me. I tried to pretend it didn't matter, but it did. I didn't know if I had it in me to set aside my feelings for duty.

Could I pretend to not have feelings for Zane?

Could I hide those feelings when he was around?

Could I allow myself to feel for someone else?

Mom and Rose had made the ultimate sacrifice for me, and I wanted to be selfish. I wanted it all. Love. Happiness. And to not get killed. Supposedly the only way to do that was to marry Zander and join our families—the Ravens and the Crows.

So I was constantly told.

But every time I was near Zane, it was harder and harder to deny the need to be closer to him and to keep the feelings I couldn't control from sweeping over me. I tried to think of TJ's safety and the responsibility bestowed upon me. It was scary thinking about the number of people who were relying on me.

An upheaval was in the works, and I was at the core.

*Joy.*

My union with Zander could be the key to ensuring peace between sectors and keeping the allows from destroying our world. If the hallows joined forces with the defiant reapers, we were all royally screwed.

It would have been easier if Zander wasn't a decent guy.

He just wasn't the one I wanted—the one that made my heart patter.

I cringed, thinking I might be strapped to a loveless marriage. If I wasn't so hung up on Zane … if I could give Zander half a chance … if my soul hadn't been linked to Zane's … None of it mattered. I couldn't change the past, but my future was still undecided. There had to be a way to govern the sectors without having to give up on love. Things might have always been done in such an order, but maybe it was time for a change. New Raven. New rules.

I swallowed the urge to puke as I ran, wondering again what had possessed me to think jogging down the beach in the middle of the day was a brilliant idea. There was a good possibility I might pass out if I didn't stop soon. My skin was clammy and overheated. Slowing to a walk, I glanced at my phone. I had lasted thirty minutes.

And I couldn't say I felt any better.

Plunking my weary butt onto the sand, I let my heart rate return to normal. The scenery was breathtaking—glittering waters, all blue skies, and pretty breezes. It was a day meant to be enjoyed instead of hidden away, and I needed the breath of fresh air to clear my head.

My phone dinged. It was Parker.

*What up, home slice?*

I smiled at the screen and replied. *Has anyone told you today you're lame?*

*Not today. And this is why I miss you so much.*

*I bet you say that to all the girls.*

Thirty seconds later: *Only you, Pipes. Everything okay there in never-never land?*

My fingers swept over the touchscreen. *Depends on your definition of okay.*

*I talked to your dad. He told me about your grandma. Why haven't you called me?*

My heart dropped. I glanced out into the ocean, munching on my bottom lip. *So many reasons—none of which you would actually believe.* Rereading his last text, I ignored his question, more concerned with the fact that he had talked to my dad and that my dad knew Rose was dead. I'd been trying to reach him for days. *You talked to my dad?* I responded.

*Yeah. I'm worried about you.*

Anger whirled through me. My life was tragically falling apart over here, and my dad didn't have the decency to call me. What was his deal? As much as I wanted to lash out at someone, it wasn't Parker's fault my dad was a class act douchebag. **Don't be. I'm fine. Really.**

**When will you be home?**

Of course he would assume now that Rose was gone I would come home. What was I going to say? This was the reason I'd been avoiding Parker for the last week. Too many questions I couldn't answer, not without him thinking I was taking the A-train straight to the loony bin. **Idk. Things are ...complicated here.**

**Do you want me to come and help?**

I choked. That was the last thing I wanted. **Nah. It's just BS paperwork.**

**Don't forget about me. K?**

**Like I could ever forget you, Parks.** He was the only thing normal and real in my life. **I've got to go. Call u later.**

As I stared down at my phone, I wondered when or if I would ever see Parker again. I scowled. A pang of regret and guilt hit me in the chest, and before I had a second to sort through what I was feeling, a dark shadow blocked my sunlight.

I was almost afraid to turn around. Overhead, the two hawks cried in rapid succession, sending out a warning. Whoever it was had them up in arms.

"I was surprised to see you alone, but then I saw your babysitters." Aspyn dropped down in the sand beside me. A pair of pink shades was situated on top of her head, chestnut locks cascading around her oval face.

I let out a breath of relief. "Oh, thank God. I thought you might be a hallow or worse."

She laughed. "Well, that's a first. No one's ever mistaken me for a ghost. And what could be worse than the dead determined to make chopped liver out of you?"

My nose crinkled. "I could think of two things."

She placed a slim finger to her lips. "Let me guess. Zane and Zander?"

I shuffled my shoes, burying them in the sand. "Bull's-eye."

"I don't see how that's a dilemma. It sounds more like an opportunity." Her mischievous smile twinkled. "Want to trade places?"

"If it was possible, I might actually take you up on it."

"You like to run?" she asked, eyeing my gear.

My lips quirked. "Only when my life is in shambles."

"Got some excess energy to burn? That I understand. It will get easier once you learn to control your powers. I bet one of your *dilemmas* might be able to help you burn through it."

Heat rushed to my face—not because I was embarrassed, but because I was envisioning what it would be like to throw all this amped up energy into lip-locking with Zane. "I'm trying to avoid a catastrophe, not enflame it."

She dug her fingers into the sand behind her and leaned back. "My way sounds more fun ... and it looks like you could use a little fun. I doubt you'll have much time to yourself soon."

"I don't remember signing up for summer school, but it looks like I've been enrolled in reaper combat and the history of banshees."

Her glossy lips arched. "I enjoy a little one-on-one."

I bet she did. Aspyn was the type of girl who was sexy without even trying. If I did or said half the things she did, I would look like an idiot. "I'm going to suck at this, you know," I said, thinking about how much I was going to embarrass myself. "I possess no athletic skills whatsoever."

"Kissing is a sport. I bet you're good at that."

My eyes narrowed. "Is sex the only thing on your mind?"

She stretched out her legs like a lazy cat. "I'm an eighteen, unattached, hot female. Obviously, it's all I think about when I'm not thinking about destroying souls."

Kicking off my shoes and socks, I crossed my legs. "What's it like being a death reaper?"

"Intoxicating. Empowering. Sexy."

*Sexy? Really?* Sexy wasn't what came to mind when I thought of death. And then I thought of Zane. Okay, I concede death could be sexy if you looked like Zane. I lowered my lashes. "I think I get the point. You love your life. But do you ever think it's because you've never known any other way?"

She looked out at the horizon, the gentle breeze picking up pieces of her hair. "When I was about five maybe, I remember seeing a summer girl about my age visiting with her family. She was on the beach hunting for seashells, and I sat watching her, thinking she had the most beautiful blonde hair. I desperately wanted hair like hers. She was so spirited and free, running up and down the beach, completely clueless that death waited around the corner. Her mom sat a few feet from me on a beach towel, soaking up the sun and watching her daughter frolic and giggle. I was still very young, but a reaper nonetheless. It was the only time I wanted to trade places with another human."

"It was her soul you were going to take, wasn't it?" I asked.

Aspyn nodded. "She was the only soul I relinquished." I expected a hint of remorse in her voice, but it sounded like she was relieved that the girl had lived.

Captivated by the story, I asked. "Why did you let her live?" It went against the natural order of life and death reapers were supposed to uphold.

Distress came into her clear gray eyes. "Because her mother asked."

That shocked me. A reaper didn't disobey the laws of death, and I couldn't help but wonder what the consequences were for doing so—something I was sure to learn. "Who was she—the little girl?"

Her gaze held mine. "It was you."

Whoosh. The air left my lungs. It felt like I'd been sucker punched. "That can't be. I-I … oh my God." My eyes searched her face. "You're serious."

There was no hesitation as she spoke. "As soon as I realized who you were, I felt ashamed. I envied you. Even then. I made a promise to your mom that I would never tell a single soul, living or dead that I'd seen you that day. It was a promise I kept."

"Why didn't you tell me sooner?"

"What? That I almost took your soul thirteen years ago? I wanted you to like me, not hate me, Piper," she said.

"But you're telling me now." Suspicion clouded my tone.

She shrugged. "Because we're friends. And I won't lie to you. It's not the kind of friend I am. I will always tell you the truth, even if it's going to hurt."

I could appreciate that; actually, I needed it. Someone I could turn to when the rest of the world was sheltering me or trying to protect me. It was still a shock, hearing how close I'd been to this world and never knew, and it made me wonder how many other times in my life I'd come close to brushing death.

I probably didn't want to know.

# CHAPTER 6

I was certifiably a crab-ass when I woke up the next morning, groggy and coffee starved, if the restless moments I had last night could even be considered sleep. I blamed TJ for my shitty night. Over and over my mind spun, searching for the right words to tell my brother he had to go home, that he had to leave Raven Hollow … and me.

TJ might play the tough guy, but I knew deep down how much he depended on me.

Rubbing the gunk from my eyes, I swung my feet over the bed. I thought about changing out of my comfy sleep shorts and T-shirt. Instead, I pulled on a pair of cute heart-covered socks that reached my knees.

I closed the drawer to my dresser and caught a glimpse of myself in the mirror. Holy. Cow. I looked like a hot mess.

My hair was knotted in an untidy bun, and there were dark circles under my green eyes. Yep. Today was definitely going to be a lazy day. I wasn't fit for company. Meandering into the bathroom, I washed my face and teeth. I was about to go hunt down some coffee when a flash of red caught my eye.

I did a double take.

*Tell me I'm hallucinating.*

Zoe stood in a pair of red shorts on my balcony, smiling with two cups of coffee. Behind her was Zach, leaning on the banister with a lazy grin—the dynamic duo. I blinked a few times, before I realized this was no sleep-deprived hallucination, and walked to the double doors, slowly opening them. "To what do I owe the pleasure?" I asked.

Zoe handed me a cup and swept past me. "School is in session, sweetcakes."

My caffeine-addicted brain only processed the fact that she was offering me my fix. It wasn't until after I scalded my tongue on the first sip that I realized she had said something. I struggled to recall what those words had been. One stuck out, and it was enough to make me groan. *School.* My day of binge watching *American Horror Story* and vegging out on an entire bag of Doritos had just backfired. "You're joking, right? It's summer vacation."

Zoe grabbed a set of textbooks and notebooks from Zach and set them on my desk. "And you've missed an entire lifetime of reaper law and order. You're about to get a crash course."

I tapped my thumb against the white paper cup. "And you both got stuck with the daunting task. Sorry." I didn't know anybody who wanted to tutor for the summer.

"Don't sweat it," Zach said, spinning the desk chair around and straddling it. "It beats working at the Black Dog. And under all Zoe's hairspray and mascara, she's really a nerd at heart."

Zoe scowled at her twin. "Not all of us fail so easily."

"Is there going to be a test?" I asked drolly.

"An oral." Zach added with a smug smile.

I fought the grin that tugged on my lips.

Zoe whacked him on the back side of his head. "Shut up, sexpot. Not every word has to be turned into something sexual."

"Yeah, it does," he muttered. "I'm a guy."

"And that explains your IQ," she huffed, planting her butt down on the edge of my unmade bed.

Zach frowned.

As entertaining as the twins were, I'd been kidding about the whole test thing, but this sounded worse. "What kind of oral?" I asked, joining Zoe on the bed.

She beamed, and I immediately knew I wasn't going to like this. "At the ceremony. The elders and overlords will be eyeballing you—judging you—waiting for you to make the teeniest of mistakes."

I felt the color drain from my face. "What ceremony?" This was news to me. Nobody had said anything about a ceremony. It sounded formal. I hated formal.

Zach flashed me another smile. "The one where you're crowned by the divine as the new White Raven. And you can bet your butt they will also be announcing your engagement to Zander. The wedding of the century."

If I didn't know better, I would swear Zach was enjoying this, watching me squirm. "Please tell me I haven't woken up yet, that my hair really isn't this messy, and I'm dreaming this whole thing."

"You, my friend, are very much awake. Here, let me show you." Before I knew what Zoe's intent was, she pinched me.

"Ouch," I shrieked, glaring.

"See. Not dreaming."

"Thanks for clearing that up," I grumbled, rubbing the flabby skin under my arm.

"But don't worry. That's what we're here for—to make sure you don't make a fool of yourself." Grinning, Zoe settled back into her spot on the bed. I thought about pushing her off.

Oh, goodie. Their confidence in me was overwhelming.

"Before we get to the nitty-gritty stuff, let's start with the basics," she said.

"No chance I can finish my coffee before the lightning round?" I asked, taking a swig from the cup in my hand.

Zoe watched me under lush, long lashes. "Reapers are angels, but we serve death. We're the essential ingredients required for death to occur. Whether a human life ends from an accident or through natural causes, we are in charge of their souls. And each sector plays its part in maintaining the natural order of things. What are the four sectors?"

This I actually knew. "Death, soul, phantom, and banshee."

"And they are each represented by?"

I twirled the paper coffee cup in my hand. "A black crow, blue sparrow, red hawk, and white raven."

"Obviously, crows are the deadliest," Zach added.

I rolled my eyes. "That goes without saying."

"Crows," Zoe interjected in her best teacher voice, "are the only reapers who can destroy a soul. And I mean destroy. No Heaven. No Hell. The majority of the souls we reap are hallows—malevolent souls that refuse to leave this realm peacefully. We're considered assassins. The essences of the souls we take fortify our powers, making us stronger. Unlike some of the other sectors, Crows are born reapers."

Zach leaned forward in the chair. "A Soul Reaper governs the souls between the human world and the afterlife. A simple touch sends their soul to either Heaven or Hell. Soul Reapers do not, however, possess the power to make a soul go with them. Sparrows is the only sector with mixed blood, meaning not all are born. Some are chosen."

My brows furrowed. "Chosen by who?"

"By you," she said.

I squeezed the cup, splashing a few dribbles of hot coffee on my hand. "You've got to be kidding me."

"Did you burn yourself?" Concern etched into the lines of Zoe's face as she passed me a napkin.

Setting my addiction aside, on the table, my back straightened. "Spilled coffee is the least of my concerns. Can we back it up a minute? I'm a little confused over the part where I choose who becomes a reaper."

"Someone has to do it."

"Why does it have to be me? How do I even decide such a thing?"

Her shoulders rose and fell in a shrug. "Beats me. I just know it falls under your jurisdiction, babe."

"Wonderful. Another thing I get to fumble through." As teachers went, Zach and Zoe kind of sucked. It gave me the heebie-jeebies imagining someone's destiny in my hands. I didn't want to play God. Could I turn just anyone into a reaper? Like the elementary school bully, Melissa Turner, who used to constantly pick on Parker? I'd have to give this more thought.

"You're getting off track," Zoe said. "We have stuff to learn, like your two bodyguards outside for instance."

Zach rolled his eyes. "This is supposed to be about Piper, not you trying to get a date."

"You mean Agent Lame-o and Agent Killjoy patrolling the grounds?" I supplied to be clear.

"Phantoms," Zach corrected. "Hawks can assume any living form, animal or human, and they mark a human for death. Their orders come from Death himself."

I folded my legs pretzel style. "Your father."

"The one and only. We don't interfere with humans' lives, not until we're needed. We have the power to kill before their time, but it's forbidden. Of course, not all reapers follow the rules. Rogue reapers, as you know, exist. They seek power and profit, often working with higher beings. Each sector has an overlord, someone who supervises the reapers under their command. There is a pecking order of power. White Raven at the head, followed by Black Crow, then Blue Sparrow, and lastly Red Hawk."

Why did I have to be at the top? It felt wrong. I knew virtually nothing. How could I be fit to govern a community?

"Don't look so forsaken. Your power comes naturally, as does your ability to rule. A banshee's voice—*your* command—is almightiness. All reapers must heed your call. But your greatest power is the ability to create other reapers. The uniqueness of a banshee differs from one Raven to another. The gifts of your mother or grandmother will be different than yours. It's what makes the White Raven such a mystery. Not even the elders know what you will be capable of."

"I don't know if that is better or worse—not knowing what I can or can't do."

"You'll be tested in training with Zane. He'll help you figure out what your strong suits are, where your powers excel."

"Zane," I echoed. "He mentioned something the other day," I quickly added to cover up the dreamy quality that might have entered my voice. Could I be any more transparent in my affections ... or more lame?

Her lips twitched. "Now suddenly I have your attention."

"I don't see what all the fuss is with *Zane*." Zach gooed over his name in his sad attempt to imitate a thirteen-year-old girl. "He isn't the only Hunter with skill."

I was not a pathetic fangirl oohing and aahing over Zane Hunter. Okay, fine. I did have moments where the sight of him made me think I was going to swoon like I was in a 1950s film.

Zoe gave him the reaper stink eye, and in my book, it was more effective than the everyday stink eye. "Like she had a choice," she retorted. "If she did, she wouldn't have picked any one of you douche-canoes."

I busted out laughing. Once the laughter started, I couldn't control it. I clasped my gut, my cheeks aching. "That was the funniest shit I've heard in days," I said when I was able to speak coherently.

Zoe set her coffee cup on the floor and looked me in the eyes. "I'm going to give you a bit of friendly advice. When you first came here, I thought it was cute and cheeky that Zane instantly intrigued you. And I might have even encouraged you, but only in fun. I swear, Piper, I had no idea what you were to Zane. If I had known ... honestly, it wouldn't have made a difference. The link between you and Zane can't be controlled or reversed. I know it sucks some serious dookie and is screwing with everyone's life. I just want you to know that I will support you no matter what. Zach and I both will." Her eyes moved to her brother who was spinning in the chair. She cleared her throat when he didn't say anything. "Right, Zach?"

"Whatever you say, Zoe."

"Imbecile," she muttered under her breath. "Do you see what I have to live with? Being the only girl in a house full of no brains and all muscle?"

"We all have our struggles. It means a lot to me, having your support. Can I ask you a question?"

"Anything," she replied.

"Oh boy," Zach said. "Way to open a can of worms."

"What would you do?" I asked, ignoring him.

Her sapphire eyes weren't dancing with their usual laughter. "I can tell you that I don't envy you. Not in the least. It's hard to think about the situation objectively, considering we're talking about my two older brothers." Her face puckered. "But let's say we were talking about Liam and Chris Hemsworth. Now there is a perfect dilemma to be sandwiched between."

No arguments there.

"And the world's balance was more or less dependent on my choice. Easy," she continued. "I'd have my cake and eat it too. Marry for duty and have a lover."

I should have been floored, but I wasn't. "Let me get this straight. You'd marry Liam, but take Chris as your lover?"

Zach snorted, shifting his tall body in the chair. "I can't believe I'm even hearing this."

Zoe ignored him. "No. You got it backward. I'd marry Chris, but take Liam as my lover."

"Yeah, that's so not an option for me. I have a feeling neither Zane nor Zander would go for that."

She pressed her lips together. "Most definitely not. They'd destroy each other before sharing something as important as you."

My shoulders slumped as I drew in a breath of air. "I don't have it in me to live a double life and be torn in half. I would screw it up somehow."

"I wish I had the answer."

"No matter what, someone gets hurt."

"Welcome to my world. Fate's a hag." A hint of her Gaelic accent peeked through.

I dangled one of my legs over the side of the bed. "I think your world needs to step into the twenty-first century. What happens if I refuse to marry Zander? I'm not saying I will. I'm curious. What's the worst that can happen?"

Silence descended over the room.

Not encouraging.

"An uncontainable uprising of Death's greatest weapons," Zach supplied.

That secret bubble of hope I was harboring crashed and burned. "That seems a little extreme."

"You asked," he muttered, seeing the crestfallen expression on my face.

"Even the greatest man can be clouded by the insatiable need for power," Zoe said. "And reapers aren't exactly considered good, so it's not hard for us to be tempted. As more and more of the elders die off, the push for change becomes louder. It's getting to the point where the voices can't be silenced, and as the word travels with the promise of power, more and more reapers are joining the uprising."

"And those voices think annihilating the Raven line is the first step to gaining more power," I concluded.

Zoe's eyes brightened. "You got it, girl. No one has more power than you."

"That's the joke of the century," I muttered.

She adjusted the thin white strap slipping down her shoulder. "Give it a week and I'll be saying I told you so. If anyone can bring out your powers, it's Zane."

That's what I was afraid of.

––––––––

THE TIME HAD COME. I could hear the bells of doom ringing in my ears —*dun, dun, duuuun*—taunting me as I readied myself to tell TJ he was leaving. But first, I needed to make a call I'd been dreading for days. I couldn't send my brother away without knowing he would at least be okay and taken care of. A sense of loneliness overcame me. I took a few deep breaths before stiffening my jaw. It had to be done.

Groaning, I hit the contact for Dad and waited for the line to ring. I didn't know if I would be more disappointed if he didn't pick up or if he did. My stomach sunk when I got his voice mail. Shocker.

"I grow tired of talking to your voice mail, Father. This is important. I need you to pick up TJ and take him home. I don't think I need to tell you why, other than it's not safe. Call me." My fingertip pressed the end call button, and I tossed my phone aside. That hadn't gone quite as intended, but onto the next dirty deed.

I rolled off the bed and meandered through the halls, taking my sweet time as I gathered the right words. There was going to be nothing easy or pretty about this conversation, so the plan was to be straightforward. I was going to come right out and tell TJ he had to go.

Plans never went as I expected.

My knuckles rapped on the door to his room. And I waited. And waited. My knocks got louder to no avail. Finally, annoyed and more than a little bit concerned, I turned the handle, relieved to find it unlocked, and let myself in.

*He better not be lounging around in his birthday suit or doing some equally gross teenage boy thing.*

The jerk was kicked back on the bed with his earbuds in and the tunes cranked. I could hear the music from across the room. His sandy hair looked like it could use a deep conditioning, and his room smelled like three-day-old pizza and sweaty socks.

I fought the urge to gag and pinch my nose.

Teenage boys were so gross.

I kicked the frame of his bed with the heel of my shoe and crossed my arms, waiting for him to get a clue.

His eyes popped open, big chocolate saucers. "What the hell, Piper!" he yelled. "Get out of here."

I snorted. "I'd like to see you make me." Okay, that was a totally childish response, but sometimes I needed to get down to his level for him to hear me.

He ripped the headphones from his ears, bolting upright on the bed. "What gives?" His voice returned to a normal volume. "Did you come to annoy me?"

"Pack your crap," I said, glancing around the pigsty he lived in. "You're going home."

"We're leaving? But I thought—"

"You thought wrong. Dad is meeting you on the main island in two days to take you home." *And better flipping be there.*

"Just me?"

"Yep. For now," I added. It was probably cruel giving him false hope, because something told me that when I said good-bye to TJ, it would be for good. Our worlds were no longer parallel.

"No freaking way. No. Not happening. If you're staying, then so am I." His belligerence was anticipated. "Summer is not even over," he argued.

"Under the circumstances, there's no reason for you to stay."

"Good thing you're not the boss of me."

"But Dad is," I countered.

He stuck out his bottom lip in a pout that used to be adorable when he was four. "It's not fair. You get to stay so you can make out and play tonsil hockey with your boyfriend, and I get sent back to live with Dad."

Again pangs of guilt hit me. If the roles were reversed, I would be pitching a fit. "I don't have a boyfriend," I argued.

He gave me a look that clearly called me a liar. "What I want doesn't matter, does it?"

I crossed my arms. "Of course it does. Believe it or not, I'm doing this for you."

"That is such a parental cop-out. When did you become so lame?"

*Ouch.* He was lashing out, and I couldn't blame him. I would take it as long as it got him off this forsaken island. "Look, TJ, I'm sorry," I murmured, genuine regret in my voice. "But I've got to stay and take care of a few things. Don't you want to see your friends?" I asked, hoping to give him something to look forward to.

His puppy eyes brightened a bit. "But you're coming home?" he asked, scooting to the end of his bed so his legs swung over.

I chewed on my lip, trying to find a clean spot to stand. This was the hard part. I had no idea when I would go home again ... if ever. Loose wisps of hair tickled the back of my neck as I nodded.

*Liar. Liar. Liar.*

My subconscious could be such a downer.

"Whatever," he said sarcastically. "It's not like I ever get a say in anything about my life." He stuck his earbuds back in, flopped down on the bed, and went back to ignoring me.

"Glad we had this talk," I mumbled, venturing over the scattered filthy clothes, a skateboard, and empty bottles of Gatorade to make my way to the door. At least he was staying hydrated while he holed away in his room.

*Two days*, I told myself. *He will be safe and off this island of death.*

What could happen in two days?

# CHAPTER 7

Because I had nothing better to do on a Saturday night, I flounced around my room, gathering all the discarded dirty clothes. I needed to do some monotonous work, like laundry. With my earbuds in, pumping classic eighties rock, I padded down the hall in my socks and dumped a load into the washer. Since I was already on a roll, why stop at laundry?

Why not make a night of it?

*Woo-hoo. Domestic party at the manor. Come one; come all. And don't forget to bring the disinfectant wipes.* If Parker could see the club-hopping, angry-at-the-world girl now ... he would think I was on drugs.

Breaking out the Windex and Endust, I started to go to work on my room, leaving no spot untouched, all the while singing completely off-key. *"Love is like a bomb, baby, c'mon get it on. Livin' like a lover with lah lah phone ..."*

Who actually knew all the lyrics word for word? I might not, but when it came to classic rock, I fully committed. Using the bottle of glass cleaner as an imaginary mic, I slid across the floor in my best Tom Cruise *Risky Business* move. I killed it. *"Pour some sugar on me, ooh, in the name of love. Pour some sugar on me, c'mon fire me up."*

Warmth spread down my neck. *Man, it's hot in here.* Tugging my oversized T-shirt over my head, I spun around in nothing but my bra and locked eyes on Zane.

A shriek rose up my throat and echoed over the room.

"Don't stop on my account. You were on a roll," he said in a deep, amused timbre.

My foot slipped on the newly polished hardwood, and my butt cheeks smacked the floor. "Holy hell," I said, clutching my shirt to my chest. "Are you trying to kill me?"

"Did you just break your butt?"

"No, but I'd like to break yours," I growled.

Leaning a hip against the wall, his eyes twinkled. "That was quite … I'm not sure what it was, but I don't think I will ever get it out of my head, though my ears are still ringing."

I wished I had something else in my hand other than my T-shirt to throw at his head. "Hardy har har. Are you going to help me up or just laugh at me all day?"

He pushed off the wall and lent me a hand. Without hesitating, I placed my hand in his. Electricity shimmered down my arm. There was no denying the attraction, and when I was staring at him, I didn't care if it was our souls or something more—the pull wasn't going to let either of us go. I wasn't sure how much longer I could resist, especially if he kept looking at me like that.

"Nice getup." His eyes swept down my body. He took a step forward, putting me in the same breathing space as him.

A flush crept over my body, not missing a single part. I glanced down and hissed, completely forgetting I was standing in front of Zane half naked. Heat stained my cheeks and my head snapped up. "I hate you."

The tips of his fingers airily trailed up my arm. "We both know that's a lie."

I smacked his hand away. "And if it is … what are you going to do about it?" I was challenging him. I knew it. He knew it.

Zane didn't disappoint.

The smugness stretched across his face. He reached out, pulling me up against his chest. "Is this what you had in mind?"

We didn't have the luxury to explore what could bloom between us— if *we* were even a possibility. Yes, the physical attraction was explosive, but it took a whole lot more than desire to make a relationship work. Outside the bedroom, I wasn't sure Zane and I could function. I spent as much time thinking about ways to hurt him as I did ways to get him alone.

Fire snapped in my eyes. Visions of me leaping into his arms and Zane kissing me senseless danced in my head. "Not quite," I murmured.

"How about this?"

I tried to ignore the cool fingers sliding over my ribs, leaving behind a blissful numbness. My eyes were drawn to his lips. "I never would have taken you for a tease." I tried pulling back, but his hands were suddenly secured at my hips, keeping me from putting even an inch of space between us.

Wowzers. He smelled so good, like a mix of frost and the ocean breeze. My heartbeat sped, thudding in my ears.

One of his hands slid to the small of my back, and a spark ignited at the touch of skin against skin. His heartbeat quickened with mine. "What makes you think I'm teasing?"

Because he still hadn't kissed me yet. I raised a brow, outwardly calmer than my insides. "I don't know. Why do you keep touching me?"

"I want to, even though I shouldn't." His warm breath stroked my chin.

I swayed toward him, my skin trembling under his touch. Not a good sign. What I should have done for both our safety was stomp on his foot and demand he get out. My heart and body overrode my rational mind. "What are we going to do about it?" I asked.

His head dipped and our lips met. My shirt slipped through my grasp, falling to the floor as my mind clicked off. What did I need clothes for? All the closer I could get to his mind-blowing abs.

Our chests touched, and suddenly I was kissing him as if we were going to become one soul. I no longer cared if he answered the question, only that he was making me feel all the feels. Oh God, I sank into his lips, tasting the increasing seduction that sparked rapidly.

His fingers pressed against my back, pulling me closer to him and changing angles. I was lost. Floating in a space where sensation ruled, blurring the mind and enchanting the body. I surrendered to the sensations he drew inside me, giving myself absolutely to his lips conquering mine.

The softly lit bedroom transformed. Gray shadows silvered at the edges with moonlight. Every tender touch, each deep kiss reached my singing soul. I could only imagine he felt the same. His arms wrapped around me, cool and comforting—a herald of safety. I drew in a death breath, letting the dark scent of him surround me.

"We can't do this, Piper," he whispered, grazing his lips along my throat, lacing conviction.

"Yes, we can," I muttered, covering my mouth with his in another kiss. "If you stop kissing me, so help me, Zane, I'll assassinate you." I scraped my teeth over his lower lip, in case he got any ideas, but his willpower surpassed mine.

He pulled back slightly, and I could see a war waging behind his eyes. It only took seconds to realize it was a battle neither of us would win. A range of emotions surged through me. Frustration. Shame. Need. Guilt. Anger. Yet overpowering them all was the fear he would let me go.

Zane straightened, coming to his full height. A muscle popped out at his jaw as he tried to gain control of his emotions. That made two of us. As long as we were touching, it became increasingly difficult. His hands dropped from my waist, and he looked away, dragging his fingers through his hair. "This can never happen again. I can't—"

Regret eked inside me. As much as I wanted to hate him, I couldn't. I understood, but it didn't stop the swell of anger. I had to take all this hurt out on someone. "You've said that before." Practically every time we'd kissed. It was getting old.

"I know. And I'm sorry. I don't want to hurt you, and if we keep doing this, it will only cause you more pain."

I hit him with a dirty look. "This connection between us sucks. I didn't ask for this."

"It's not something that can be turned off, Piper." He picked up my shirt from the ground and tossed it to me. "You should put this on."

I caught the shirt and roughly pulled it over my head. "Whatever. We'll pretend this never happened. I'm going to blame it on the after-effects of Rose's death. Obviously, I'm not in the right state of mind." My hands became animated. "In fact, you should stop showing up in my room whenever you get an itch."

His brows pulled together. "Look, I'm not saying we can't be friends, because we're going to be family whether we like it or not. And I made a vow of duty. No matter what, I'll be in your life."

The vow.

I'd almost forgotten about that. The sworn bond that allowed him to sense when I was in danger. How many different ways could Zane and I intertwine our lives? All but the one I actually wanted.

"And what if I don't want you in my life? What if it's too hard?" I started to turn around, but before I could take a step, he was in front of me. I swore he did that to get under my skin.

Zane's eyes flashed. "You're a terrible liar."

"And you're a terrible friend."

"I deserve that. But it doesn't change the fact that you *do* want me."

Taking a deep breath, I struggled with my temper. Anger was the only outlet to release the flare-up of hormones he enticed. One minute he was telling me to stay away, and the next he was kissing my brains to mush. "Why are you here? Or did you just come to torment me?"

His blue eyes were bright as he stared at me. "You make it seem like I take sick pleasure in hurting you."

I raised a brow. "Don't you?"

He snorted. "Hardly. You're not the only one who suffers. We just deal with it differently. I can admit that I want you more than I've ever wanted anything in my life. You're beautiful. But ... your safety comes before my wants."

My mouth opened, but nothing came out. Hearing him admit that he wanted me took my breath away. Yes, I felt it, but hearing the words had an entirely different effect on my body. I swallowed. "What about what I want? Doesn't that count for something?"

He grinned. "I thought you didn't want me."

I rolled my eyes. "If we're going to keep things in the friend zone, you have to stop doing that."

His cool breath washed over my heated face. "What?" he replied, feigning ignorance.

It wasn't cute. "I don't know. Whatever this is you keep doing. Flirting with me. Giving me those looks. Touching me."

"It's a lot harder than it sounds," he murmured in all seriousness.

Eventually, something was going to have to give. We were either going to have to admit what was brewing between us or stop seeing each other, because I wasn't positive how much of the yo-yoing I could handle. Looking at him, my heart toppled, and I didn't see how we could be only friends. The feelings I had for Zane were deepening by the day, the hour, the minute.

"You never told me why you came," I said, changing the topic before my lips decided to go back for seconds ... and thirds.

He backed up a few steps, giving us both air to breathe. "Tomorrow your training begins. I wanted you to understand what will be expected of you and how we're going to avoid merging our souls."

"Can't wait," I grumbled, walking to the double doors and stepping outside. The summer night air was what I needed to clear the last remnants of Zane from my head. I lifted my face, letting the silvery moonbeams wash over me. "What's the plan, Teach?"

He stood beside me on the balcony overlooking the gardens. "We'll be around other reapers who are training and sharpening their skills. As long as we make sure you combat against them, we should be okay."

"But not you?" I asked, turning my head slightly toward him.

He looked dangerous under the moonlight. "No. I will be there to instruct you, guide you, but using our abilities at the same time could expose the link between our souls."

And for reapers, it was all about the soul. It might have sounded like a piece of cake, but I learned that the easier something appeared, the more difficult it actually was. "Right. That would be disastrous. Why?"

"In the eyes of all the sectors, you're engaged to Zander. We must not do anything to entice doubt of your commitment to him."

I hadn't even come to terms with it. Here's to hoping those acting skills I learned in sixth grade drama class would come in handy. "And you think we can do this?" His confidence would put my rising anxiety to rest.

"I believe in you."

That made one of us. "Won't people think it's strange that I'm suddenly training?"

"Not at all. It's expected of you. You're the next White Raven. It's stranger that you haven't been training since birth." Zane's eyes flitted to the shadows seeping among the gardens below. "Time is essential. Like most secrets, they become exposed. It is only a matter of time before the sectors learn of Rose's death. Already there are whispers."

I was screwed.

"When you say *combat*, are you talking Jackie Chan?" I couldn't see myself as a fist fighter. I was more a hair puller.

"You have got to learn both offensive and defensive moves if you are going to battle against hallows. They aren't bound by the same laws of nature humans are. You need to learn to be faster, smarter, and lethal."

"In case you haven't noticed, I'm not a ninja."

He grinned. "Not yet, Princess."

*Grand.*

Like twilight, a serene silence descended between us. I have no idea how long we stood there, leaning on the banister, our arms brushed up against each other. An hour? Two? It didn't matter, because I felt an internal harmony I'd been missing my entire life. And here it was beside me in a six foot two, dark and dreamy form. Moonbeams framed my face as I glanced over at Zane. Where I attracted light, he was all darkness. Shadows congregated around him, swathing him in midnight.

"It's late." His voice broke the stillness, a trickle of his accent sneaking through. "I should go."

I nodded, because I was afraid if I opened my mouth, I would ask him to stay. And even more afraid he would say yes.

As he turned to leave, a thought occurred to me. "Hey, what is the origin of your accent? I can't figure it out, and it's driving me bonkers."

His poetic lips curved at the corners. "Is it now?"

I didn't know if I liked the troublesome look that flashed in his eyes, but my blood started to sing. Then he was gone, leaving me wondering. *Damn him.*

Friends my butt.

# CHAPTER 8

**B**uzz. *Buzz. Buzz.* My alarm went off, announcing my day of training perdition was about to commence. After a quick change of clothes and a trip to the bathroom, I jumped into my jeep and headed to the Black Crow. Standing outside the seaside country club, I bit my lip, contemplating going home to binge watch Netflix with TJ.

Since telling TJ he was leaving Raven Hollow, he pretty much gave me a wide berth, grunting at me if we passed in the hall. I think we were both avoiding each other. I had my reasons, and I could only assume he was still pissed at me.

I shifted on my feet, squinting at the sun as I stared at the gray, weathered boards of the barn-like building. The Black Crow sign swung with the wind, its metal links squeaking as it moved back and forth. There was a distinct scent of salt in the air, and if I inhaled deeply enough, I could get a whiff of the freshly baked muffins from the bakery.

"Thinking about ditching?" a deep voice murmured in my ear behind me.

Ignoring the goose bumps skating down my neck, I gradually spun around. "At least I know you can't read my mind."

A slow, wry smile teased Zane's lips. "I'll only come after you."

I stared up at him, the sunlight highlighting his striking features. "That won't be necessary. So, is there like a secret, underground lair?"

Zane's lips pursed. "Come on. I'll show you."

"Lead the way." I pivoted on my heel, following Zane. Inside, rustic beams were exposed across the vaulted ceilings. The place had a sort of beachy southern charm to it—rustic chic as my mom would have said. We walked past the bar area toward the back of the club where the employee offices were located. Although the Black Crow had plenty of history to see, I couldn't take my eyes off Zane.

His dark locks were windblown as if he'd been out working on the docks. The sleeves of the Black Crow T-shirt he was wearing were cut off, emphasizing the strength in his arms. Just as my thoughts started to stray to less than friendly thoughts about Zane, we came to a door with a keypad on the wall. The buttons lit up in neon red as he punched in a five digit code. A series of clicks followed right before the door swung open to a narrow hallway.

He held the door open for me. "There's no need to be nervous," he said as I passed by, brushing his arm.

A thrill went through me. "I just don't want to make a complete jackass of myself."

His usual smugness oozed from his half smile. "Princess, that's inevitable."

In a jerk reaction, I punched him in the arm. "Thanks a lot. I feel so much better."

Unfazed, his grin only widened. "Save it for the ring, Rocky."

The hall led to a circular steel room with a set of stairs that led to what I guessed was a combat floor. A computer hub lined the wall to my left. Around the upper level was a sequence of large arched door-ways, opening up to other areas of … I had no idea what went on in those other areas. "What is this, the Batcave?"

"Something like that."

My gaze roamed to the other occupants in the room. I recognized only a handful, excluding my arrogant instructor. Aspyn was stretching her long legs on the mat. She caught my eye and winked.

Venus, the ginger skank, was whispering to a group of girls huddled below in a corner. We'd never officially been introduced, but I didn't need an introduction to know that Venus and I would never be friends. We both wanted the same guy. Her eyes went straight to Zane, glimmering with elation, only to turn to disdain when they landed on me.

*Wonderful.*

Another enemy. Just add her to the long list of reapers who wanted me dead.

I felt everyone's eyes on me the moment Zane and I proceeded into the room. We hadn't started and my head was already beginning to throb.

As we eased down the stairs, I let my hand trail along the metal railing. The lower level was cool and smelled slightly of my school gym. Not what I would consider a pleasant scent. And the memories associated with gym class were ones I'd rather never relive. Cushioned blue floor mats covered most of the floor and squished under my tennis shoes. We wove in and around reapers, careful to not disturb their routine or get accidently popped in the mouth by a flying fist. If anyone was going to get hurt, it would be me. And it was going to be something as simple and stupid as tripping over my own feet.

I should have been paying more attention to where I was going. As we passed Venus and her rotten groupies, I stepped on my shoelace, tangling my feet, and came inches from face-planting into the mats. A sharp pain shot over my ankle, and I winced. "Dammit." As first impressions went, I'd knocked it out of the park. Was it possible for me to start this day over?

Zane struggled and failed to keep the amusement off his lips. He extended a hand. "You okay?"

I burned him with a scowl and ignored the help, pushing myself up. "There was an invisible bump or something on the mat. I swear."

"Uh-huh," he stated, finally stopping at an empty spot in the corner. "You ready?"

I snorted. Did I look ready? My heart was jumping out of my

chest. Securing my hair into a ponytail, I cleared my throat. "So, um, what do I do?"

Zane smiled smugly. "First"—he tweaked the end of my nose—"we need to teach you the basics. Lesson number one: Never lose sight of your target."

"Thanks," I said drily. "I'll try to remember that."

"You have an overabundance of enemies now and learning to fight and how to use your inherited gifts will be crucial," he continued. "Even though I've taken an oath to protect you, I might not always get to you in time."

I nodded. I fully understood the danger I was in, and I could admit there was a sense of security and empowerment in the idea of being able to handle myself with more than snappy words.

He took a breath and backed up. "Now hit me."

"With pleasure." I took advantage of the moment and plunged forward, curling my fist and then hurling it into Zane's gut. *God, that felt good.* At least it did for about two seconds before the pain started radiating down my hand, but I kept a stiff lip.

"You hit like a girl, Princess."

I angled my head to one side. "How about that? I *am* a girl, in case you haven't noticed."

"Oh, I noticed," he said low enough for just my ears.

I felt myself blush and irritation flared deep inside me. "I need a few moments to warm up."

Zane chuckled, and he stalked forward, his face losing all amusement. "Warm-ups aren't a luxury in the real world." He slipped into predator mode and circled around me like a wolf. In the space of a blink, he was completely shrouded in darkness, and I broke the first rule: *Never lose sight of your target.*

I had failed.

A shadow licked out, morphing at Zane's command into a thin, sleek blade and slapping at my ribs. I shrieked, glaring as I felt the sting of absolute coldness thrash my skin. It was worse than frostbite. "Dammit, Zane, that hurt!"

He reappeared from the darkness with a humorless smile. "A piece of advice: Don't get hit, Princess."

Glaring, I stabbed him with a series of daggers. How was this going to make me a fighter? For a moment, I was tempted to tell him to bite me and stalk right out the door, but I swallowed my pride and faced him. Regardless of the welts I would have in the morning, I could take a few cuts and bruises if it meant saving someone I loved or myself.

"Stop thinking and let your natural instincts react. Thinking, even for only a moment, can get you killed." He crooked two fingers. "Again."

Bunching my muscles, I gave a feeble yell and lunged. He struck out with a sword formed from the shadows he manipulated. It cleaved through the air between us. I felt the burn on my forearm before I realized I'd been hit—a bolt of ice searing across my right arm.

I hissed, cradling my hand against my chest. "You asshole. I can't believe you cut me."

"I warned you."

For two and a half hours we practiced, and I'd only been able to hit Zane a handful of times and lost count how many swats I took with his shadowy weapons. I got hit a lot. The sting went through my clothes, but my butt wasn't as bruised as my pride. Disaster came to mind.

Anger came and went, flaring up each time Zane managed to smack me, leaving behind the icy marks of failure. I tried switching from defense mode to offense and back to defense in hopes of giving my skin a break. But it didn't matter. Zane adjusted, only attacking more.

"You're not playing fair," I said, finally snapping.

He folded his arms, the shadows humming behind him. "Fair? I thought I was clear. This is a lesson, not a game. Hallows don't play fair. They play to kill."

Fine. Point taken. Tired and cranky, I was ready to call it a day. I pinched the bridge of my nose, my ribs throbbing. "So far, all I've learned is how to take a beating … and that I'm probably going to die."

Zane's lip curled into a snarl. "That's not going to happen."

I wished I had his self-assurance. "Not even you, the dreaded Death Scythe, can predict my future."

He grabbed the tip of my chin between his fingers, examining my face. "You need to eat, gain your strength, and then sleep. We can pick it up tomorrow."

"Thanks, Mom," I snapped. "If I didn't know better, I would think you enjoy zapping me with your darkness."

"You're not quitting on me, are you?" he baited.

That was it. *Buckle up, buttercup. You just flipped my bitch switch.* Nails extended, I flew at Zane, intending to smack the calm expression off his face.

He snatched my wrist with one hand, midair, before it cracked across his cheek. The rage that had ignited inside me simmered at the surface as I stared him down. With a flick of his wrist, he tugged me closer, but I didn't go willingly. I struggled and cursed like a bloody rock star.

"What took so long?" He folded his muscular arms, stretching them across his Under Armour shirt.

I glared. "For me to realize you're a dick?"

There was a satisfying grin on his lips that made me immediately want to scratch his eyes out. "Nah. I think we both know you already figured that out. I was talking about the moment you let go and just reacted, allowing emotions to rule your actions."

My senses were buzzing from the anger and because Zane was still touching me. I stepped back, breaking the connection.

"Feelings are powerful, but they can also be dangerous if you don't know how to control them. There is *knowing* how serious this is and *believing* it. If I had wanted to, any of those hits could have ended your life. I could have taken your soul and absorbed your powers. In a fight like this, you can't afford to lose." The depths of his blue eyes said more than his words. He didn't want to lose me.

I swallowed a lump of emotion. He was right. I had much to learn.

I WASN'T sure what woke me. The cawing of a crow, the howling of the wind from off the oceanfront, or the funny smell that tickled my nose, but as I blinked, my room was quiet. I rolled to my side, glancing out the windows. The curtains were drawn and moonlight streamed in, casting gleaming shadows over the dark wood floors. I'd learned that things, both living and dead, lurked in the shadows.

As I swept over the room, I came in contact with eyes the color of dew-covered moss. An eerie sense of familiarity joined the nausea that began to roll through me. I clutched the blanket to my chin, reminding myself to breathe. Yes, there was someone in my room. No, it wasn't Zane. I was beginning to think my security system was fatally flawed. Two reaper break-ins this week.

Pushing the tangled hair out of my face, I sat up, squinting in the dark. The reddish glow glimmered in the darkness. "Crash?"

He took a long drag on his cigarette. "The one and only, doll." He exhaled, a billow of smoke filling the air.

*Glad we got that settled.* As I stared at him, his hip leaning against my dresser, I wondered if I was dreaming. This was the first time I'd seen Crash since that day in the parking lot when he'd offered me a smoke. "Um ... did I summon you?" It was a bad habit I'd recently acquired.

"Not that I know of. I couldn't sleep."

I tried not to be creeped out and keep my calm, but it was too late. "So, you thought it would be a good idea to break into my bedroom?"

With a flick of his finger, he dropped ash from his cigarette on my floor. "I was bored."

"Usually, when I'm bored, I don't invade other people's homes in the middle of the night. I mean it's"—I glanced at the clock—"three o'clock in the morning." I'd only been asleep for a few hours, being the night owl I was.

Everyone was wound up, waiting for a feud to break out between sectors, waiting for the restless spirits to descend upon us in a chain reaction the reapers couldn't control, waiting for me to take command. Was that why he was here? If so, which side did Crash stand on? Mine? Or the rebellion's? My mind started to go off in multiple tangents. Had something happened? Was Zane okay?

"What's wrong?" I asked.

He shook his head, wisps of his blond hair falling over his forehead. "Not what your pretty little head is thinking. Your boyfriend— or should I say boyfriends?—are just fine. Although, that's more than I can say about myself once they find out I was here."

I glanced sideways at my dresser, wondering how long it would take me to grab the blade I had hidden in the top drawer. I was pretty paranoid these days. "Okay, why exactly are you here?"

Crash's eyes met mine with a wealth of concern I had never expected to see on his scruffy face. "Have you seen Estelle?"

My curiosity was piqued. What on earth would he want with Estelle? And now that he mentioned it, I hadn't seen her in days, probably before Rose's death. "I'm sorry. If you came all the way here looking for Estelle, it was a waste of your time. As far as I know, she hasn't been to the manor in days."

Crash glanced out the window, letting out a weary sigh. "Damn."

I loosened my grasp on the blanket, letting it fall to my waist. "Is she missing?" This was unexpected.

"She hasn't been home in two weeks, which usually isn't cause for alarm. Reapers are known to come and go wherever the spirits call. But it's not like her to leave for so long without checking in."

"Estelle's a hawk." I racked my brain, trying to recall if I'd seen the mark on her wrist.

Pulling another long drag from his cigarette, he nodded. "She's my sister."

This was one of the strangest conversations I'd ever had in my PJs, and lately, that was saying something. "Why come see me?" I had my suspicions … dark and disreputable just like Crash.

One of his bushy brows arched. "You're a banshee."

I glanced down at my hands. "Uh, right. You want me to like summon her or something?" Wow, that sounded extremely lame. Time to shove my head under the covers and pretend this whole conversation never happened.

A nefarious grin started to spread on his lips, as if he knew what was going on inside my head. "Or something," he said.

I felt the need to be honest. "Sorry to have wasted your time, but you totally picked the wrong banshee. I have yet to master the whole beckoning of reapers." I could probably summon Zane in my sleep, but anyone else, not so much.

"You have power, Piper—a hell of a lot of power. Seeking one reaper should be a piece of cake. I suggest you start figuring out how to use your abilities before you find yourself in another unsavory situation. Rumors travel faster than truth."

I tilted my head to the side, watching him. *Did I sense an undertone of a threat in his words?*

He flicked his cigarette, crushing it into the floor with his boot and extinguishing the stick. "I'll give you a few days to sharpen your skills, and if Estelle hasn't popped up, your goons won't be able to stop me from finding you. We all have our special abilities."

Goody gumdrops. A threat and an ultimatum.

Before I could tell Crash to go suck a lemon, the veins around his eyes turned scarlet, cascading over his face. This was nothing new, a trait I was beginning to expect from reapers, but then his form began to ripple, liquefying and becoming transparent. I mean, I could literally see through him. Gawking, I edged forward on the bed, watching as Crash's body morphed into ... a snake?

Disgusting.

Stupefied, I blinked, suppressing the urge to squeal and run around the room like a chicken with its head cut off. My body shuddered.

I guess that explained how Crash was able to get inside.

So much for Zane's vow of duty. I thought he was supposed to get some kind of homing signal when I was in trouble. Or was it just only when someone had a blade to my throat?

I doubted I was going to be getting much beauty sleep after that. Since I knew I wasn't going to be able to go back to sleep, I shot out of bed and padded across the room. I checked every window and door, securing the locks. Even then, I was frazzled, so I did the one thing that calmed me at the wee hours of morning. I drew.

I flipped through my sketchbook, looking at how my drawings had changed. What used to be kickass anime girls with colorful hair and wicked blades had transformed into fifty shades of Zane.

I sighed.

# CHAPTER 9

"You look tired" were the first words out of Zane's mouth the
following day.

Gah. I wanted to throttle him. Today was not the day to
mess with me. Not only was I sleep-deprived and cranky—waking up
at the butt crack of dawn did that to me—today was also the last day
TJ was going to be on the island. I kind of wanted to throw up. "I
didn't sleep well."

Zane stretched, like a panther. "Too busy thinking about me?"

My short laugh came out louder and crazier than I'd intended.
"Not quite. I had a visitor last night."

"You never told me you were having a slumber party. And I wasn't
invited." He put his best put-out face on, but he looked ridiculous.

I pursed my lips. "*If* I was going to have a sleepover, I'd rather it be
you than Crash."

That got his full attention. About time. His gaze sharpened, the
hue of blue in his irises darkening. "Crash was in your room last
night?"

"Uninvited, I might add, just so we're clear." I scuffed my foot on
the mat, lifting my lashes to meet his sinister gaze. "And what the
heck? Where were you? Didn't you get my damsel-in-distress signal?"

"I was working," he stated flatly, steely eyes circling the room. "And I never sensed that your life was in danger."

It was easy to forget sometimes that when he said *working*, he wasn't talking about down by the docks. He had been reaping souls. "Who kicked the bucket?"

"A guy on the main island," he answered before his eyes found mine. "And stop trying to distract me. I'm going to kill him," he growled more to himself than me.

My sigh was audible. "I'm trying to stop you from going commando. It was no big deal." Or so I kept telling myself. "He was looking for his sister."

"Estelle?" The doubt in his voice went up like a red flare.

I nodded. "I guess he hasn't seen or heard from her in days and is worried. He came to the manor looking for information. I didn't have any."

He stared at me like I'd grown two heads. "And he just left … without trying to hurt you?"

I crossed my arms. "I'm still here."

"That's the point. It makes me wonder what he's up to."

"Does everyone have to have an objective?" I countered. "Could it be possible he is just worried about his sister?"

"He's a reaper." Zane's voice, grim and dark, made my blood freeze. "Not to mention a Hawk."

It seemed the phantom reapers had bad reps, but so did someone else … "And what makes him less of a threat than you?"

"I'm far more dangerous, Princess. But his father is the sector overlord, an elder, and very vocal in his aspiration for change."

My stomach pitted in tight coils. "Oh."

In this situation, it paid to know who your enemies were. I needed to learn who was who within the sectors, who abided by the laws of life and death and who wanted to rip my heart out. I needed to fully immerse myself in this world. I needed to push myself harder.

"The bastard's lucky he's not here," Zane seethed. I thought I detected disappointment.

Suddenly, Crash was the least of my worries. "Forget about Crash.

I'm here to be a ninja or some crap. So, what are we waiting for? Teach me. Everything."

Zane leaned a hip against the nearest wall, eyeing me. "Everything, huh? Where did this urgency and eagerness come from? Yesterday, I had to all but drag you in here."

I shrugged. "You reminded me how much I have yet to understand." *And lose.*

Dressed from head to toe in black, he took a step forward, shoulders squared and feet planted. "Then let's do this, *Princess*." His tongue rolled over the irritating nickname, goading me as the shadows trailing on the walls closed in around us.

"Oh, for the love of God. Please tell me I'm not going to spend the day dodging your sadistic methods of combat. I don't think my body can handle the torture, and so help me, if you tell me not to get hit, I'll cut off your balls."

He pinned me with a look that made me want to roll my eyes. "Lack of sleep makes you feisty. Good. You'll need it." He was suddenly in front of me, his fingers lifting up the end of my shirt, exposing my back.

I smacked at his hand. "This is not the time or place to cop a feel, comrade."

His hand dropped back to his side, eyes twinkling. "No marks. Your skin is as creamy as a newborn baby's ass."

"Oh, 'cause you've seen so many babies' butts."

"You heal. No harm done, except your pride."

"That's what you think," I mumbled. "My pride's just fine, but you could use a few blows to the ego. Then maybe you'd be less of a jerkface."

A black brow curved. "Let's refocus your energy. And you'll be happy to know I thought we'd try something different."

I squirmed in my workout gear, wondering why this sports bra was so constricting. My boobs couldn't breathe. "Right, because I did so exceptionally before."

His lips twitched, watching me fidget. "We need to figure out what supernatural abilities you have … other than being a smartass."

I kept my eyes on his and saw them sparkle a serene blue. "Well, that's easy. I'm not sure there's much I can do, except get myself in trouble," I mumbled.

"Not entirely true," he said. "You managed to take down a hallow on your own, absorb a reaper's soul, and you have no problem summoning me."

Yep. I had done all of that. "You're forgetting one key factor. I didn't do any of those on purpose."

He gently grabbed my arm, turning me toward him. "Whether you consciously meant to or not, some part of you knows what to do. We just need to get your mind to tap into that part."

I raised my head. "I'm trusting you."

Zane's eyes burned bright. "I'm the only one you can trust."

"As much as it hurts me to say it, you're right. Okay, Zaney, tell me what to do."

He blinked once. Then twice. I swear I saw him counting in his head before he spoke. "So, we know you have random bursts of power usually driven by strong emotion."

Yeah, like my life being threatened. "That's helpful. I still have no idea what I'm doing."

"Fear and rage seem to be triggers."

"I've no shortage of either emotion."

"That's what we're counting on," he said.

This time I rolled my eyes.

"As much as I would love to get in the ring with you, we need a guinea pig—another reaper for you to spar with and test out your control." He scanned the room, searching for an idiot dumb enough to let a novice like me experiment with possibly life-threatening powers.

But it was a logical idea, considering under no circumstances were we supposed to use our abilities together. Things happened, kind of like when they crossed streams in *Ghostbusters*.

Tension flitted through Zane. His eyes turned to slits, glinting with anger, and I knew something bad was about to go down. My body braced for God only knows what, I turned around, and the pressure that had been building in my chest deflated. A whoosh of air expelled from my lungs.

It was only Crash.

I'd been expecting … who knows, but bad habit guy wasn't it. "You gave me a heart attack," I said to Zane, whose eyes were zeroed in on Crash like he wanted to cause him severe bodily harm.

"Did I hear you're looking for—?"

Crash went from standing in front of us to being flat on his back in a span of two seconds. Zane was looming over him, ice crackling in his eyes. "I should kill you."

"What is your deal, mate?" Crash croaked.

"*My* deal?" Zane roared, teeth ground together.

Crash was on his feet again with Zane in his face. So much for flying under the radar. We now had the attention of the room, and my first response was to crawl under the mat or lock myself in a locker. I tucked my hair behind my ear, uncomfortable with all the eyes staring at me … as if I needed any more attention.

I wasn't looking for trouble, but trouble had a way of finding me. "Zane." I sighed. "We don't have time for this. We need to get to the *important* stuff."

I didn't know a whole lot about Crash other than he was rough around the edges and Zane disliked him—immensely. It was enough, however, to know those two traits didn't mix well, like oil and vinegar.

Zane spun around and fixed me with a glare that would have made most people shrink. "Piper, mind your own business."

"How is this not my business?" I barked.

"I'll deal with you in a minute." Eyes snapping in restrained anger, he gave Crash a humorless smile. "I warned you once to stay away from her. And you know I don't give second chances."

Crash backed up a step or two, but there was nowhere to go as he hit a wall. "So am I to assume you won't give me two seconds to explain?"

"You got that right." Zane sidestepped me as his hand curled into a fist and sunk into Crash's gut.

Groaning, Crash doubled over. "Is it necessary to hit me with such a glacier punch?"

Zane had this chill to his powers that froze blood. I shivered, thinking how cold he could be.

"I'm the son of Death. What were you expecting? Warmth and fuzzies?"

"I can see you're in a mood, but I can help you," he rasped. "You need me."

I held my breath, slightly afraid of what Zane might do next.

"Not *you*," he replied without hiding his distaste.

*Oh snap.*

Crash's smirk didn't budge as he straightened up, obviously aware Zane wanted to wipe his scruffy face across the floor. His gaze swept the room. "I'm the only one available."

There was something in his tone that suggested he knew more than Zane was comfortable with. I blinked, and Zane loomed over Crash, his back jammed to the wall. "Let's get one thing straight. I. Will. Never. Need. You."

In my school, if a fight was about to break out, everyone stopped and gawked. Nothing happened here. The volume didn't change, and no one batted an eye.

I cleared my throat, cutting through the heightened tension as the two meatheads glared in an epic stare down. "Guys, I'm not going to learn jack shit if you can't go two minutes without puffing out your chests and having macho moments."

Neither one of them reacted at first, and after what felt like a lifetime, Zane poked his finger into Crash's chest. "Good thing this isn't about you."

I assumed that was his way of saying we would accept Crash's offer to help, though I wasn't entirely sure there wasn't something in it for him.

Crash's green lantern eyes twinkled. "If it makes you feel better, I won't hurt her ... much."

Zane cursed, and I moved, blocking him from decapitating Crash. Standing between them probably wasn't the safest place, but in the heat of the moment, I didn't see how I had a choice. Someone had to keep these two from tearing into each other.

Turning my head, I glared at Crash. "Gee. Thanks, douche-canoe."

A spark of humor winked in Zane's eyes.

Crash's lips pursed. "Do you make that stuff up on your own?"

I sighed, my patience being tested. "It doesn't matter. Let's get started doing ... whatever it is I'm supposed to do."

The muscle below Zane's jaw throbbed. "Fine. Crash, you know what to do."

Before I even had a chance to respond, Crash moved, and from the corner of my eye, I saw Zane flinch. This wasn't going to test just me; it was going to test us both.

My blood pressure rose as my eyes fought to follow Crash's movements, but I was no match for his speed. As he bounded over the mat, white smoke swirled, blue light shimmered, and Crash became an animal.

A roguish-looking brown wolf with gold eyes threw back his head and howled. The ground shook under my feet, tipping over the water bottle I'd placed next to me on the floor. There was no denying the tremble of magic that shimmered in the air.

My mind was saying this was ridiculous. I'd never seen a wolf outside of a zoo, let alone a human turn into one. He bared his teeth. They looked very real. And very sharp. My heart flew into my throat. I didn't think Crash was going to hurt me, but the point of this exercise was to force my powers to the surface, and I guess we were going with fear as the trigger.

I gave Crash props for his commitment.

As the wolf stalked toward me, my instincts were screaming for me to run, fast and hard, but I kept my feet planted. I rolled my neck, loosening the tight muscles. *This should be fun.*

Half a scream escaped my mouth before the beast barreled me down, my back slapping hard against the mat, enough to stun me, knocking the wind from my lungs. Ignoring the pain pulsing throughout my body, I twisted and kicked. My reflexes sharpened. I stiff-armed the wolf in the muzzle as he snapped his jaw at my face.

An agonizing screech ripped from my throat.

"Use your inner strength, Piper, to stop him," Zane instructed.

No matter how much I bucked, the beast wasn't going anywhere. He was too big, too muscular. He had a paw on either side of my head, drool dripping from the corner of his mouth onto my neck, and the heat of his pants lapped over my face. I couldn't see a way out of this predicament. But that was my first problem. I was thinking like a human, not like a banshee.

And that was the moment I ceased my struggles. My poor body was spent anyway and welcomed the release. I used what energy I had left to lift my hand. Fear coated the back of my throat, but my wits slowly returned. My hand stretched out, locking onto the center of the wolf's underbelly. I was sweating and whimpering, but I held steady.

My whole body tensed with shock as prickling white tendrils of power radiated down my arm and past my fingertips. The wolf threw its head back, a mangled howl unleashing from its mouth. I watched enthralled as the white ribbons wove from my skin onto the wolf's, swarming his heart. Crash's animal form went stiff.

"Piper," Zane warned in the background.

I heard him, but his voice was as distant as if he was on the other end of an alley, but I understood why he was cautioning me. If I weren't careful, I could take Crash's soul. That was a sobering thought.

With more effort than it had taken to paralyze the wolf, I disengaged my fingers from the wolf's silky fur, but even as I let go, something was building inside me. It scared me. His head lolled to one side, and the weight of his lifeless body crushed mine. Unable to take the pressure building inside me, I screamed. Long and loud. *Whoosh.* Air expelled from my lungs in a force I didn't know was possible and hit the wolf in the chest.

His body went flying backward and landed several feet away. I scooted up, inhaling a shaky breath and staring at the unmoving animal form of Crash. My hands were trembling, not because I was afraid the wolf might wake, but of myself, of what I'd been able to conjure. I wasn't even sure what I'd done, but the magic of being a banshee sang in my blood.

I watched as the wolf's lean, yet robust, body wavered and slowly turned back into a man. "Holy crap," I whispered, stumbling to my feet. Several other curses were let loose.

Zane's smile was infectious, the little specks of blue in his eyes vibrant and alive. "Like a dull knife sitting in a drawer, you just needed to be sharpened up."

I didn't know whether to hate him or thank him.

Crash sat on the floor, appearing to have been knocked into a stupor.

*Clap. Clap. Clap.*

The sound came from behind me. I lifted my head, turning it over my shoulder to see a grinning Zander saunter down the metal staircase. He looked as if he'd just come from a business meeting, dressed in khakis and a button-down blue shirt, the sleeves rolled below his elbows.

"Wow. That's one heck of a sonic boom you got there," he complimented. "I think that's a first. I've never seen anyone actually force a shifter to change back to their human form."

*Is that what I did? Compelled Crash out of his wolf form? Huh.*

"She's a quick learner once she gets her bearings," Zane said. There was a hint of pride on his lips.

Zander's sky-colored eyes landed on mine. "Death will be pleased to hear you're progressing."

"Are you in charge of giving him my daily report?" I asked slightly snippier than I'd intended. In my defense, I was kind of shaken up. My hands trembled faintly.

"Weekly. Not daily."

With Zane I could always tell when he was being a smartass. I wasn't there with Zander. Or maybe I took Zander more seriously. Either way, a puzzling look furrowed my forehead as I sorted out how to respond.

"I'm kidding," Zander said before I gave myself a brain aneurysm.

"You done for the day? Or did you want to wipe Crash's face with the floor once more?"

"He's going to be okay, right?" I asked, glancing down again at Crash, who was staring off into la-la land. My fingers and arms were still tingling with a power that both frightened and thrilled me.

Zane gave a half-hearted shrug. "He'll live, if that's what you mean. And if he doesn't, no one will miss him."

My eyes tapered to a glare.

"He's joking," Zander assured me.

"Is he?" I mumbled, unconvinced.

"We can't really be sure, can we?" Zander winked.

"You'll want to do him in yourself, brother, once Piper tells you what Crash was up to last night," Zane blabbed.

I clenched my jaw. What a nark. "People in prison get shanked for less."

Amused, Zander started walking backward toward the stairs. "Then for Crash's sake, she better fill me in on the way."

The mysterious Irish lilt in his tone piqued my interest. "On the way where?" I asked.

"You'll see," he said.

Any place would be better than here. I was done with the training yard. "Now might be a good time to tell you I hate surprises." I glanced over my shoulder at Zane before we left. He was looming over Crash. Shadows surrounded him, so I couldn't see his face. As much as I wanted to get out of here, I thought twice about leaving him alone with a dazed Crash.

# CHAPTER 10

"How's it going? The training?" Zander asked when we were comfortably sitting in his car, a convertible of sorts.

"Just peachy," I answered, hanging my arm on the window ledge. "My butt has become quite acquainted with the mats."

Zander laughed softly. The balmy breeze played with the curls at the nape of his neck. "We've all been there."

Reaching behind my head, I tugged the hair tie from my ponytail and shook out my hair, letting the wind whip through it. "I find that hard to believe."

"Are you kidding? When we were growing up, Zane made it his personal mission to best me at everything."

That I could believe. "He does seem like a try-hard."

Zander laughed, and it was a nice sound. Just nice. No tingles. No heart palpitations. No blood rushing. Those were only reserved for the rare times Zane truly let go.

He pulled up to Inside Scoop, a local ice cream shop. Nothing fancy, only a walk-up window with outdoor seating, but the lack of bells and whistles had no impact on the taste or the local joint's popularity. TJ and I had come once for a nighttime treat. My little brother had a weakness for ice cream. I had a weakness for anything sweet. I wasn't picky.

"This *is* a nice surprise," I said, smiling.

His gaze flicked to the left, meeting mine. "I figured you deserved a treat. And it gives us a few minutes alone."

For more than a moment, I'd forgotten that Zander and I were supposed to be *seen* together. The smile on my lips lost some of its luster, but I kept it firmly in place. Then I saw the buckets of creamy goodness and my stomach rumbled. Any feelings I had about Zander and me took a back seat to ice cream. There were so many choices. Mountain berry, coffee and donuts, and my personal favorite, ooey gooey butter cake. I settled for a cherry vanilla waffle cone dipped in chocolate sprinkles. What was ice cream without sprinkles?

I trailed behind Zander as he steered us away from the cluster of empty tables and toward a spot under a tree. If it hadn't been for the fifties music playing softly in the background, the silence between us would have been unbearable.

Things were already strange between us. He was my fiancé, and I knew next to nothing about him, other than he was a reaper and had an extraordinarily hot brother—none of the little things like what his favorite color was or his favorite food. I didn't even know his middle name.

I dug into my cone like a girl who starved herself. Apparently I had worked up more of an appetite than I thought. And man was it delicious. He dipped his spoon into a cup of some strawberry shortcake concoction, and I wondered if he was the kind of guy who was okay with sharing food.

Glancing up, I found Zander watching me with a hooded smile. "What?"

"You have a little something just here," he said, using his index finger to indicate a spot below his lip.

I rubbed at my mouth. "Better?"

"Not quite." Smiling, he extended his arm, brushing the pad of his thumb at the corner of my lip. "Sprinkle."

Heat crept across my face. "Thanks." It was a different sensation having Zander touch me. There wasn't the instant zap that happened with Zane. This was much, much more subdued, but enough to tell me he wasn't human.

"We've never really gotten a chance to *talk*," he said between bites. "I know things have been crazy since you got here, and I imagine you must feel like your entire life has been shaken up in a cement mixer."

"That's one way of putting it," I said, taking a lick off the side of my cone, though my appetite seemed to have vanished thanks to my stomach being full of knots.

His back was pressed up against the tree trunk. "I don't want things to be weird between us or for there to be any misconceptions."

I could respect that and gave him props for being the kind of guy who was up-front. It was a quality I admired. "I don't want that either."

"Things are complicated for us. We never had a say in our future. Both of us are expected to do our duty. I'm not going to sugarcoat it and say it doesn't suck that you have a bond with Zane. I want you to know that I understand what is between you and him."

My lashes lowered, fanning over the tops of my cheeks. "At least one of us does, because it confuses the hell out of me."

He gave a short laugh. "I can see how it would. Even without the link between your souls, Zane is not an easy person to understand."

"Good, so it's not just me."

"No," he said, smiling. "My brother is … complicated."

I frowned. "That's putting it nicely."

He chuckled. "I guess it is. You're much easier to talk to when you don't have that wall up."

My tongue darted over the rim of the cone, licking a dribble of ice cream before it ran down my hand. "It's difficult to trust people. Lately, I never know who is going to stab me in the back. Literally."

"Understandable, considering who you are. But I hope, over time, I will earn your trust. I can be an ally if you let me. And a friend."

"I would like that." Seeing as we would be spending the rest of our lives together, it seemed wise that Zander and I be friends at the very least. It would make the years to come easier on both of us, and maybe … we would find more. However unlikely it seemed at this moment.

"Good. Then I would like to make a promise to you, and I hope you will do the same."

I was listening. I owed him that much.

"I won't lie to you, and I ask you to do the same. Even if you think it might hurt me or make me angry, I'd rather us be open and honest."

"I can do that."

"There is a lot of pressure on both of us, pressure neither of us asked for. And before things go any further, I need you to know—"

"Oh God," I interrupted. "You're in love with someone else?" My mind was jumping all over the place.

He chuckled. "No, Piper. There is no one in my life right now. What I was going to say is that I won't hold you to our engagement."

Air stalled in my lungs. "Huh? I don't think I understand."

He twirled his spoon around in the cup. "I've been thinking about it, about us, about our future. And I can't be the guy that you're stuck with. The guy you're forced to marry out of duty. I don't think either of us wants to be the runner-up spouse."

"Zander, I—"

"No lies, remember?" he interrupted.

I nodded, closing my mouth.

"Look, I'm not saying we call it all off and cause an outright panic or worse. I'm just saying you take a little time and think about what you want. And no matter what your choice is, I will support you and stand by your side. Friends?"

"Friends." He was impossible to dislike. I sat up a little straighter. "Do you honestly think there is a way to stop the uprising without us marrying?"

"I don't know. But I am willing to take the risk. For you," he said.

Feeling slightly off kilter, I asked, "Why would you do that?"

"Believe it or not, Piper, you have more people that care for you than you think."

"And your father is okay with this?"

Zander grinned. "Hell no."

The bubble of hope inside me that had been escalating deflated.

"Don't look so glum. He might be Death, but you're the White Raven. Whether you believe in yourself or not, your word is the ultimate ruling. And when do children ever do as their parents say?"

Zander had given me a lot to think about, though it was something I'd already been considering. Another way. "You're a good guy. Too good."

"That proves how much we don't know each other."

I didn't have the heart to tell him there was only room for one bad boy in the family, and he didn't qualify.

---

I WAS A GIRL NO MORE. From the evening my mother had died, my destiny had been sealed. Bound by blood and oath to protect what I was—a banshee—and rule. Come hell or high water, I was going to do my best to make Rose and my mother proud.

Even with the knowledge of what I was and the power still tingling on my fingertips, a part of me wanted to end my time on Raven Hollow—the girl inside me yearning for home, the familiar scents of cinnamon and apples, the worn couch in our small family room, and knowing Parker was downstairs if I needed a shoulder to cry on.

Yet, for the first time, both the woman and the banshee craved to be stronger. The taste of power was still warm in my blood and trembled to fully embrace what was mine by birth and right.

Still buzzing, I needed to feel free, not cooped up in the manor. So I steered my jeep toward the ocean in search of seclusion and myself.

The water, the quiet, and the gentle rocking of the waves reminded me of the last time I'd had a truly happy day with my mother.

She'd looked beautiful, I remembered, the firelight casting a glow over her skin. The whole family had been there, including Parker, sitting around the fire on our roof deck, roasting marshmallows and listening to my parents take turns telling tales of their youth—how they met and such.

I'd never imagined in less than a month she would be gone from my life forever. Killed by the very thing she'd run from—had hidden from me my entire life.

A prickle skirted down my spine as I dug my toes into the sand, resting my chin on my knees, and a great need to see her one last time overwhelmed me. The water lapped over my feet, and I stared into the deep blue ocean.

My mother smiled at me.

I blinked.

Her shining emerald eyes shone over the calm waters. Those eyes became her face, and then she was walking out of the sea-foam straight toward me.

"Mom?" I asked hesitantly. I knew to not always trust my eyes. I'd had a similar vision once, which turned out to be a Red Hawk hell-bent on killing me.

The Hawk had met an unfortunate demise, and I'd taken her soul.

I slowly pushed myself to my feet, careful not to make any sudden movements. "Is it really you?" I choked, disbelief clouding my eyes. I expected any second for her pretty face to morph into someone else's.

She nodded, her face glowing in the moonlight.

"How is this possible?"

"Your powers and your great need to see me brought my spirit." The sound of her sweet voice was just as I remembered.

Tears wanted to come, blurring my vision of her as she wavered in front of me. I willed them away, needing to see her clearly. Blonde hair fell freely down her back, her eyes filled with love. And the power I never knew she possessed surrounded her. I felt it.

"Why did you never tell me what I was?" It was the one question plaguing my mind, but I never thought I would get the chance to ask.

The lines she always used to complain about around her mouth softened. "Oh, my love, my sweet girl. I wanted nothing more than to keep you from this world, and it was naïve of me to think you could escape destiny. Or that I could run from mine."

Motherly instinct to protect her daughter, I understood, but I had always thought our relationship had been more than that. She had been my best friend. "Why didn't you fight them, fight to stay with me?" I didn't know the exact details of what had happened the night she'd been murdered, only what the police had told my father, but I realized now, it wasn't the truth.

"If I could have, I would have given up more than my life, more than my powers. So much more to save you, Piper."

"I miss you so much."

I felt her lips on my cheek, her warmth as she enfolded me in her arms, and her scent, light and floral, flirted with the air. For just a moment, I closed my eyes and was a child again.

My chest ached. "I don't know what I'm doing."

In the mists of the ocean she glowed, silver-edged, veins white like mine. "Remember you are not alone. I am ever with you, in your blood, in your heart, in your power. You will know what to do when the time comes. Trust your heart."

My heart? What was she saying? "I want to be brave and strong like you and Rose. I will be, for TJ. I will protect him. I swear it. But I'm scared. I don't want to fail."

"We all have fears and regrets. Use that fear to harvest your powers. You're not just a banshee. You're the White Raven."

"Everyone keeps telling me that, but I don't know what being a banshee means."

"I renounced my heritage, refused what was mine by right. I can only say how sorry I am for hiding what you are. I wanted to give you a happy life, free from death and the darkness for as long as possible. I wanted to give you the light, my daughter. And when the time came, I would have let you choose." She held out her palm, her veins shining through the mist.

I joined my hand with hers, feeling a quick jolt of energy. "I don't think I would have chosen this."

She smiled. "And what of Zane?"

My eyes widened. "You know about Zane and me?"

"I can see what is in your heart. Your soul calls to his. Together you're more powerful. You'll protect each other. Trust what you are. It is enough."

It seemed so simple. A wave rushed over my ankles, splashing up over my legs, and just like that, the vision was gone, as was my mom. Seeing her disappear again was painful, but it had been an opportunity I'd never thought I would have, at least not while I was still breathing.

*I will be brave*, I thought, staring at the surf washing up on the sand at my feet.

Turning my arm over, I studied my wrist—the mark gleaming bright under the high moon. I would be strong. And one day soon I'd be strong enough to lead. But I still longed for more time. The vision had come and gone too quickly, so many questions unanswered. Was my mother implying I should go against the oath Rose had made to unify my bloodline with Zander's? Was she telling me to find a way to be with Zane? Trust my heart, she had said.

My heart wanted Zane. There was no doubt about it.

I stood overlooking the water, the shine of it now gleaming under the fullness of the moon. I thought about my mom, the sound of her voice, the scent of her hair, and my heart pinched.

As I started back to my car, I heard the high, sharp cry of a hawk, a reminder I was never truly alone. Except tonight, her words would also stay with me. Smiling to myself, I touched the amulet, which had been hers, now hanging around my neck. It was cool against my skin and carried the image of a raven.

"I will get stronger," I murmured, my voice drowned out by the waves, and then started the trek back to the jeep.

# CHAPTER 11

**D**oomsday.

At least that was how TJ felt. He stood on the manor's porch like a sad puppy dog, and the emotion in his brown eyes tugged at my heart. I was an anxious wreck. So far today I'd bumped my knee into the dresser—twice—got shampoo in my eyes, and spilled hot coffee down my shirt all before noon. It was going to be that kind of day.

TJ dragged his duffle bag across the driveway. "This is total bullshit."

"Welcome to life," I mumbled, jumping into the driver's seat of my jeep. "At least it's a beautiful day," I said.

TJ tossed his bag in the back seat, shaking the car. "Who cares if the sky is blue?"

I scowled. "Are you really going to sulk and complain the entire way to the ferry?"

He hoisted himself into the passenger seat. "Is the sky blue?" he said drily.

I stuck the key into the ignition. "Smartass." The windows were open wide, letting the balmy breeze dance over my face. "It's going to be a scorcher today." Already I could feel little beads of sweat gath-

ering along my hairline. And if I had to fill the silence with meaning-
less chatter, I was going to torture us both. I understood he was salty,
but I didn't know what else to say. It might have been better to keep
my mouth shut, except I didn't want the last conversation with my
brother to be about nothing.

"At least you get to enjoy it. The rest of my summer will be filled
with smog."

"Stop acting like a tool. I would give anything to be going home," I
said wistfully.

TJ leaned his arm out the window, watching the landscape fly by.
"Good. Let's trade places."

"You want to be a girl?" I asked, hoping to draw a smile. I was
disappointed.

He continued to gaze at the scenery. "Now who's being lame?"

I sighed. "Trust me. I won't be lying out on the beach getting my
tan on."

He finally looked at me. "I know. It's just we haven't been separated since ..."

Since Mom died. I took my eyes off the road, glancing at him. "I
know. I'm not happy about it either."

"Dad's going to be there, right?"

"If he's not, we're disowning him," I said, hoping my unease wasn't
audible.

He let out a feeble laugh.

It was the longest and shortest ride of my life. My brain couldn't
seem to make up its mind whether I wanted to hurry up and get this
over with or drag out the good-bye. Shifting the car into park, I took a
long look at TJ, preserving his face in my memory. For once, he didn't
have an ill-humored comment.

Reluctantly, we climbed out of the jeep, neither of us in joyous
spirits. I didn't know who dragged their feet more.

Boats scattered the harbor, bobbing and gliding over the water.
The sea was a soft, dreamy blue with frisky waves that rolled up
against the docks. Any other day, I would have taken a moment to
appreciate the sheer tranquility and beauty of the ocean and the

endless rumble of the surf, but today it was a bitter and lonesome song.

Crows winged overhead, circling and diving in the sky. A long shrill pierced the air. We stood side by side, gazing out into the foggy harbor, waiting to see the first light of the ferry.

"This is a summer I'll never forget," he said, leaning his hip against the pier.

"It's been life-changing to say the least."

"Hey, I just realized I'm going to miss your birthday."

Ah, yes, the big eighteen. "Please. You know how I feel about my birthday."

The smile I'd been hoping to see appeared. "Exactly my point. It's so much fun to see you squirm."

I had to tip my head back to meet his eyes, which always burned my butt. "I guess this year my wish is actually going to come true. No birthday fuss."

The horn from the ferry blasted, and my head turned out to the sea. There it was, TJ's passage to safety. As it maneuvered its way into the port, my heart plunged in my chest. Saying good-bye to another person in my life sucked. I easily forgot every horrible thing he'd ever said to me and all the brotherly pranks he'd pulled. I wanted five more minutes with my little brother.

The big boat was crowded with tourists anxious to start their summer vacations. Not that long ago, TJ and I had been on that ferry, dewy-eyed and clueless. It felt like a lifetime ago.

We waited in silence as the passengers unloaded. I glanced down at my shorts with the frayed hem, kicking the toe of my sneaker over the sandy wooden planks. "I hate good-byes. You know that. So, I'll see you later."

He opened his mouth and then closed it. Reading the expression on his face, I knew he wanted to argue again about leaving, but something changed his mind. Maybe he saw the sorrow swimming in my eyes. When he did say something, it was a childhood phrase our mother used. "Later gator."

A tentative smile played at my lips, and I lightly bumped his shoulder with mine. "Later gator." And even though I knew it would embarrass him, I gave him a quick hug and was surprised when his arms squeezed me back. I'd always been the strong one, and I held back the tears rising up in my throat.

My chest was heavy and filled with uncertainty and a loneliness I'd never felt as TJ hauled his bag and trudged onto the ferry. Each step he took brought him closer to safety and farther from me.

I sent a text to Dad, letting him know TJ was on the ferry, waiting to sail.

Pigs must have learned to fly, because he actually responded. *You're doing the right thing. He'll be safe.*

Well, that confirmed two things. My father was waiting for TJ on the main island, and he knew what I was. I didn't bother to send back a reply. In an hour or so I would text TJ and make sure he'd made it home.

I lifted my face to the sky, seeking inner strength to get me through the next chapter in my life. Alone. But never really alone, I reminded myself.

To calm myself, I breathed in slowly. Salt air. Water. And death.

*He will be okay. He will be safe.*

The ferry swayed from side to side, plugging out of the harbor and into the bay. I had planned to stay until the boat was no longer in sight, but the crowd became too much. Too much laughter. Too many happy faces.

I spun around, and in the shadows of the dock emerged Zane. Like a switch, seeing his face, the floodgates opened, a tears-streaming-down-my-face kind of emotion overwhelmed me. I sniffed, my feet automatically moving from a walk to a run, and I leaped into his arms, burying my face into the space between his neck and collarbone. The feelings I'd suppressed came pouring out of me.

He caught me in one swoop, arms winding around me as he kept me secured against him. A coolness that always surrounded him splashed over my face. After I finished bumbling all over his shirt and wiped the snot from my nose, I tilted my head back and took a deep breath. I felt a little dizzy staring into his eyes. "Thanks."

"Anytime you want to soak my shirt, Princess, I'm your guy."

There was something warmhearted and right about being in his arms. And even though it was probably a bad idea for us to be seen together, especially with me draped all over him, I didn't care. Not at this moment when I needed him most. "I'm glad you're here."

"It's for the best," he said, brushing the backs of his fingers over a teardrop trailing down my cheek.

My skin tingled from the contact. I nodded. "I know it in my head, but my heart …"

"I get it. I feel it too," he said, reminding me we shared emotions, except he was way better at hiding them from me.

I grabbed a handful of his shirt and held on, not ready to break contact. It was then I realized … "You cloaked us in shadows?"

"Don't worry. I was smooth about it. No one noticed."

I didn't doubt his skills. Not for a second. Taking advantage of the concealment, I lifted up onto my tiptoes, brought my lips to his, and kissed him. It was a quick and innocent kiss, well maybe not all that innocent. I felt the zing of it throughout my body, breathing life back into me. "Whether anyone can see it, you do have a sweet side, Zane Hunter."

His lashes lowered. "And you better keep that to yourself. I have a reputation to keep."

The corners of my mouth turned up. "I don't know whether to laugh or snort, but your secret is safe with me."

A single brow arched. "I think you're going to be okay."

I would be. But Zane was a big part of my surviving on this island. I moved out of his arms and slowly felt the sun warm my skin as he dropped the veil of darkness. The bustle of the pier came rushing back around me. My eyes went to the water, searching for the ferry. It was nothing more than a pinprick on the horizon.

Satisfied that I had done the right thing and all was well for the moment, I faced Zane and hesitated. "Do you have to go?" I asked.

His gaze dropped to my lips.

I swallowed, mesmerized by the darkening hue that leaped into his eyes.

"Piper?" someone called from behind me.

I knew that voice, but … it couldn't be. No way. It wasn't possible. Not in a freaking million years. My ears must have been playing tricks on me, because my luck couldn't be that bad. Could it?

Zane's eyes narrowed, and he stepped closer to me.

I swallowed the large lump in my throat and spun on my heel. Glancing up, I shielded the sun from my eyes, and my tummy coiled tightly. *Holy shitballs.*

"Parker?" I squeaked.

# CHAPTER 12

I nside my head, a string of inventive curse words went off, and my jaw dropped to the ground. He wasn't really here. Not in Raven Hollow. Tell me I had not sent my brother to safety only to have my best friend in the line of fire. What had he been thinking, coming here?

Granted, he didn't know what went on in Raven Hollow. He didn't know what I was. And I wasn't sure I wanted Parker to know. I liked being his *normal* best friend—the girl he'd always known. I didn't want Parker to look at me any differently. It would kill me to have him scared of me ... or worse. Parker was the only real friend I had; losing him would hurt deeply.

"Piper?" he said again with concern. His coffee-colored eyes ran over my face as if he was checking to see if I'd been bitten by a zombie. Not that I blamed him. I was acting like a moron.

Somehow I found my tongue, but my brain was slow to catch up with this new turn of events. "Oh. My. God. Parker. What are you doing here?"

His half-smiling lips turned down, the excitement shining behind his wired frames faded. "That's what I get? We don't see each other for almost two months and all I get is a *what are you doing here*? No hug?

No, *Parker, I'm so happy to see you?* Classic, Pipes. Thanks for making a guy feel special. I did just take a plane and a ferry to see you."

"No one asked you to," I snapped, feeding off his irritation. The moment the words left my mouth, hurt leaped into his eyes. I wanted to slap myself. What kind of friend was I? Parker didn't have a mean bone in his body, and the fact he'd put up with my random bursts of bitchiness all these years was a miracle. "I'm sorry. It's not that I'm not happy to see you. It's just ... I'm surprised." And scared shitless.

"I can see that." His feet shuffled on the concrete. "I heard what happened to Rose, and I thought you could use a friend."

Boy could I ever, if this island wasn't the most toxic place on Earth. An awkwardness Parker and I had never had before descended. I had to remind myself that Parker was still the same guy. It was I who had changed. Exhaling, I tried to soften my welcome. "You have no idea how good it is to see your face."

The smile I loved finally split across his boyish face, so easily forgiven. He engulfed me in a tight hug, squeezing my ribs together. "I'm really sorry, Pipes," he whispered.

He was warm, consoling, and smelled of home. I buried my face in his shirt and wrapped my arms around his neck. Parker offered a familiar comfort, so different from Zane.

*Zane!*

He cleared his throat behind me, annoyance spiking through our bond. It was the first time I recognized an emotion being something other than mine. I stiffened in Parker's arms, feeling about ten shades of red color my cheeks. How was I going to introduce Parker to Zane and vice versa? Instinct told me it was highly unlikely these two would like each other. They were polar opposites.

Parker and I had always been friends, but there had been a brief moment before my mom died that we had been moving toward something more. It never really had the chance to bloom, yet I knew Parker still harbored the hope it would. I knew his feelings for me ran deeper than just friendship.

*Oh, this should be a blast.*

Untangling my arms from Parker's neck, I stepped back, putting space between us. Parker's eyes swung up over my head, colliding with Zane's. I racked my brain, trying to recall my conversations with Parker since I'd been here. Had I ever mentioned Zane?

It didn't really matter now. It was evident that Zane was with me. Standing in the middle, I glanced from Parker to Zane and back to Parker. I felt a panic attack rising.

Zane extended a hand. "You must be Parker. I'm Zane, a ... friend of Princess." He said it in a way that implied Zane and I had in-depth conversations about Parker, totally not the case.

"*Princess*," Parker echoed as if he was trying it out for size. "Yeah, that fits Pipes to a T."

"What brings you to Raven Hollow?" Zane asked, sizing Parker up.

Parker shrugged. "Piper. She's been through hell this year."

He had no idea.

"She's a tough chick," Zane added, implying I was stronger than Parker gave me credit for.

I craned my neck and eyeballed Zane, smiling. "Did you just refer to me as a chick?" Not that I didn't appreciate that he thought I could take care of myself. A lie, but it was kind of endearing, and Zane didn't have a whole lot of endearing qualities.

He tilted his head to the side, raising a sinister brow. "There's nothing wrong with being a chick."

Whether he did it intentionally or not, the quality in his timbre oozed a sexiness that I felt all the way to my toes. "Whatever you say, *dude*." I glanced back at Parker who was frowning at my little exchange with Zane. I tucked wisps of hair behind my ear, suddenly feeling guilty.

I wanted to tell Parker to get back on the ferry and take his butt back home, but as I stared into his eyes, my resolve weakened. He was genuinely excited to see me. I'd give him two days. Max. What could possibly happen in forty-eight hours? After my birthday, I'd figure out a way to get him to leave. No matter what it took. No matter what the cost.

I was about to suggest we go somewhere quieter when a guy accidently bumped into me and I stumbled, but thanks to Zane's quick reflexes, I managed to avoid kissing the ground. "Man, there are so many people here. I can't believe you found me," I said to Parker as I regained my balance.

His brows drew together as he glared over my head at Zane for a moment and then back to me. "It's crazier than Comic-Con. I was searching the crowd for you and I swear you were nowhere to be found. And then suddenly you were in front of me. It was so weird."

"Jet lag," I reasoned.

He rubbed the bottom of his chin. "Must be."

Before he could overthink it, as Parker always did, or question why I'd appeared from thin air, I decided we needed to move this reunion elsewhere. Preferably someplace with security. Raven Manor. "Come on. Let's get out of here."

Zane's eyes hardened to glass.

I did a mental eye roll. Now was not the time to go all he-man. Whatever he had planned for today was going to have to wait. Having Parker and Zane in the same room for more than a few minutes wasn't a good idea. Not at this point. The air was suddenly clouded with too much testosterone. Especially since the veins around Zane's eyes were doing the glow thing. It was hard to not be captivated. Up close, they were sort of beautifully striking.

"Talk to you tomorrow?" I said to Zane, signaling with my eyes to lay low on the reaper mojo. Most humans couldn't see the markings of supernaturals, but I wasn't taking any chances.

Zane seemed to get it, because he nodded. "Of course." He leaned in, brushing a chaste kiss across my cheek, and whispered in my ear, "Be careful." Then he stepped back and walked away.

Only when he'd disappeared into the crowd was I able to relax. "You ready?" I asked, glancing up at Parker.

He was looking at me funny. "You two seem awfully close."

Did I detect bits of jealousy? "We do?" I shrugged and started toward the parking lot. "I guess. His family was close with Rose."

"So you've been spending a lot of time together?" He tried to sound nonchalant, but I could tell the answer was important to him.

"I guess. As you'll soon find out, there's not much to do on the island."

He climbed into the passenger seat and sighed. "Ah, I've missed Josie." Josie was the name Parker and I had given my Jeep Cherokee.

I giggled. *When was the last time I'd giggled?* "She lives on."

"Island life must agree with her."

"Probably because I spend more time walking than driving her."

Snapping on his seat belt, he stretched out his long legs and settled back. "Show me this ostentatious house you've inherited. I still can't believe it. You're rich." He leaned back in the seat, looking relaxed and happy.

I wished I felt the same. "I'm warning you, it's a bit much."

"Everything is bigger than where we live." Parker came from a single mom household. His dad had split before Parker was even out of diapers, never to show his mug again or send a dime to help support his kid—the definition of a deadbeat dad. And because of it, he was an only child. His mother was afraid to marry again. I wasn't sure who I felt sorry for more—Parker or his mother.

My family had kind of adopted Parker. He was always invited to Christmas and Thanksgiving dinner. His mom was a nurse, and her twelve hour shifts didn't always allow her to be home. She was an amazing woman and mom, who adored her son, doing her best to make sure he was happy.

Anyone who stepped into Parker's room would know immediately what made Parker happy. Superheroes, graphic novels, and action figures.

"Earth to Piper."

My fingers gripped the wheel tightly as I snapped back to the present. "Sorry. I was just thinking about your mom. How is she?"

"The same. Working herself into an early grave."

"She wants the best for you, Parks."

"I know, but I would like her to meet her grandchildren someday." His eyes met mine.

Why did I get the feeling he was talking about our possible future children? I rubbed the back of my neck with one hand, the other steering the car. The temperature had suddenly gone up twenty degrees. Thank sweet Heaven Raven Manor came into view. "There it is." I slowed the car, waiting for the gate to open.

The house glistened ivory in the sun and shimmered and sparkled through the night. I heard Parks gasp as he got his first eyeful. "It looks like a museum," he said in awe.

Coasting up the driveway, I replied, "Well, it definitely has history."

Parker gaped as the car came to a stop, unable to take his eyes off the grandeur of the house. Unfolding his body from the seat, I meandered around the car to stand beside him and bumped my hip up against his. "You want a tour?"

"Uh, does Superman wear a cape?"

Parker had an unusual sense of humor I actually found amusing. "You're a dork."

He grinned lopsidedly at me, laugh lines circling the ridiculous expression.

We strolled through the front door side by side, and although I'd passed under the entryway countless times, it never ceased to impress me. Massive pillar candles flanked the entrance hall. Vases were filled with richly hued flowers from Rose's personal garden, scenting the air with roses and lilies. The wood along the staircase gleamed under the crystal chandelier.

It was breathtaking.

I turned in a circle with my arms out. "Welcome to my humble abode."

"Why would you ever want to leave?"

My face fell, and my voice dropped octaves. "I'd give anything to go home, sleep in my own bed."

The creases at the corners of his eyes smoothed out on his face. "You miss it?"

I nodded. "Desperately." I didn't try to hide the sadness.

He tugged at the ends of my hair. "I've missed you too."

"Come on. I'll show you the rest of the house before I turn into a sobbing mess." We jabbered as we wandered, and I laughed numerous times at the pure astonishment in his eyes as he took it all in. "You can stay in TJ's room. It's completely pimped out. You'll love it."

"You okay?" he asked. "You know, after having to send TJ home?"

"How do you know about that?" I took a second to think about Parker arriving the same day I'd sent TJ home and how awfully convenient it was. Too convenient. Something was fishy, and it wasn't the high tide.

"Your dad," Parker replied. "It was his suggestion that I come here to help you sort through things. He even paid for my travel expenses."

"How thoughtful," I said drolly.

---

PARKER and I were sitting on the floor in my room like old times, a furry blanket spread out underneath us. He'd gotten settled in, had a bowl of Gracie's chili, and now we were catching up.

"I can't believe you still wear those," he said, regarding my Hello Kitty jammies.

I glanced down, holding the shirt out at the ends. "They're cute."

He gave me a cheeky grin, stretching out his legs. "Try hideous."

"Shut up." I whacked him on the arm. "I bet if they were Supergirl, you'd think they were amazing."

"Obviously."

I leaned back on my palms. "I bet your superhero collection has quadrupled since I've been gone."

"Sadly, no. The summer job hunting didn't go so well. But I don't want to talk about my lack of employment. Tell me about Raven Hollow. I want to hear it all."

I picked at the seam on the blanket. "Everything is so … *different* here," I said.

"Good or bad?"

I felt like we'd had this conversation before. Initially, "bad" was at the tip of my tongue, but I quickly retracted the word and made an inaudible sound.

He cast me a sideways look. "Are you speaking in tongues now?"

"Hilarious." He was the same Parker, and it was a reassuring feeling.

Warm brown eyes softened. "This place is like paradise. Why so glum?"

Because living in a house the size of the Taj Mahal blows chunks. Because I never knew if any minute hallows would bum-rush the house. Because none of it felt real. Not even with Parker here. Living in Raven Hollow was a nightmare or a dream, depending on the day.

Leave it to Parker to see through the fake smiles and laughs. Deep down I was a mess. I let out a shaky breath. "Because no matter how happy I am you're here, you can't stay," I said, sounding like a lunatic and not to mention a shitty friend. Desperation was etched into my expression.

Light beamed down on his sunny hair, dancing cheerfully around his oval face and emphasizing his bewilderment. "Piper, are you on drugs?"

If it were only that simple. "I wish," I mumbled.

"Okay. What gives? You're starting to worry me."

Good. He should be worried, but I couldn't tell him why. What would I say? *Parker, the world is not as it seems. There are supernatural forces living among us, reapers and ghosts. I guess all that crap you read in your comics isn't entirely crap. Evil creatures are running rampant on Earth, and I'm one of them.* He would undoubtedly think I'd started doing magic mushrooms. And by telling him the truth, I would only suck him into this world and put him in danger. Next to TJ, Parker was the most important person to me.

So as I sat there biting my lip, I knew no matter what came out of my mouth it would be a lie, and I'd rather not lie to Parker. To be honest, he would call me out on it. The problem with being friends with someone your entire life was sometimes they knew you better than you knew yourself.

"I'm sorry," I huffed, thrusting my fingers into my hair. "I'm not making any sense."

"That's the first thing you've said that made sense."

I tossed a pillow at his head. "It's been a long day. You know how I get if I don't get at least ten hours of sleep."

"Bitchasaurus rex." He tucked the pillow under his arm and pushed to his feet. "We have plenty of time to gossip like we're in a Lifetime movie. You get your beauty rest, *Princess.*"

I snatched a discarded sock on the floor and rolled it into a ball before sailing it across the room, straight for the back of Parker's head. *Bull's-eye.*

He glanced over his shoulder. "When did you become so violent?"

"I'm no princess," I said.

"Trust me. I know." He grinned and quickly shut the door before I could launch something else at his head.

*Two days, Parker. You got two days before I boot your ass back home.*

As soon as the door closed behind Parker, I went to wash my face and brush my teeth. Emerging from the bathroom, I hit the light switch, letting blackness blanket my room. I strolled over to the balcony and stood in the doorway, one leg crossed over my ankle as I leaned against the frame.

There was something bugging the shit out of me, and I wouldn't be able to sleep until I got it off my chest. Grabbing my phone, I sent my father a text. I didn't care if it was one in the morning. ***How dare you send Parker here?***

Pacing the room, I was prepared to wait, but shockingly, he replied in under a minute. ***I was only trying to help.***

My fingers flew over the keys. ***I don't need your help. Not now. Not ever. Stop trying to be a parent after you've been absent for more than a year. I can take care of myself.***

***You were always able to, even as a child.***

*What is that supposed to mean? That I hadn't needed him or still don't need him?* He was clueless, and I was hurt.

I turned my phone off. Exhausted and beat, I didn't want to engage in a text war, regardless that I'd been the one to start it.

# CHAPTER 13

A storm was coming. Not the kind of thunderstorm that raged and cracked across the night's sky, for tonight the skies were clear and the waters stayed calm. This storm roared inside my head, invading my dreams.

The small apartment lacked its usual coziness and instead felt cramped and claustrophobic. Inside, the vibrant and bold colors were muted and washed out, dull grays and bland taupes.

Nothing about the place felt like home, yet it was.

The apartment was empty. No laughter or humming. Not ever again.

I pushed at the door to my bedroom, but when the door squeaked open, it was a long, wide hallway. White marble glistened on cold floors as my bare feet padded down the hall. I caught a glimpse of myself in a large, silver-framed, oval mirror—long pale hair sweeping past my shoulders, bright green eyes that seemed to glow oddly. And my lips were red like blood.

I touched my lower lip. A chill entered the hall, causing the little hairs on my arms to stand up. Easing my head slowly to the right, I watched as a mist crawled along the marble floor, creeping toward me. In my experience, nothing good or human followed the creepy vibe I was sensing.

*Hallows.*

They were close. Breathing down my neck. Calling my name. Taunting me with my own fear. I turned to run down the hall and came nose to nose with one of the ghastly mofos. Frozen, I stared at his iridescent face. "You're in desperate need of some sunlight, dude," I said, the words popping out of my mouth before I thought about what I was saying.

The backhanded slap sent me sprawling. A bright shock of pain had me curled up into a little ball. Terror clutched my belly as I dragged myself along the floor, looking for an escape. I wasn't going to get far if I didn't get back on my feet, and there were more of them now.

Fog covered my hands and feet, increasing in density. I glanced over my shoulder to gauge how much shit I was in and gasped.

Four more figures had drifted into the hall, all faces I recognized. TJ. Parker. My dad. And … Zane. Pure panic discharged inside me, my breaths quickening. I scooted backward on my butt, shaking my head. *No. No. No.* This couldn't be. If they were hallows … they were dead. Suddenly, I lost my grip on the dream, the emotions inside too real, too raw.

My head spun and spun, blurring the four figures as they stalked toward me with leering grins of hunger and spite on their wishy-washy faces. I lost focus of the room, of where I was. Blood pumped in my veins, the blood of the hunted. And when my vision cleared, I was no longer in the white house, but outside. My fingers dug into the mossy grass, dirt gathering under my nails.

They were on top of me before I had a chance to get my bearings. But the moment I did, I fought—kicking, scratching, and clawing. I welcomed the rising tide of rage. "I'm going to kill you," I spat, no longer thinking of them as TJ, Dad, Parker, or Zane. They were hallows.

"You don't have it in you," the hallow of Zane taunted.

"Maybe not yet, but I will," I seethed, kicking out my legs and planting my feet into his gut. Edging off the forest floor, I ran to the shadows, where the air was soft and cool. There were screams in the wind, eerily not all of them mine. My breathing was ragged as I ran, tearing in and out of my throat and ending in whimpers. Fear ruled inside me until there was nothing left. No reasoning. No answers. No reality.

Brush tore at my clothes, shredding them as I darted. Then, I could run no more. My feet teetered on the edge of a cliff, rocks tumbling over the side. Winds slapped at my back with sharp bites, pushing me closer to the ledge. Below the wild violence of the sea churned, water colliding against rock. Amidst the darkness, the lighthouse sliced through air, but below, the sea was wild, churning in violence.

With nothing else to do and no other path before me, I leaped from the rocks and spun in the wind as I plunged toward the depths of the water. The dream, the light, and my fears all tumbled in with me. Zane's name rang from my lips, echoing in the wind as I fell.

Just as my feet hit the crisp water, my eyes popped open and I was staring at the ceiling. Sweat drenched my forehead, and my skin was clammy. Light poured from a full moon, casting a cool glow over the darkness. As my eyes roamed over the room, a shadow formed near the balcony doors, slowly becoming a man with spellbinding eyes burning blue.

An icy shiver glanced through me. "Zane?" I squinted in the dark, focusing on his face. "What's wrong? What happened?"

His dark waves were untamed and windblown, just the way I liked them. "I should be asking you, Princess. You called."

*Uh, what?* Confusion swirled as I sat up, and I swallowed back the fear I could still taste. "No, I didn't."

He moved, blinking to my side. Those bright blue eyes glimmered, encompassed by black veins. He brushed damp strands of hair from my face. His touch was so light. "You did. In your sleep."

I chewed my lip. *Had I really?* My cheeks burned. How many other times had I screamed his name? "This isn't the first time, is it?" I asked, peeking through my lashes.

He shook his head. "Hardly."

I groaned, ready to bury my head under the pillows. "Don't tell me I do this every night."

"Off and on since Rose passed. It's been almost nightly now since your training."

"I don't understand. Why can't I control it?" I didn't think about the covers falling to my waist or that I wasn't wearing a bra.

He shrugged. "My theory: It's because we're suppressing the link between our souls during the day, and so once your body shuts down, your soul calls to mine."

My entire body flushed at those words. *Oookay*. That was kind of hot, in a weird and twisted way. Then it hit me. "You come every night?"

With him standing over me, I could smell the ocean on him. "You make it sound a lot creepier than it is."

I rolled my eyes. "That's not what I meant. And you know it."

"I only peek in, make sure you're safe," he admitted, a smile in his voice. He sat on the edge of the bed, one leg angled in a triangle toward me. "But tonight was different."

"Different how?" I asked, because it had been different for me too.

Concern flickered across his stoic face, deepening the lines around his eyes. "You're not usually pale as a ghost or shaking." His fingers laced with mine, and immediately I felt calmer.

I hadn't realized I'd been trembling. I stared at our joined hands, and an image flashed before my eyes. It was the same picture, but my finger had a ring on it—a wedding band in the most intricate design. It was beautiful. My lashes fluttered, and it was gone.

"Your eyes aren't bright with fear," he continued, his thumb absently rubbing across mine. "Most nights you never wake up. But tonight you didn't just call my name; you screamed."

"I had a nightmare," I admitted. "It wasn't my first, but this one was bad."

"I-I sensed you were in danger, but there was no way I could get to you. You were in the one place I couldn't reach you." His fingers tightened against mine as he relived those moments in his memory. "Do you want to talk about it?" I could hear how much he wanted to know what had happened in my dream.

I wasn't the only one who was turned inside out. My gaze rose to his. The pain and frustration crystallizing in his eyes caused pangs inside my chest. I was going to go out on a presumptuous limb here, which I hoped would make both of us feel better. "I'd rather you hold me."

The look that gathered in his eyes made my body tingle. "Piper, I don't think—"

"I'm not asking for you to *sleep* with me," I clarified. "Just stay for a little bit. Nothing *has* to happen."

"That's the problem. I don't think I could help myself. Not tonight. I'm already tempted."

Okay, we could sit here and argue about it all night ... or I could do something about it. Because I really, really didn't want to be alone right now, completely forgetting that Parker was in the house. My mind was scrambled with thoughts of only Zane.

I grabbed a fistful of his shirt and pulled him farther onto the bed. "What? You were already half on the bed," I said when he glared up at me under dark lashes.

He brushed aside the hair hanging in my face. "You're impossible ... to resist."

Those sexy eyes that crinkled at the corners made my stomach topple over. We both knew I would never be able to overpower him. If he really wanted to, he could have resisted. "I'm glad."

"I want you to know this is dangerous," he warned.

I smiled. "Good thing I like living on the edge."

The mattress dipped as he moved more toward the center of the bed, making himself comfortable and leaning back. He opened his arm, an invitation I couldn't turn down. "Now that you got me here, tell me about the dream."

I snuggled my head on his shoulder, indulging myself in his scent. It was hard to stop myself from thinking about how superb his body felt pressed against mine. Lord have mercy, I shouldn't be thinking about his body at all. "It was nothing. Just a nightmare. Everyone has them."

He lifted a brow.

Right. Not everyone was a banshee and summoned reapers to their beds. I sighed, placing a hand on his chest. His heart beat steadily, reminding me he was alive. "I was being chased by hallows—nothing new—except this time, when they got close enough for me to see their faces, it was TJ, Parker, and my dad. All dead." I swallowed the lump that weaseled its way up my throat. "So were you."

His lips turned down as he processed. "You're right. It was nothing more than your subconscious expressing your fears."

Tracing lines over his shirt, I asked, "What made you suddenly change your mind?"

No hesitation. "I don't die easily."

I scoffed. "I can't believe that's what you base your analysis on."

He swung his other arm behind his head, a smug grin on his face. "It's the truth. I'm the son of Death."

I tilted my face up to make a snide comment, not realizing how close we were. The words never made it past my lips. I felt myself getting swept away by his face. Eyes of a gypsy, body of a god.

Together we were ensnared in a trance. The air seemed to spark between us. I didn't know how long we lay there caught up in each other. "You bring light into the darkness," he murmured, touching the side of my cheek as he spoke.

"I want you to kiss me," I said in the dark. I knew what I wanted and so did Zane, especially when my entire body was illuminating as it was now.

I lifted my hand in the air. He pressed our palms together, and a static bolt of energy radiated down my arms, causing the veins under my skin to glow brighter. I caught the intensity in his luminous eyes. A half grin spread on his lips, revealing a dimple deep in his cheek. "I know you do."

More than half transfixed by him, I felt a little dizzy. "What are you waiting for?"

His fingers weaved with mine as his cool eyes hooked mine, full of desire. "Piper," he whispered in a rough texture.

All my senses enhanced.

It seemed so simple to me—so natural. Zane and I were meant to be together. I was tired of fighting the universe. I was tired of pushing aside my feelings, and I could see he was too.

Zane was going to kiss me. And the anticipation was delicious torture.

He lowered his mouth to mine, mashing my lips against his. A spark always burned under the surface, and it ignited into a wild inferno. He gripped my hips and pushed me back all in one swift motion. I wiggled against him, encouraged by the breathy moan of my name.

The kiss was infinitely sweet and tender, slow at first, as if he was savoring the sweetness. He tasted of home. No quick peck. No chaste kiss. Our tongues touched, tangling. And that was all it took for things to explode.

I loved the feel of him, the muscular back, the narrow hips, and the strong hands as they glided over me with patience, lingering and kindling fires along the way. My body seemed to shimmer in the heat, glowing under my skin. He conjured a light inside me.

As I clung to him, his fingers moved into my hair, fisting the strands at the base of my neck and murmuring endearing words I recognized but couldn't understand. They reached my heart, warming my soul. I ground my lips to his as he forced my head to tilt, allowing deeper access to my mouth. Nothing mattered when Zane was kissing me. Time ceased. Responsibilities forgotten.

He demanded everything, all of me, and I surrendered into the dark and light we solidified between us. I curled my hands into his hair, pulling closer as my body arched into his. "More."

But it wasn't enough. Would never be enough.

I wanted more than stolen kisses. I wanted all of Zane, heart and soul. Being with him and in his arms like this only reinforced what I knew in my heart. There was no way I could marry Zander when my feelings for Zane were so damn intense. Now I needed to figure out how I was going to get out of this farce of an engagement without hurting anyone or jeopardizing the balance of the universe.

Fun times.

Our lips separated, and he stared down at me. "Do you feel any better?" he whispered.

My body warmed in a hundred places, close to feverish. I'd say I'd made a full recovery. "I feel like I've been to both Hell and Heaven in one night."

"We keep complicating things. I don't know how to stay away from you."

"I don't want you to." But I could see the resolve in the lines on his face. Things were not going any further. My body was aching for his touch.

He moved closer, extending an arm, and I curled against his body. "This is bigger than just you and me," he said.

I wanted to stay like this, tangled up with him all night. Having him here beside me was enough. It's all I wanted. I nestled my head in the space between his shoulder and neck. "I know, but for tonight, can it just be us?"

He murmured something Celtic against my hair as he spoke. "Try to get some rest, Princess," he added.

How was I supposed to sleep when my innards were still buzzing? I smiled, placing a hand over his heart. Before I knew it, I'd drifted back to sleep in the deepest, calmest rest I'd had in weeks.

---

IT WAS the scent of coffee that roused me, that and a husky laugh. My eyes fluttered open. I was half lying on top of Zane, my head resting on his shoulder and a hand balled on his shirt, as if I was afraid he might leave in the middle of the night. There was this complete harmony inside me, and I didn't care about my morning bedhead or bad breath. I stretched, not ready to fully wake from this satisfying haze of sleep.

And I might not have had a knock not sounded on the door,

followed by Parker's voice. "You better be up, Pipes. It took me almost an hour to find your room."

My eyes locked with Zane's. *OhmyGodno.* Then I shoved him over the side of the bed, dumping his ass on the ground. "You've got to get out of here," I whispered frantically.

He glared up at me from the floor, sexily rumpled from sleep. I couldn't believe he'd stayed all night. I couldn't believe I'd pushed him out of the bed. If Parker found us together …

"Piper?" Parker called again. "Are you okay? Did you fall out of bed?"

"Uh. Um, hang on," I yelled, jumping out from under the covers, my eyes darting over the room. Zane had stood up, eyes thinned to slits. "Hurry," I whispered, pushing at his back and steering him to the balcony. "Get out of here before he sees you."

"Would it be the worst thing if he did?" Zane grumbled, not bothering to lower his voice.

I covered his mouth with my hand. "Shh. He might hear you."

He took a nip out of my palm, and my eyes darkened. I hated seeing him go, and if Parker hadn't been banging on my door right now, I would have dragged Zane back to bed and kept him hostage for the entire day. Shaking my head, I opened the door and shoved at his chest. "Go." Quickly closing the door with Zane smirking on the other side, I glanced over his face one last time before I whipped the curtains in place, covering the glass.

FML.

# CHAPTER 14

"Piper?" There was genuine concern in his voice. He was probably on the verge of busting the door down.

I padded across the room and threw the door open. Parker stood with to-go cups of coffee in each hand. I ran my hand over my hair, pushing loose strands out of my face. "Sorry, I had to pee."

If Parker thought I was acting completely crazy, I would agree with him. My head wasn't on straight, and I was blaming Zane. Parker handed me a cup, stepping into the room, and glanced around. "I know how you can't function without this and how much you love to sleep in."

I let the paper cup warm my hands. "Thanks."

"Were you talking to yourself? I swear I heard voices."

"It was probably the radio." The lie rolled off my lips, but I quickly turned to more concerning matters. "You went out on your own?" Panic tripped over my heart. He could have been hurt—easy pickings for the hallows or someone who wanted to cause me pain.

"Yeah, early riser and all." He took a sip of his drink, which I was a hundred percent sure was straight black coffee. "You were right. This place is … quaint."

Quaint wasn't what came to mind when I thought of Raven Hollow. Terminal. Toxic. Prison. "Parker, you should have woken me up."

"And risked your morning wrath? No thanks." He took another swig from his cup. "You know, there are people who drink real coffee and then they're those who drink sugar and cream with a dash of coffee."

"Hey, there is nothing wrong with cinnamon dolce," I argued.

He scrunched his nose. "Yeah, if you don't mind Christmas vomiting up in your cup."

I took a sip. "Mmm, it's perfect. Thank you, by the way. For the drink."

Leaning a shoulder on the nearest wall, he smoothly asked, "So, what are we doing today?"

I bristled. "Um, well. I kind of already have something planned for today. I didn't know you were coming."

"That's cool. I'll just tag along."

I choked on my coffee. "It's not a big deal. I'm sure you'll be bored out of your mind, and I will only be gone a few hours. You could explore the manor. Take a swim. Walk the beach." Anything, as long as it kept Parker away from the Black Crow, where I was supposed to meet Zoe for another riveting lesson.

Parker was used to accompanying me anywhere. He was like a puppy, always following behind me. "It doesn't matter where we go. I came to see you."

Internally, I groaned. There was no way I could say no, not without raising suspicion, or making me feel extremely guilty. Dammit all. "The country club."

"Excuse me?" He pretended to clean his ears out. "I don't think I heard you correctly."

I rolled my eyes. "If you make fun of me, this froufrou drink is going to end up on your head."

He laughed. "I wouldn't think of it. What are we doing at the *country club?*" he asked in a hoity-toity voice. "Not that I have anything against membership-only clubs. I'm just having a hard time imagining the Piper I know rubbing noses with the elite."

"It's not like that. Trust me. And Rose was a member." She'd been more than a member.

The mention of Rose had the expression on his face sobering. "I still can't believe it. I know you harbored some intense feelings toward Rose, but it sounds like you were beginning to let her in. And I know how hard that is for you."

I took my coffee and sat down on the window seat. After what happened with my mom, Parker had been the only person I could open up to. This time, it was different. Maybe it was me that had changed, but regardless, things had shifted. Parker couldn't be my crutch, and I felt the pain of another loss. "I don't think I can take losing another person I care about."

"You're the strongest person I know, Pipes," he said, seeing my crestfallen face but misreading the hurt.

I fiddled with my cup, not looking up. "If anything happened to you—"

He sat down beside me, putting a hand on my knee. "I'm not going anywhere."

I swallowed. As long as he was on this island and near me, he wasn't safe, but I couldn't tell him that. Knowing Parker and his good guy attitude, he wouldn't leave my side, even if the world were collapsing around us. "I forgot how awesome it is having you around," I said, a half smile on my lips. Parker had this way of making me feel better, making me feel like I could do anything.

His face relaxed. "You're probably the only person in the world who thinks I'm awesome."

"Then the rest of the world sucks. How many times have I told you that?"

"I've lost count."

"Okay, you know what? Change of plans. We're going to spend the day together, doing whatever you want to do." I surrendered, even though I knew it was going to bite me in the ass.

"Are you sure? I know you have responsibilities to take care of."

"One day won't make a difference." Or so I hoped. "Give me ten minutes, and then I'm all yours."

He beamed, the sun lighting up the side of his face as he looked up at me. His boy-next-door smile and puppy eyes could melt hearts of mothers everywhere. He was the type of guy parents wanted their daughters to date. Wholesome. Honest. Dependable. My Parks.

As soon as I was alone, I sent a text to Zoe, letting her know our lesson was going to have to be rescheduled due to Parker being in town.

*Boy BFF Parker?* She texted back.

*The one and the same.*

*Oh goody. Fresh meat.*

I scowled at my phone. Parker was not meat of any kind, especially to Zoe. *Off-limits.*

She sent me a pouty emoticon, along with, *Don't be a boy hog. You can't have them all.*

It seemed like I was ensnarled with three guys, but that was never my intention. I didn't even know how I ended up here. *It's not like that.*

*Uh-huh. Have fun. TTYL.*

I rolled my eyes. Didn't she understand I didn't want Parker mixed up with this part of my life? I was a complete mess. My life was a mess. Parker shouldn't be here. I shouldn't be a banshee. And I didn't know what to do about any of it.

This was wrong.

I *should* go tell Parker I'm not feeling well and insist we stay home. But I couldn't bring myself to squash his enthusiasm.

Foregoing makeup, since I'd wasted five minutes texting Zoe, I tossed on a pair of shorts and ran a brush through my tangled curls. My eyes glanced over the rumpled bed as I was about to set out. It was hard to believe less than an hour ago I'd been fully absorbed with Zane. I could still smell him on my skin, a scent that lingered.

·  ·  ·

PARKER and I spent the whole day goofing off and exploring the island. It was refreshing seeing the seaside town from his perspective. Everything was cute and charming, where all I saw was death and disaster. He thought it was so freeing being at the edge of the world. I'd never felt more caged, the reminder of who I was never far as my shadows squawked overhead. It was both a nuisance and a comfort.

"The birds here are crazy," Parker commented, glancing up. "Those two black crows have been following us all day."

I stubbed my toe on the pier. "Ouch. Dammit," I swore, hobbling on one foot.

He grinned. "It's nice to know some things never change."

"What? Like me being a klutz?"

"Exactly."

I scowled. "You better watch yourself or you're going to end up wet with a mouth full of saltwater."

Parker looked over the side of the pier. "I'd rather not take a dip right now. Fish freak me out."

I laughed. "Don't tell me you're afraid of the ocean."

"I'm not afraid. I just don't like squishy, slimy things." He had this horrified look on his face.

"Does that mean you don't want sushi for dinner?" I teased. Parker hated sushi.

His skin tinged slightly green, or it could have been the waning light. "I think I'm gonna hurl."

Looping my arm through his, we started down the pier toward my car. I'd had a carefree day, and it had been long overdue. Zoe and Zach cornered us just as we were hopping into Josie, giving me such a fright I almost punched Zoe. "Zoe, you were two seconds away from a bloody nose."

"Hello to you too, girlfriend." She leaned into the window, a curve to her cherry lips. Dark curls framed her slender face, tumbling over her shoulders. "And you must be the BFF."

Parker's eyes bulged behind his glasses. I couldn't blame him. Zoe was drop-dead gorgeous. If he didn't get all tongue-tied around her, I might question his manhood. "P-Parker," he faltered.

Zoe studied him from head to toe, taking in his manga T-shirt and worn jeans. "Cute. You're definitely coming with us. I need a distraction."

Parker's cheeks heated in an adorable way that made me want to pinch the sides of his face. "Zoe," I growled. "What are you talking about?"

"It's your birthday in"—she stuck her head into the car, glancing at the dash—"five hours. Zach and I are here to ensure that your eighteenth birthday is one you'll remember. You deserve it, because with it comes a hefty price tag."

"What do you have in mind?" I asked, skeptical of any idea the twins had. They could take double trouble to a new level.

"There is a rave tonight at Atmosfear screaming your name," Zach said, eyes twinkling. "Perfect for a wild birthday night."

Ugh. They knew my weakness. I nibbled on my lip, thinking about Parker. The smart thing to do would be to go home and have a quiet night watching movies with Parker. But the idea of going to a club sparked a longing. Bright lights. Pumping bass. Dancing. A chance to let my hair down. I turned to Parker and raised my brows. "It's up to you."

Zoe turned her violet-blue eyes on Parker, batting her insanely long lashes. I didn't think there was a guy who could resist that look. Even I was a little bit awestruck. "Of course he wants to go, don't you?"

Parker was putty in Zoe's paws. His lips lifted into a grin. "Pipes' birthday. I wouldn't miss it."

"Pipes," she squealed in excitement. "You even have an adorable nickname for her." She grinned. "Well, that's settled. Let's go have ourselves a little fun. What do ya say, Parks?"

I groaned.

Parker drooled.

"Meet us there in an hour. Oh, and ditch the birds," she whispered, eyes rotating to the sky.

Easier said than done.

.  .  .

FORTY-FIVE MINUTES LATER, I'd dug out a pair of dark jeans and a red crop top. I was adding the finishing touches of makeup when Parker appeared freshly showered in my doorway, wearing a new manga T-shirt.

"Wow. You look … different," he said, his whiskey eyes running over my face.

"How so?" I asked, curious to know what he saw. Physically, I thought I looked the same, except for the little white raven on my wrist, but Parker shouldn't be able to see the mark.

He shrugged. "I'm not sure. Did you cut your hair?"

I shook my head. "Nope."

"I don't know, but whatever it is, it's definitely working for you." He stared at me for another moment. "You look … really, really great."

I stood up, slipping my feet into my favorite pair of midrise boots. "Was that a compliment?"

"Don't let it go to your head."

I grinned. Seeing Parker like this made me think of old times. How easy it would be to slip back into a life before Raven Hollow. And I realized for tonight that was what I wanted—one bomb-ass night like the many Parker and I had had together.

However, that burst of nostalgia didn't last long. As we got back in my jeep, doubt slithered inside me. I was beginning to wonder if I was making a gigantic mistake. Parker at Atmosfear? This club wasn't like the others in Chicago. It was a club filled with reapers, some of the most deadly beings on Earth. I must be insane.

"What are we waiting for?" Parker asked as I spaced out.

*For pigs to fly.* I stuck the key into the ignition and let it rip. The entire drive to Atmosfear, I half expected a fleet of hallows to appear out of nowhere and play chicken with my jeep. But the streets were free of angry ghosts, at least for tonight.

Zach and Zoe met us a block outside the club. Parking in the heart of the island was a hassle, especially in the height of summer. "Are you sure this is okay? Safe?" I whispered to Zoe.

"Lighten up. Have fun. What could possibly happen? You're

surrounded by the most lethal weapons. And Zane's been ordered to keep an eye on you tonight."

"Just peachy."

Her lips split into a grin a second before she skipped in front of me, lacing her arm through Parker's, and led him down the alley. "You coming, Pipes?" she called over her shoulder.

*Oh, for the love of God, someone shoot me now.*

# CHAPTER 15

A t a first glance, Atmosfear was like any other club—liquor poured from the ceilings, bright lights flashed in time with the bass, and partygoers filled the dance floor. From personal experience, I knew this particular club was a supernatural sanctuary. This time when I strolled through the metal doors, I knew I wasn't drugged or drunk. The marks glowing on their wrists weren't a figment of my imagination, but reaper identification.

I glanced down at the inside of my arm, thinking the little white raven stood out like a beacon. But the vibe of the club put me in the birthday mood. It was a weird feeling knowing I was one of them—hell, I was the leader.

Zach came up between Zoe and me, putting an arm around both of us. "Girls, try to behave. I'd rather not have my face messed up tonight." And then, with those words of wisdom, we watched him get lost in the crowd, looking for some girl to prey on. The Hunters' charm was legendary.

"You ready to let out your inner stripper?" Zoe asked, shaking her little tush.

"Inner stripper?" Parker said, leaning in near my ear. His voice tickled the hair on my neck. "I'd pay to see that."

I elbowed him lightly in the gut. "Not tonight, you won't."

"We'll see. If there is one thing I've learned about going out with you, Pipes, it's you never know what may happen."

I rolled my eyes, not because what he said was preposterous, but because it was true.

Zoe's dark eyes gleamed at Parker. "You and I are going to get along just fine."

That's what I was afraid of. I wasn't sure how I felt about Zoe taking such an immediate liking to Parker.

"What kind of place is this?" Parker asked, taking in the scene. And what a sight it was.

I held onto the railing, surveying the sheer energy of the room below. "A very different kind of place," was my answer.

He bumped his shoulder lightly into mine. "Not so different from a few of the sketchy joints you've dragged me to. At least I'm not getting the serial killer vibe."

I glared at him.

"What's with the VIP treatment? You some big shot now?" He was teasing me, but ...

I choked.

Zoe's smile widened, and she laughed.

I hadn't noticed until Parker said something, but I was drawing unwanted attention. More whispers. I could only imagine what they were saying, and it was becoming clear that my days of hiding were numbered. I was going to have to step up into my official roll as the White Raven soon.

"Uh-uh," Zoe sung. I didn't like the texture of her tone, like I'd done something wrong.

Tingles danced along my skin. *Oh boy. Here comes the fun.* My eyes aligned with Zane's as he walked toward me, a silent, watchful shadow in the dark club. Everything from his cool eyes to the chill in the air surrounding him was a warning. He was a formidable force I had yet to understand. A good head taller than most, he stood out in the crowd for an entirely different reason than I did.

But damn, he looked good. And that was the honest to God truth.

Zane in dark jeans and a black V-neck T-shirt stretching across his broad chest was absolutely mouthwatering. His hair tumbled over his forehead, and he had a half grin on his face.

I hated how often my cheeks flushed, but I couldn't take my eyes off him or stop thinking about last night. Nothing had happened, but what was unnerving me was how much I'd wanted *something* to happen. And I couldn't get the image of him sleeping next to me out of my head.

I knew the second he noticed Parker beside me. The smile on his face went glacier, his body tensing and then relaxing, as if determining that Parker wasn't a threat.

For a moment, no one moved.

"What's he doing here?" Zane said.

Parker stiffened beside me, and my hand itched to smack the eyeballs out of the back of Zane's head. It was hard to believe this was the same guy whose arms I'd spent last night wrapped in or how quickly he could go from sweet to douche. "Don't be a jerk," I hissed.

Too late.

Parker and Zane were in the throes of a heroic stare down.

"Asshole," Parker coughed under his breath.

Zoe laughed, amused by Parker.

Zane widened his stance, biting back a growl. I flattened my hands on his chest and pushed him backward toward the nearest dark corner. "What the hell was that?"

A muscle popped at his jawline. "This is no place for a human, Princess."

"Don't you think I know that? Besides, he can't see anything, right? No reaper marks. No trouble."

"Let's hope not," he said skeptically.

"What is that supposed to mean?" I countered. My hands were still pressed to his chest. I dropped them when I realized I was still touching him, but I did so regrettably.

He sighed. "It means some humans see past the veil of life and death. Some have a stronger intuition and are able to open their minds to the possibility of the world beyond this one. It can also depend on how much death has touched their souls. If someone has had a near-death experience or lost a great love, it tends to unlock parts of their minds, allowing them to see what is normally hidden."

Fan-freaking-tastic.

I hadn't expected to be at odds with him so soon after last night. It made the afterglow I'd been riding all day dim. "Well, he doesn't seem to think anything is out of the ordinary, so I guess I lucked out."

His eyes stayed on me before he nodded. "Stay out of trouble, will ya?"

"I'll try." As I turned to leave, I stopped, angling my body back toward him. "You don't need to babysit me tonight."

A rueful smile quirked his lips. "I'll stick around all the same."

My stomach tightened, and a chill moved through my blood. One step forward, two steps back. That was the definition of my relationship with Zane. "Suit yourself."

As I spun around to rejoin Parker and Zoe, Zane grabbed my arm. "One more thing in case I don't get the chance later." He leaned down, sweeping his lips across my cheek. "Happy birthday, Princess," he whispered in my ear.

I shuddered and instinctually leaned toward him, but he'd already moved back. I stumbled a little, losing my balance. His lips curved.

Dazed and somewhat irritated, I made my way over to Parker and Zoe. As soon as I was within yelling distance of Parker, he jumped all over me. "I don't get it, Pipes. You're a smart girl. What are you doing with a douchebag like that?" Obviously Zane rubbed him the wrong way, but I couldn't blame him.

I blinked. "We're not together," I said, but his eyes were still brimming with doubt and anger. "It's complicated, okay?"

"Whatever." Parker was having none of my lame excuses.

"Look, I don't want to fight with you. Can't we forget Zane and have a good time?" Not that I could ever truly forget about Zane. It wasn't possible, not when we were in the same room, but Parker didn't know that, and I sure as hell wasn't going to tell him.

He downed the drink next to him at the bar. "It's a good thing it's your birthday."

"That's right. Now, let's dance." I tugged on his hand. "Come on. You know you want to."

Zoe was frowning at me from her seat at the bar. I think I'd just stolen her dance partner, but since I *was* the birthday girl, I deserved first dance.

Pulling Parker onto the floor, I told myself to ignore Zane, to pretend he wasn't here. I slipped around the bodies, searching for an open space. The club was packed tonight, and I loved it. Letting the music rule me, I stepped up to Parker and draped an arm around his neck. I started to move, but unlike most adorable dweebs when they danced—they kind of stood there and let the girls do all the work— not Parker. For a geek, he could move.

My perfect partner in crime.

Loosening his muscles, he quickly picked up the beat, matching his rhythm with mine. I swayed with the music and then whirled in a circle. Pleasure brought a rosy glow to my skin. I knew my body was luminous, a reaper by-product. Parker didn't seem to notice. I'm sure the strobe lights helped, but I was happy to see the joy in his eyes.

Or maybe I was mistaking joy for something more ...

His hands settled on my hips. "You still got it."

My mouth, unpainted and soft, curved up and teased out the dimples on my cheeks. "I forgot how well we move." The words came out raspy, like I was trying to sound sexy but failing miserably. So not my intention.

I didn't know how many songs we danced to. That was the thing about places like Atmosfear; you got caught up in the music and hours flew by. All around us, bodies glistened with sweat and people laughed. When I glanced around, it was like a rainbow—the guy to my left with a purple Mohawk, the couple beside us whose veins shimmered red, and the girl behind me who looked like a living Rainbow Brite.

For the first time, Raven Hollow felt like home. Maybe it was that I'd finally accepted who I was. Maybe it was having Parker here, a piece of my old life. Or maybe it was a combination of everything. Parker. Zane. Atmosfear. Me.

Parker's head lowered, his forehead pressing to mine. His long lashes fluttered against my cheek, and I giggled. The next thing I knew, his lips were on mine. I couldn't say I was surprised, because deep down I knew he had a crush on me. Maybe it was more than a crush. What surprised me was I didn't push him away immediately, which Parker took as encouragement.

His lips pressed more firmly to mine. There was nothing wrong with Parker's kiss, and actually this wasn't our first. I remembered it being just as sweet ... except it didn't steal my breath away. There was no jolt of power rushing through my veins, heating up my blood. I didn't lose myself, forgetting the world around me.

He wasn't Zane.

And if I could think of Zane at a time like this, no one's kiss but his ever would be enough. He'd tarnished me forever. Kissing Parker made me think this was the calm and pleasant future Zander and I had to look forward to. No toe-curling, heart-pounding, body-surging lip-locking. After the other night, I wasn't sure I could settle for anything less.

It was a sobering thought.

As gently as I could, I broke off the kiss and stared into Parker's wonderstruck gaze. "Parker, we can't," I said, placing both palms on his chest to keep him at an arm's length. It wasn't my motive to hurt him, but I would hurt him all the same. The knowledge splintered a piece of my heart, but it was unavoidable. I refused to lead him on, to ensnare another in this twisted triangle I found myself in.

"Why not?" he asked, leaning in to make another attempt for my lips.

I was having none of it. He might have caught me by surprise before, but not a second time. I pushed harder against his chest. "Parker!" Alcohol and the ambiance of the club made him bolder than normal.

"What gives? I thought you had feelings for me."

"I do. Of course I do," I assured him. "You're my best friend—"

"Don't you dare pull the friend card," he said. "What about the, *Parker, I miss you*s or the *I love you*s?"

All around us, people continued to bump and grind, but I didn't care. Most of them were oblivious to the squabble quickly turning into an inferno. "I meant them ... as a friend."

"That's such bullshit," he snarled. "I know it. You know it. I don't understand. What happened? One day you're into me and the next you're not? I gave you time because I thought that was what you needed."

"It was," I said in a small voice. I wasn't sure he'd heard me.

"And now you've decided you don't have feelings like that about me. Is it because of him?" His finger shot in the air toward the back of the club. Distaste rolled off his tongue. Any ideas I had about Parker and Zane being friends were quickly becoming unrealistic.

I swallowed. "Who? Zane?" It was a stupid question.

He thrust frustrated fingers through his unkempt sandy hair. "Oh please, don't play the innocent act with me. I'm not an idiot or blind. I've seen the two of you together. You have a thing for him."

Tension settled between us like a well-worn blanket. He was right, but it was way more than a thing. "It's not that. I'm engaged," I blurted out, and my hand flew quickly to my mouth. I swear the room went silent, but mostly it was in my head.

He blinked, shaking his head in confusion. "What?"

"I'm engaged, Parker."

He looked like I'd cracked him across the cheek with my open palm. "You're shitting me."

"I wish," I muttered, knowing nothing I could say would soften the pain on his face.

"I don't see a ring," he stated, eyes darting to my fingers and back to my face. "How can you possibly think you're in love with that douchebag? You deserve so much better."

I shook my head, taking a step forward. "I'm not engaged to Zane, Parks." But boy did I wish I were. It would have been believable.

Confusion clouded his whiskey eyes. "Then who? If you're making another lame excuse because you don't have feelings for me, just be big enough to tell me. Don't lie to me."

I wanted to stick to as much of the truth as I could without revealing what I was. "I wouldn't lie about something like this. I swear. It's Zane's brother, Zander."

"He has another brother?"

"Yeah," I replied flatly.

"Now I know you're lying. Zane, I could have believed. You've been making googly eyes at him and fawning all over him since I got here. It's sickening."

"I do not make googly eyes."

He crossed his arms. "At least admit how you feel."

"Fine. I have feelings for him. Is that what you want to hear?" I yelled.

Hurt slashed across his eyes. I reached out, intending to lay a hand on his forearm, but he stepped back. Pivoting, he stormed off the dance floor.

"Shit," I swore to no one in particular. "Parker!"

He didn't even break his stride.

# CHAPTER 16

How did I ever find myself caught in a love tangle? Not with two guys, but three? WTH? In high school, I couldn't even get a date to prom. I felt stupid as shit. I could have handled the situation with more care. Parker was my oldest friend, and it wasn't his fault my feelings had shifted in a big way. Or that I was as unavailable as someone could get.

I was afraid of losing him.

Without a second thought, I took off after him. *Where did he think he was going to go?* I caught a glimpse of the back of his shirt as he barreled through the doors. The last thing I wanted was Parker running around the streets of Raven Hollow at night. Alone.

Pushing my way through the crowd, I had both hands on the metal door when I felt someone following me. It didn't stop me. Outside, the sky sparkled like crushed diamonds in space, and the air was cool and clean as the mountains. Yet it wasn't the unexpected crisp air that caused my skin to goose bump. "Zane, I don't need your help," I said over my shoulder, not slowing my pace.

He ambled out of the shadows and into my line of sight. "Of course you do."

"You'll only make things worse."

"Tough shit," he said, sounding a bit sharper than normal.

"You don't understand. I hurt him." My voice caught as the fast techno beats faded in the distance.

"Oh, I saw. The whole club saw. Anyway, he's a big boy, Princess."

I stopped in my tracks, and it took him a step or two farther to realize we weren't shoulder to shoulder. "I wouldn't expect a jerk like you to understand."

He wore that damnable knowing expression. "A jerk, huh? You didn't think so last night."

"Argh! You're driving me crazy." My eyes scurried along the street in front of me. Buildings lined both sides of the intersection, but there was no Parker in sight. There were, however, quite a few intoxicated partyers stumbling around, making me slightly nervous. "Where the hell did he go?"

Zane never got the chance to utter the snappy comeback on the tip of his tongue. Out of nowhere, a figure flew from around the corner and bum-rushed him. At first I thought it was a hallow or a reaper. But … *it couldn't be.* My eyes widened in disbelief. *Parker?*

Sure as shit. Parker's fist shot in the air, zooming past Zane's cheek as he sidestepped out of the way. I blinked, about to intervene, but Zane beat me to it. He had Parker pinned against the wall, his eyes going smoky, the veins circling them the color of ink.

I stood there for a moment with my mouth hanging open. What was going on? I felt like I'd walked into an alternate universe. Someone must have slipped something into Parker's drink. He was never aggressive or physical. My eyeballs couldn't believe what I was seeing. Feeling seven shades of awkward, I stood there dumbfounded, as two very different guys for whom I cared deeply, just different kinds of deep, fought each other.

Zane pressed his forearm into Parker's chest. Parker groaned in pain as he pushed against his restraints.

"Zane! Let him go," I finally said.

"I'm keeping him from hurting himself," he replied.

Parker didn't seem to mind or notice his feet weren't touching the ground. "This is what I don't get, Pipes. What do guys like him have that I don't?"

Zane's eyes roamed down to Parker's shirt and then back up. "For starters … fashion sense and a decent haircut."

"Zane," I snarled. "Shut up."

"What? He asked," Zane retorted.

Parker laughed, but not in a good way, more like he was about to lose his shit. "You don't deserve her."

Zane narrowed his eyes. "That, we can agree on."

If Parker noticed anything odd about Zane's eyes, he did an impeccable job of hiding it. "She was mine first," he barked.

Zane growled.

"Whoa," I said, stepping up so I was in both of their faces. "Hold it right there. I am not, and will never be, someone's possession. Is that clear, you Neanderthals?" I glanced back and forth between them. I contemplated knocking their heads together to get my point across, but by the looks on their faces, I doubted it would have made a difference.

They ignored me.

Parker rolled his shoulder, but it did no good. He wasn't going anywhere Zane didn't want him to go. "Get your hands off me," Parker hissed.

Danger shadowed Zane's face. "Why? So you can make a fool of yourself?"

A thread of fear finally showed in Parker's eyes.

Wow. This was not the kind of birthday I'd had in mind. Fighting with my best friend. Zane and Parker butting heads. What next?

I decided it was time to call it a day and hoped tomorrow this would all be a bad dream.

A girl can fantasize.

It became clear bringing Parker had been a mistake. The knowledge of that mistake was painful. I was making them in abundance, one right after the other. "Okay, here's the deal. Parker and I are going home, and I'm going to try to forget this night ever happened."

Footsteps echoed down the side street behind me, but I didn't think anything of it, not until the breath from my lungs turned cold, billowing in the air. My eyes immediately found Zane's, and I saw the same alarm register in his.

Hallows.

*Oh, goody gumdrops.*

"I think your birthday surprise just arrived," Zane muttered drily.

Time stopped, and the hairs on the back of my neck rose. I looked up, knowing what awaited us. Or so I thought.

Estelle stepped out, under the streetlight, her almond-shaped eyes twinkling under the glow. There wasn't an ounce of warmth or kindness, emphasizing my confusion. Behind her were a few Caspers—the not-so-friendly ghosts.

"Estelle?" I said stunned. "Where have you been? Crash has been looking for you."

"Ah, the devoted older brother. He worries for nothing." I didn't like the sneer in her voice and neither did Zane.

He dropped Parker to his feet, positioning himself in a way so he stood between Estelle and me. "Considering the kind of company you keep, I'm thinking he has a right to be concerned."

"That's the thing." Static crackled in the air, and a reddish-white light radiated from Estelle as the four hallows closed in ranks behind her. "You never know what you have until it's gone. Mortals always take advantage of life."

My stomach twisted. "You and I both know I'm no mortal."

"Piper?" Parker rasped. "What the hell is going on?"

"Oh, I know," Estelle said. "You're the White Raven."

*Well, shit.* There went my element of surprise.

I'd been warned that rumors had been circulating about my newly gained status, but there was something in Estelle's hazel eyes that led me to believe she knew more than she was letting on. It made me leery. Revealing I was the White Raven was risky, but in order to keep Parker safe, I was willing to take the risk. "Am I supposed to be impressed you figured out my secret?"

Her lips curved in a sickening grin. "It was never much of a secret. Not to me. One Raven down and one to go."

I felt the shock of what she implied quake through me—Zane's and mine—it jolted inside me. "Y-you killed Rose," I accused, hardly believing it was possible. My brain stopped functioning. Estelle had been a friend; at least, I thought she'd been.

But as I let the idea simmer, all the cracks and missing pieces came together.

Parker's head was bouncing back and forth, trying to understand what was happening.

Zane's jaw locked, and his stance changed. He was coiled tight, ready to strike. A chorus of hisses rang from the four ghosts at her side. Things were getting hot up in here.

Estelle clucked her tongue, eyes on Zane. "Don't get any ideas, Death Scythe."

"All I've got is ideas … on how to kill you. And I promise you, if you touch her, I will kill you," he said darkly.

"Kill?" Parker echoed. "He's not serious, is he?"

Estelle pretended as if Parker didn't exist. "No, I don't think you will. It's why I brought these guys. To keep you busy."

He flexed his fingers. "Only four? I'm offended."

Once the disbelief wore off, the force of it slammed into me, burning a hole of outrage and anger so bright I knew my entire body was lit up like the Chicago skyline. My ears roared with uncontained fury. Someone was calling my name, but I was past the point of hearing.

Her hazel eyes darkened, turning the color of coal, and I knew from the flickering of her outline what was about to happen next.

Death shrouded Zane as he stepped in front of me, easing me behind him in one smooth motion. His muscles coiled beneath his skin. "Piper," he cautioned.

The second his skin touched mine, clarity filtered through the red haze. I took a deep breath to calm my pounding heart. Right. We needed to be smart about this. There were more of them than us, and plus I had Parker to consider. I couldn't go ape-shit on her like I wanted to. It didn't change the fact that I had a score to settle with this bitch. Not to mention, I was still learning. Estelle had the advantage here.

But I had one thing she didn't.

Zane.

He locked eyes with the bigger hallow. "We can stand here all night making googly eyes at each other, or I can start the massacre, because I *will* take your souls."

"Okay, I'm out of here," Parker informed us. "There's no way I'm going to be a part of whatever this is."

"What are you doing?" I mumbled to Zane under my breath.

"Ending things before they get out of hand. Stay back with What's-His-Name, and"—his icy eyes flashed to mine for a moment, a multitude of unspoken words, but all he said was— "don't die."

"*Die?*" Parker squeaked.

Then the murderess attacked.

She was a phantom reaper and had the ability to transform into whatever her black heart desired. I wasn't sure what she was, but it didn't matter when she shot a green ball of what looked like plasma directly at my head.

Zane wrapped an arm around my waist, tugging me against his chest. He spun, shielding me with his body. I pressed my face into him, clutching his shirt. There was no place I felt safer than in his embrace.

A cool mist traveled over my body as a series of intense bolts of light shot over our heads. "Stay down," Zane instructed and took up a fighter stance.

Parker was huddled down beside me, his hands over his head. "Oh God, Pipes. The world is under attack."

A dry, raspy laugh echoed down the road. "Your pet is funny. I promise to make his death painless, unlike yours."

Just thinking about Parker dying left a metallic taste in my mouth. "I hadn't realized you were a psychopath," I snapped.

Zane stretched out his muscles, pure power radiating off him. He took off, speeding toward the four rabid spirits like a bullet to the brain. As I followed his movements, my eyes lost him from time to time. His form moved in and out of the shadows.

By the time he reached the hallows, Estelle had shot off another round of fireballs. I pushed Parker to one side and threw myself to the other, letting the light whiz between us. Parker, in his less than coherent state, skidded across the ground, but I wasn't worried about a few cuts and bruises. I was worried about his soul.

Slick tendrils of pitch-blackness expelled from Zane, wrapping around the throats of two hallows. Knowing his skills, I figured he could handle the ghosts as long as they didn't phone a friend.

And that left me with Crazy Pants. My pulse was all over the place, and since I lacked Zane's awesomeness, I decided to use the one weapon I had. My voice. "I don't understand. Why are you doing this?" I asked.

"I thought it was obvious. Power. Control. Power. Blah. Blah. Blah. You get the idea," she answered.

Heart pounding, I backed up against a wall, keeping her eyes focused on me. "Not really." I could hear the scuffling and fighting, but I was afraid to take my eyes off her.

"That's your problem. You lack vision."

I'd thought Estelle was trustworthy. She had been the first person to make me feel at ease. This girl in front of me was a stranger. I didn't know how to talk to her or what the right words were. It felt like no matter what I said, I was putting my foot in my mouth. "Fuck you."

A weak and demented smile crossed her lips. "You know, I'm not going to enjoy killing you as much as I did Rose. It's a pity. I actually liked you."

Parker flinched, and it was enough to remind Estelle he was there. *Dammit Parker.*

Because I needed to keep her focused on me, I moved away from Parker, drawing her eyes to me. "Too bad I can't say the same."

Her eyes flashed, and the veins around them darkened to a deep red.

So much for reasoning. I moved away from Parker, closing the distance between Estelle and me. I didn't know why it hadn't occurred to me before. Newsflash. I was a freaking banshee.

I screamed—as loud and sharp as I ever had. The sound vibrated into the night, carrying over the entire island until my throat went dry. I had no clue what I'd just done, but it felt significant.

Estelle let out an exaggerated breath. "You shouldn't have done that."

Assuming it had actually worked, it would be only a matter of time before reapers should descend, answering my call. "You didn't give me much choice."

Evidently, it was too much to think she'd retreat. I'd cornered her. *Checkmate, bitch.* In a matter of minutes, the street would be overrun with Death's most lethal weapons.

I knew not all stood by my side. Hell, most of them didn't even know I was the White Raven, but that was all about to change. I was going to show my true colors and deal with the consequences later ... if I could keep myself alive that long.

Estelle had other plans.

My gaze flicked to see Zane absorbing the soul of one of the hallows. He had another one tied up and restrained with shadow bonds. How he'd done that was a mystery to me. But the third ghost was barreling straight for me.

"Piper!" Zane's voice snapped me out of my terrified daze.

The ghost bulldozed into me, just dying to do some damage. My head slammed into the back of the brick wall. Starbursts radiated throughout my vision as sharp pain exploded at the crown of my head. He came in for round two, and I managed to lurch to the side, narrowly avoiding having my brains splattered all over the building.

And then something snapped inside me.

Light welled, encompassing every cell in my body. There was a heady rush of power building from the center of my chest, flowing to the tips of my fingers. I knew that feeling, what it meant, and I was powerless to stop it. His soul was mine.

The strangest thing happened. Time seemed to turn sluggish, yet I could see everything crystal clear. Suddenly, it clicked. Time hadn't stopped. I was moving at inhuman speeds, seeing the world around me in a different measurement—a sensory heightened awareness.

Arching back, I slammed both my hands onto his chest. I wanted to hurt him. Badly. A pulse of light shot down my arm, ramming into the hallow. His mouth formed an O, a silent scream on his lips, as he was thrown back several feet in the air. The hallow splintered into fragments of smoky light like a broken mirror. This was who I was. It hit me then—what I could do, what I was capable of. No longer was I frightened of the power inside me. It defined me.

Spinning around, I concentrated on who I was and the energy inside me. The wind around me kicked up, swirling in dangerous patterns. Above, the dark sky moved with restless, ominous clouds. The games and taunting were over.

I wet my dry lips, ready to kick Estelle's skinny ass.

A high-pitched cry pierced the night. *Parker.*

With wild eyes, I glanced behind me, and my worst fears came true. Estelle had Parker in her traitorous clutches, a blade pressed to his heart. Eyes wide and frantic, a panic seared my flesh. The bright white light surrounding me flickered. "Let him go," I pleaded. I would beg on my knees if that was what it took for Estelle to release him unharmed.

Her eyes gleamed with the satisfaction of triumph. "And lose my advantage? Please. I think not."

I could probably take her out—one quick blast of my light—but what if she moved or I missed and hit Parker? I didn't want to take the risk. "It's against the rules, Estelle. We don't interfere with death." My voice was shaking.

She dug the blade deeper against Parker's chest so it went through his stupid manga T-shirt. "Who said I was interfering? How do you know I don't have orders to take his life? Maybe it's his time."

I knew she was trying to screw with my head, implying that Roarke had ordered a hit on Parker. Why would he do that? It became obvious this wasn't going to end well—for her. "Fine. Have it your way. You hurt a hair on his chest, and I'm gonna drop you like third period French."

Reapers were fast, determined, smart, and deadly. I needed to remind myself I was all of the above. Maybe I wasn't cunning and skilled in dark arts like Zane, but I wasn't helpless either.

Wind rushed over my face, blowing back my hair. Zane's eyes met mine as I beseeched him. If we linked up, aligning our souls, Estelle didn't stand a chance. He knew what I was asking. With a slight tip of his head, simultaneously we moved.

Our hearts picked up together, and my soul surged as his darkness collided with my light, but before our souls fully synced, Estelle flicked her wrist.

And my world went black.

"No!" I screamed.

But it was too late.

Her blade punctured Parker's flesh, and I watched helplessly as his eyes went wide with bafflement. Then the pain registered, fracturing the light in his eyes. She discarded him to the side like he was nothing more than trash. My best friend landed in a heap a few feet away from me, twitching for a few seconds and then going still.

"Parker!" My blood chilled, hardening to ice, while his soaked the ground.

A breath later she was on me like ugly on butt. I responded quickly, leaping up and kicking her in the belly. It was surprisingly firmer than I expected, and the skank recovered like she didn't feel pain. She grabbed me by the hair, a complete bitch move, and jerked my body back against her. I gave a muffled cry and felt her hands at my throat.

If she rendered me unconscious, my soul was as good as toast.

Panic surged in me again. It seemed to be the emotion of the night. You'd think I would be used to getting the snot beat out of me. I wasn't. Unlike robo Estelle, it still hurt. A lot.

If I could just break out of her death grasp …

I lifted my arms, now encased in a bright light, in the air. I spread them wide and let loose a jolt of power so strong the impact almost knocked me on my ass. It raced like a torpedo down my fingertips, hitting Estelle in the chest. "I told you not to mess with me."

She fell to the ground, and I pounced. I did what had to be done. My hand shot out, covering the center of her chest as my knee dug into her stomach to keep her from getting any funny ideas. This ended here. Sow. Reap. Estelle's harvest was over.

I never wanted to kill someone. Never. Until now.

I siphoned the essence of life from her body. As soon as I felt every last drop of her soul resonating inside me, I fell backward on my butt, laying my elbows on my knees and my hands on my temples. A brightness filled me from the inside out, but the elation was as short-lived as I remembered.

*Parker!* "Oh God," I muttered, scrambling across the ground, oblivious to the gravel cutting into my hands and knees. "Parker!" I screamed, the sound curdling in my throat.

# CHAPTER 17

I didn't want to believe that was blood I was seeing. Parker's blood. It oozed down the side of his temple, trickling from his lips. The front of his shirt was soaked in the sticky red stuff. I felt the color drain from my face. Zane was beside me as I trembled, my hand stroking Parker's sandy hair. His face was so pale; his lips a deathly shade of blue. This couldn't be happening. Not again.

"Zane?" My voice shook as I begged for his help, blood and tears streaking down my face.

"He's gone," he said as gently as he could.

"No," I croaked out, horrified at what he was saying. My chest was rising and falling, but it felt like I'd stopped breathing.

He pulled me into his arms, but I resisted, fighting until my arms went lax. "We don't interfere with death. You know the rules," he said, sounding remorseful. His fingers moved into my hair.

"Bullshit," I cried. Tears burned the back of my throat, making my voice hoarse and raw. I could barely breathe. My gaze flicked up. "I don't care about the stupid rules. This is Parker. I can't lose him."

His finger moved along my bottom lip, catching the tears with the pad of his thumb. "There's nothing *I* can do, Princess." It hurt him to say it, because it would hurt me.

Sobs clogged my throat, rendering me speechless. Just like that, I was supposed to give up. What was the point of being a reaper? All doom and gloom. *Screw the rules.* I wasn't letting him die. I wasn't giving up.

Moving out of Zane's embrace, his words played over and over in my head as I stared down at my hands covered in Parker's blood. No matter how much pressure I applied to the wound, the blood kept flowing. *There's nothing Zane can do. There's nothing Zane can do.* My mind ran over the words on repeat. It was too sickening to think I'd never hear Parker's laugh again, never see him wear another one of his ridiculous manga shirts, never see him smile or be able to tell him how much I needed him in my life.

And then, it clicked. I knew what Zane was trying to convey. It was up to *me* to save Parker.

My eyes snapped to Zane's. Was I misinterpreting what he was saying but not saying? Was it really possible for me to save Parker? He lifted his brows in a you-can-do-this expression.

If there was even the teensiest chance, I had to try. Only one problem … I had no idea what I was doing, no idea where to start, no clue if I had it in me. *Deep breath.* Through the fog of dismay and trepidation, a bit of reality seeped in, and a voice sounded in my head. Not Zane's. Not mine. *Oh God, I've gone crazy.*

*"You're not crazy,"* the voice responded. *"But if you don't listen to me, Parker is going to die. For real."*

"Rose?" I murmured, my eyes shifting left and right.

"Piper?" Zane whispered in concern. Talking to my dead grandma might be cause for alarm, if I was anyone else.

*"Who else would it be?"* the voice said.

*"Of course it's you,"* I said in my head, assuming she could hear me.

*"Now listen. Each second you waste is precious and will end up draining more of your power."*

Enough said. I wasn't going to question how she was able to communicate with me—maybe later when I could think beyond Parker's blood. *"What do I do?"* I asked, desperate for hope.

*"When you took that traitorous reaper's life, you inherited all her souls,*

*including Parker's. You're going to restore his soul and heal his body."* She stated it so matter-of-factly.

*"I just can't twitch my nose and make it happen."*

*"The key, Piper, is believing you can do it."* I could hear the exasperation in her tone. *"Now lay your hands over the center of his sternum and summon your light. His soul is gone. When you touch him, you will be able to feel the emptiness. Instead of extracting his soul, you are going to fill his body with your light, until your lifesource is pumping in his veins. This is your legacy."*

I did as she instructed, placing my palms on his chest and harnessing the power that was a part of me. It came quicker and with less effort than ever before. A network of silvery white veins grew until I was glowing from head to toe. The air around me shimmered as if it was raining glitter. With a burst of energy, my vision clouded, producing a white filmy light behind my eyes.

Each cell of his soul warmed into his body, giving him life. There were voices and whispers in the background, but I closed my eyes, concentrating on the sublime static releasing from my skin. I held on as long as I could.

As my lashes lifted, my light flickered out, and Zane's face took shape. His eyes were bewildered, mouth hanging open as he stared at me. Time stopped, along with my heart, waiting for a sign of life, wishing with all my might. Then it happened; the sharp inhale of air filling Parker's lungs was music to my ears.

Zane was staring at me. "Holy ..."

"Shit," I finished.

His fingers raked through his hair. "Do you know what you've done?"

*I did it.* I'd brought Parker back from the brink of death, restoring his soul. "I can't believe it." I didn't care how many rules I'd broken, only that Parker was going to be okay ... mostly.

"Believe it, Princess. You gave Parker his life back. I didn't think that was possible."

Surprised by the shock in his voice, I had to ask, "But you had a hunch, right?" He was the one who had more or less planted the seed in my head.

He shrugged. "I wouldn't even call it a hunch. More like a really long, long shot."

"Well, I didn't do it alone. Rose came to me."

"I heard you say her name."

She saved Parker. Looked like I owed Granny big time. Guess I was marrying Zander after all. It was what she'd wanted.

I glanced down. Parker's chest was rising and falling in steady breaths. I placed my hand over his heart, needing to feel it beat. My fingers ran over the torn material where Estelle's blade had pierced. There would be a scar on his chest at the entry point. The sight stoked a fire of pain, anger, and regret. My fist clenched, but knowing Parker, he would think it was cool—a war wound or adventurous story to tell his grandkids. I sighed. He would be able to have grandkids now.

Parker's eyelids fluttered open as he regained consciousness. "Why am I covered in blood?" His voice was hoarse.

I laughed, a hysterically maniacal laugh, and threw my arms around his neck. "You're okay," I whimpered. Stupid, girly tears of relief clouded my vision.

He wrapped an arm around me. "Don't cry, Pipes. I'm sorry I acted like a jerk."

I pulled back, pressing a finger to his lips. "Shh. Don't talk." For the first time since Parker left the club, my body relaxed, and it was then I sensed them.

Something happened inside of me. Like a switch being flipped, I was keenly aware of the reapers surrounding me. Zander, Zoe, Zach, and Aspyn stood at the intersection among others, their eyes taking in the scene before them. I didn't know how long they'd been standing there, but my guess was long enough to see me perform a miracle.

The cat was out of the bag.

There was a new Raven in town.

I hoped they didn't except me to give a speech, because I didn't think I could form a coherent thought after everything that had happened. And by the looks on their faces, they needed more than a hot minute to catch up. Heck, I was going to need at least a year to process this. Maybe a decade.

I assumed most of them had put two and two together after seeing an act that could have only been performed by a banshee—specifically the White Raven.

Zander crouched beside me. His dark hair was combed back. "You okay?"

I met his questioning glare. "Yeah. Can you get us out of here?" I was beginning to feel the aftereffects, and I wanted nothing more in the world than to go home. Or faint.

"I was planning on it. That was quite a show you put on."

My hand lifted to the side of my head as I tried to make the world stop spinning. "Ugh. How bad did I screw things up?"

A sympathetic grin teased his lips. "Don't worry about that now."

Parker sat up, his eyes examining me in a way that made me fidgety. "Pipes, w-what's wrong with you?"

Zane and Zander both went still beside me.

The gears in my head wound. Parker dying had changed everything. And in that split second, I realized I could no longer hide what I was. This was the moment I'd dreaded since Parker stepped off the boat. My greatest fear was he would no longer look at me as his best friend. "If you value your life, Parker, you'll keep your questions until we're alone."

His eyes were big, but understanding dawned as he noticed all the attention we had on us. With a slight tip of his head, Zane and I helped Parker to his feet. There was an enlightenment inside me as we walked through the crowd, a pulsating that gathered in my veins, growing with each heartbeat.

I couldn't explain it, but as I passed each person, I got a sense of who they were, and it went beyond what type of reaper they were. Another puzzle for another day.

Although I knew he wasn't thrilled, Zane climbed into the back seat with Parker, who looked like he needed a year's worth of sleep. Zander held out his hand. "Keys please."

Normally, I was pretty stingy about letting other people drive my jeep, but I didn't even argue, dropping the keys into his palm. I slumped into the passenger seat. As soon as I let my muscles relax, it hit me like a ton of bricks. The exhaustion was overwhelming, draining me of energy. I was barely keeping my eyes open, and the gentle hum of the engine was soothing, a mundane sound, but I needed something ordinary to ground me.

"Do you know what you've done?" Zander whispered, breaking the comfortable silence.

I dropped my head on the back of my seat. "Which disaster are we talking about?"

His dark eyes tapered. "How many others are there?"

"This is Piper," Zane mumbled from the back. "The possibilities are endless."

I scowled, closing my eyes and running my fingers through the tangle of knots in my hair. "So I've made a few mistakes. The world hasn't ended … yet."

"When word gets out you killed Azrael's daughter, it will only add fuel to the rebellion," Zander said.

I winced. "She had a few screws loose. What was I supposed to do? Let her chop me up into little bits and rob me of my soul?"

"No," he said. "But there will be retaliation."

"Can't wait," I muttered, cocooning myself in my arms.

"Where the hell was your detail?" Zander growled.

"Where were you?" Zane shot back.

My temples throbbed. The questions and bickering were turning my headache into a serious migraine. I was slightly concerned for my safety. Zander was more focused on arguing with Zane than keeping the jeep between the lines. Or maybe I was seeing double.

"How could you let her do this?" Zander spat out.

I choked on a laugh of outrage. *Let me?* When were they going to understand I didn't answer to them? Funny thing, they answered to me.

Zane almost flew into the front seat. "She didn't have a choice, Zander. Her life was in jeopardy," he rumbled, defending me.

"So many things could have gone wrong. Actually, I don't know if it could've been worse."

Duh. It could always be worse. I could think of two things off the top of my head. Zane and I could have publically merged our souls. And Parker could have died.

Zane glared. "It can when I come up there and kick your ass."

"Mature," Zander replied.

"Stop!" I yelled, throwing my hands in the air. "Can someone wave the white flag, at least for tonight? Placing blame and hashing it out isn't going to change the outcome. What's done is done. We all knew I couldn't hide forever. Already others are suspicious. I guess now they'll know there's a new White Raven."

Zander's hands rotated the steering wheel. "I hope you're ready for this."

"Me too." I looked over my shoulder at Parker to make sure he was still breathing. I felt like a new mom on her first night home with her infant.

"He'll have questions, Piper. How do you know he can be trusted? That he will keep your secret?" Zander asked.

"I've known Parker almost my whole life. He'd never betray me or intentionally cause me harm." He loved me. Well, he had. I sounded far more confident than I was feeling. "If anyone can believe in the paranormal, it's Parker." He spent more time living in the world of comics and manga than reality. Reapers really weren't that far of a stretch from guys who wore tights and capes or gunslinger girls with awesome hair.

"I hope you're right."

I bit my lip. "Do you really think your father ordered Parker's death?" I couldn't fathom why he would do such a thing.

Zander kept his eyes on the road, but I saw his jaw pop. "I promised I'd be straight with you. I don't know, but I wouldn't put it past him."

"Why?" Maybe Roarke wasn't the man I thought him to be. I mean, sure he was Death, but what would be gained by Parker's death?

Zander had a theory. "To push you into being a banshee and accepting your responsibilities. By threatening someone you care deeply for, it would force you to awaken what is laying inside—the abilities you subconsciously suppress because you're not ready to handle them."

"He would do that?"

"I think we can agree that people will do just about anything when their backs are pushed up against the wall."

Well, crap on a cracker. It didn't change the fact that I was salty as heck. Staring out the window, I thought about the constant different directions my life took. From day to day, I never knew what awaited me, what trauma, what challenge, or what frightening surprise.

I could cheat death—bring a soul back from the brink of death. Kind of epic. But I couldn't take two minutes to bask in the ambience of being awesome, because I was sure shit would hit the fan tomorrow.

---

I LIFTED the blue plaid blanket, tucking it up to Parker's chin. The color in his face was slowly returning to normal, but his body still had to be in shock. "You need rest," I told him. If he was awake, he had time to think, and it had been a long night. I wanted to crash for at least twelve hours, but from the look in his eyes, I wasn't going to escape so easily.

He put a hand over mine. "Don't leave. Not yet. I need to know what happened. What's going on with you? You haven't been yourself since you got here."

My heart went down south. I'd hoped for some time to collect myself, to figure out what I was going to say, but he was right, I wasn't the same.

He watched me struggle to figure out what to tell him. "Someone tried to kill me tonight, and I think I have a right to know what's going on. Tell me, Pipes."

He did deserve the truth. And Estelle hadn't *tried* to kill him ... she *had* killed him. I took a deep breath. "Okay." It was a good thing we were by ourselves. Zane and Zander would have had a conniption. I sat on the side of the bed.

Intrigue gleamed in his face. "Does this have anything to do with Rose or your mom?" he asked, sitting up higher in the bed.

I nodded. "Yeah, it does."

His brows drew together. "I saw her ... I think."

"Who? Rose or my mom?"

"Rose," he said after a moment of struggling to recall.

"What do you remember?" I asked, afraid of his response.

"I-I ... I'm not sure. It seemed like a movie. I was there, in the film, and then suddenly I was spectating, seeing everything from above. That girl had a knife. She attacked us. Oh God, I think she stabbed me. D-did I die?"

I shook my head. "You're not dead, Parks."

He wasn't convinced as he rubbed the center of his chest. "After she stabbed me, I felt such coldness. My veins filled with ice. Then I was floating, and there was a woman. She was iridescent, not quite a tangible force. Does that make any sense?"

I nodded, twiddling my fingers together. "More than you know."

"I'm not sure, but it was as if her soul wasn't tethered to Earth. She held my hand, telling me it was going to be okay, that you were going to save me. She was an angel, ghost, apparition ... definitely something unnatural."

"Rose," I whispered.

"I remember when you went through a phase where you thought you saw ghosts." He released a breathy chuckle. "It wasn't a phase, was it?"

I fiddled with the chain around my neck. "Not exactly, but I didn't know that. Not until recently."

He inhaled and exhaled slowly, taking it all in. "This is really freaky, Pipes. I watched you from outside my body."

I swallowed, already knowing what he'd seen. Too much.

"You touched me." His eyes met mine. "You were glowing, swathed in a white light. What is going on? Even now, when I look at you, there's something different about you. Tell me I got a concussion or something stupid."

"If I told you it wasn't real, would you believe me?"

He stared at my face, a heavy pause in the air. "No," he stated.

My heart turned over. "I didn't think so."

"I don't understand. Why would anyone want to hurt your mom or Rose? Hurt me? There's a connection, isn't there?"

Parker was too smart for his own good. "This is going to sound crazy, but I swear I'm not making this up."

"I trust you. I know you would never lie to me." Blood rushed to his face. "But you're starting to freak me out."

"You get stabbed in the heart and now you're suddenly freaking out? I think at this point, I'd be past the freaked out stage and into completely ballistic."

"Oh, I'm getting there. But I'm trying to play it cool, keep it together. You seem nervous." His fingers interlocked with mine. "You know you can tell me anything. Nothing you can say will change how I feel about you."

I was counting on that. "You say that now …"

Under his weary gaze, he studied my face. "What has you so afraid that you feel as if you can't talk to me? I know you."

My eyes lowered. "You shouldn't have come here, Parker. It's not safe."

"I think we've established that. I'm sorry, but I'm not abandoning you." His fingers tightened on mine.

Pulling my legs up, I tucked them against my chest. "I'm different. I think you see that."

The silence seemed to stretch for an eternity before he spoke. "What are you?"

This would be one of the most difficult challenges I'd ever faced. I'd assumed it would be a weight off my shoulders, not sandpaper scratching my throat. Each time I opened my mouth, nothing came out. The sense of vulnerability I was feeling left me unsure. "It's hard to explain."

"Since when have you ever been at a loss for words?"

I took a shaky breath. "I'm a reaper," I blurted out.

# CHAPTER 18

There. I'd said it.

Parker stared at me hard. "A scythe-wielding, black-cloak-wearing reaper?"

I did a mental eye roll. "I know it sounds crazy. Half the time I can't believe it myself."

"You don't look like a reaper," he said, pointing out the obvious.

"A banshee more specifically. And what am I supposed to look like?" I challenged.

"I don't know. Gray-green skin, wild eyes, and electric hair—you know, as if you stuck your finger in a power outlet."

I pressed my lips together. "I'm sorry to disappoint you, but you know fantasy rarely looks like real life."

"Are you sure I didn't hit my head?" He rubbed at the back of his hair, looking for a bump. "If you're screwing with me, I'll never forgive you."

It would have been easier if he had been knocked out or had a concussion. He might not remember anything then. "I told you that you wouldn't believe me."

"Who said I didn't believe you? I know what I saw. And I'll agree it's far out there. I mean, we've seen some pretty messed up shit in the city, but nothing like this. You're my best friend. I've known you my whole life. How did I not know what you were?"

"That is a question I've asked myself a gazillion times," I said. "How did I not know? Why didn't my mom tell me?"

"Your mom?" he echoed.

I nodded. "She knew, Parks. She knew the whole time and never once told me. It's one of the reasons we never saw Rose."

He had the same initial reaction I'd had. "Why would she keep something like this from you?"

I gave a one-shoulder, nonchalant shrug, pretending it didn't bother me when we both knew it did. "I guess to protect me."

"It would make sense. She loved you." He squeezed my hand and then released it.

"I know, but it doesn't erase the pain of being lied to your whole life."

The expression on his face softened. "No, I imagine it wouldn't, especially for someone like you."

"What the heck does that mean?" I countered.

"You feel everything deeper. Love. Hurt. Betrayal."

My lips pursed. "I never really thought about it."

"I know you don't like to talk about her, but what happened to your mom, was it because of who she was ... a"—he swallowed —"reaper?"

I blinked. "Sounds weird, doesn't it? I can barely wrap my head around it. At times, I think I'm living in an Alfred Hitchcock film."

And so it began. Parker started bombarding me with as many questions as he could, asking about all aspects of reaper life. He wanted to know what it was like, how I felt, what I could do ...

There was curiosity and enthusiasm in everything he asked. Biting my lip, I could see the interest growing as I answered his questions. And it made me nervous. I didn't want Parker any deeper into this world than he already was. The knowledge of what I was, what I could do, put him at risk.

He sat up straight, rattling off question after question. "When did you find out? How did you find out? Why didn't you tell me?"

"Hold up. Take it slow, okay? You've had a helluva night. Let's not overdo it. I almost lost you." A tear dropped down my cheek.

"Don't cry," he whispered. Guys and tears. They made them all uncomfortable as hell.

I tipped my chin, retracting the well of emotions. "I'm okay." I waited until he was reclining on a mountain of stark white pillows before I answered his questions. "I only found out what I was a few weeks after I arrived. Zane told me. And I didn't tell you because I was afraid you would look at me differently. I didn't want to lose you." My voice trailed off. I'd come so close to losing another person I loved. Was this my destiny? To love and lose it all?

"You can't scare me off that easily. Even if you have horrible taste in guys and scream like a banshee."

I cracked a smile. If he could joke about it, I knew things were going to be okay between us ... except for the kissing part. We'd deal with that another day when he was stronger and wasn't recuperating from coming back from the dead. "Don't ever die on me again."

He grinned, but it faded too quickly. "You mentioned Zane told you?"

I nodded. "Yeah, he's sort of a reaper—a death reaper. His father is *the* Grim Reaper."

"That explains a lot," he mumbled.

I lightly pushed on his shoulder. "Believe it or not, he isn't all bad."

Parker made a noise of disbelief. "That might be a topic we can agree to disagree on. What's the deal with the two of you? And don't tell me you're just friends. I can accept that you might be a reaper, but no way can I accept that you don't have feelings for him."

"It's complicated."

"I gathered that. You're really engaged?"

I nodded, glancing down at my hands. "Like I told you earlier, to his brother, Zander. Rose arranged it before I got here. It's supposed to *solidify* my place by marrying the firstborn son of Death. Things aren't precisely all moonlight and roses between the sectors."

"But ..." Parker prodded, knowing me well.

I reached around my neck and pulled at the dainty silver chain. "I don't love him. I always thought I would marry someone I was deeply in love with. It might sound extremely girly, but I want to spend my life with someone who gives me more than lukewarm feelings."

"And you love Zane," he said, filling in the blanks.

"Love is a strong word. I'm figuring it out. Some days he makes me want to string him up by his balls."

Parker chuckled. "I'd pay to see that."

"But we have this connection I can't deny." My intention wasn't to hurt Parker, yet no matter how I delivered the news, it was going to be a spear to his heart. I knew how he felt about me, but lying to him would only prolong the inevitable.

His long lashes swept down over his hazel eyes, and when they met mine, my heart turned end over end. I hated that I made him hurt. I only ever wanted to protect those I cared about. "Do I even want to know what kind of connection you're talking about?"

"Probably not," I replied. "But you asked for details."

He wrinkled his nose. "I did, didn't I?"

Sitting down alongside him, I stretched out my legs. "Our souls align. We can synchronize them."

"What does that mean?"

"Uh, it's still to be determined. We can merge our souls, which allows us to do all kinds of insane things."

"Don't stop now."

"Well, we can share power, communicate without talking, and who knows what else."

He adjusted his glasses. "This connection goes deeper though. Your emotions are tangled with his."

"It's messy for sure," I mumbled, my eyes glancing at the clock. I might be a night owl, but Parker certainly wasn't. "It's late. I should let you get some sleep." I moved to stand up, but he laid his fingers over mine, stopping my movements.

"Wait. Don't leave just yet."

There was something in his voice that gave me pause, and I think I understood. He didn't want to be alone. I couldn't blame him. The idea of going back to my own empty room was unappealing. Death had a way of making you want to appreciate life. "Scoot over," I said, peeling back a corner of the blankets.

He moved to his left, and I climbed into the bed next to him. I rested my head on the pillow, turning on my side so we were face to face. "How did you save me?" he asked.

I rested my head on my hands. "In all seriousness, I'm not sure. I have these abilities I don't quite know how to control. And if it wasn't for Rose, I wouldn't have been able to save you."

"Looks like I owe Rose a thank you. Any chance you can arrange that?" He lifted a goofy brow.

I let out a dry laugh.

"I was totally kidding," he assured me, staring at the ceiling.

"The less you know, the better, especially for your safety. It's dangerous."

He shook his head. "Oh, no you don't. You can't tell me something like that and leave me hanging. It's pretty clear that danger is imminent."

I shifted my head on the pillow, finding a comfortable spot. "Exactly. That's my point. Danger lurks around every corner."

"For who? You? Me?"

"All of the above. There are malevolent spirits whose souls stay here on Earth for a number of reasons, but mainly because they have unfinished business with someone from when they were alive. The longer they remain here, the greater their destruction. You being in Raven Hollow puts you at risk."

His shoulders relaxed. "You can't get rid of me that easily. I'm not afraid of ghosts."

"You should be," I huffed. "Things are unsettled between the different sectors. There is strife among us, and with the kind of skills reapers possess, things can escalate. It's why I'm still here and engaged. By joining my bloodline with Zander's, it offers me protection and a commitment to what I am."

"Will you show me how it works?" he asked.

"I'm still learning."

"You seem to be doing just fine. You did save my soul."

True, I had. What was the point of having powers if I couldn't have a little fun? "I'm sure I've broken about a thousand rules tonight. What's one more?" I closed my eyes and inhaled. In my mind, I pictured the light inside me, flowing from my fingers to my toes until it vibrated and hummed. It was Parker's gasp that had my eyes fluttering open.

The white light picked up blond highlights in his sandy hair. "Holy. Shit. At least you never need a nightlight."

I laughed, rotating my hand in the air. It shone in the darkened room. Not everything about being a reaper was as gloom and doom as I'd thought.

---

I ARRIVED EARLY for my training the following morning, leaving a sleeping Parker safely inside Raven Manor. Zane was engaged with another reaper, Dean. At least that was what I thought his name was. A quick glimpse at his wrist revealed Dean was a Crow.

I'd come to be leery of anyone who wasn't a Crow. As I stepped down off the stairs into the training area, I expected the stares, the questions, and the intrigue on everyone's faces. It still made me uncomfortable, enough so that I thought about walking right back up the stairs and out the door.

And then Zane caught my eye, daring me to walk out. He was goading me. If I turned and ran with my tail tucked between my legs, he would come after me. That would embarrass me more, so I raised my chin.

Seeing Zane and feeling his darkness swell into the air made me want to tap into my power and exploit it. It seemed the more I used it, the stronger the pull was. I remembered the dizzying rush of bliss. Zane only intensified the feeling.

Turning away before I did something foolish, I spotted Aspyn sitting with a group of girls, and since it looked like Zane was going to be tied up a while longer, I headed in their direction. Normally, I'd steer clear of cliques. Giggle fests and hair braiding parties weren't my thing, but I got the impression reaper girls were quite different than high school girls. So I hoped.

"Well, look who the cat dragged in," Aspyn said, grinning. Her long hair was tied high on the crown of her head, emphasizing her cheek-bones. "That was quite the spectacle last night. I'm glad to see you're not hiding out at the manor."

I wrinkled my nose, slightly terrified of being bombarded with questions. "Not my style."

"Girls, this is Piper, the new White Raven." With a smile that said she was up to no good, she eyed me. "Piper, this is Kourtney, Calista, and Taby—the bitches."

I smiled.

"You're so lucky to have Zane as your mentor," a little pixie said—Calista, I thought. I had a hard time seeing her as a reaper. She didn't look like she could hurt a fly.

It was a relief that the first question out of the gate was about Zane and not about how Rose had died. "He's definitely intense. And surprisingly, when he's not being an asshat, he's a pretty good teacher."

The table erupted in giggles. "Zane is one of the toughest ..."

"Roughest," Aspyn added.

"Baddest," Taby chimed in.

"Hottest ..." Kourtney's lips curled.

Calista's hands wrapped around a Gatorade bottle. "Swoon-inducing—"

*Good God.* "I got it. Every female on the island has a hard-on for Zane." And that earned me another round of giggles.

"Except you," Aspyn provoked.

What game was she playing at? She knew I had a thing for Zane, but that was all she knew. "I'm impervious to jagoffs."

Aspyn twitched her little nose. "What a sasshole you've become."

"Trust me, this is nothing new," I mumbled.

"You're so much cooler than I'd thought you'd be," Kourtney said.

"Thanks, I think."

Aspyn's red lips twitched. "Don't look now, but a six-foot-two hunk of yumminess is coming this way." Of course everyone at the table went on high alert. I swear there was a uniform sigh from the table as all eyes glanced behind me.

"Are you done slacking off?" His voice was dark and husky.

I put my hands on the table and slowly turned around. Zane loomed over me, wearing jogging pants and a sweaty T-shirt plastered to his chest. His expression was an impatient one, but by God, his sweat smelled like it should be bottled and sold as cologne. It was doing ridiculous things to my brain. "What did you say?" I asked, shaking the haze of hormones from my head.

His eyes were pinned to mine. "Let's get out of here." He more or less growled and grabbed my hand, tugging me to my feet.

Aspyn laughed. I glared over my shoulder at her. She winked, and the other girls' mouths were gaping. I whipped my head back to Zane, his hands still twined tightly with mine. "Where are we going?"

We'd reached the top of the stairs. "Out. I can't work with you trapped inside that room."

"Oookay. What did I miss?" I struggled to keep up with his long strides.

"It's hot as Hades in here," Zane rumbled. "And I need air before I do something reckless."

"Reckless?" I squawked. "Like singlehandedly slay a dragon, or merge our souls in front of a room full of reapers?"

He frowned in a sexy, brooding way. "Does it matter?"

I jerked my hand out of his as soon as we were outside. The sharp July sunlight was warm. "Will you stop pulling me around?" I crossed my arms, feet planted. "You still haven't told me where we're going."

"Somewhere with lots of space. The beach. We need the privacy."

"I'm not going to lie. You're sort of making me nervous. Did Craig beat the big bad Death Scythe?"

"Piper," he said in low, chilling voice. "We need to *talk*. I figured you'd prefer privacy, unless of course you want to freely talk about what happened last night with a room full of reapers."

I didn't know what was happening or what was unfolding between us, but things were intensifying. And knowing us, this conversation was going to get loud. Although I didn't want a crowd, being alone with him at this point made me nervous ... and a bit excited. "I'm not going anywhere with you."

"Get on the bike, Piper." He handed me a helmet.

I had no sooner stuck out my chin when his hands snaked around my waist. The moment my back hit his chest, I went still in his arms. Oh so familiar tingles radiated down the base of my neck, but times a hundred. I wasn't prepared for the intensity.

As soon as the helmet hit my head, I started breathing again. His arms released me, and he threw a leg over the motorcycle, tilting his head to the side. "Don't make me chase you."

I wouldn't give him the pleasure. Annoyed, I yanked myself onto the bike behind him. I barely had time to secure my arms around his waist when the bike took off like a bullet.

I buried my face in his shirt as we went flying down the road. The trailing wind hinted of the sea, growing stronger as we approached a secluded section of the island. My legs vibrated under the roar of the engine, and I tried not to think about how good it was to be holding onto him.

The beach was remote, and I could see nothing but surf and sand, annoying seagulls, and the occasional sailboat. It was beautiful, but not even the beauty of Mother Nature changed my sour mood.

Swinging my leg off the bike, I strutted onto the beach and planted my butt into the toasty sand. "Well, you got me here. Talk," I said as his shadow fell over me.

Easing his weight down beside me, he squinted against the sun's beams. "What did you tell him?"

He meant Parker. No clarification was needed. I bit my lip, hesitating. "I told Parker everything."

"Dammit, Piper!" he cursed, his ragged voice sending the seagulls flying away.

I wasn't going to let him make me regret my choice. "There's no need to yell. Let's tone it down a notch ... or ten."

He tensed. "That's not how this works. You're making it nearly impossible for me to keep you alive."

I had a feeling this was only going to escalate, but it didn't stop me from speaking my mind. "I never asked you to be my bodyguard."

"Trust me, if I could undo the vow, I would." The words exploded from him.

And for a second, I was afraid he'd broken the vow by just wishing for it. A pang hit me in the chest, but I kept my face blank. "What crawled up your ass?"

His gaze turned to the endless ocean, projecting guilt and pain. "Forget it. Let's just get this out of the way."

"Screw that." I pushed his chest, craning my neck to look up at him. "You're not going to shut down on me. If you have something on your mind, say it. I am not going to train with you while you have a chip the size of Pluto on your shoulder."

"Have it your way."

Finally, we were going to get somewhere.

A muscle ticked in his jaw. "My *problem* is your irresponsibility with your boy toy."

*Boy toy?*

"Zander was right," he continued. "You endanger us by flapping your yap."

*Here comes crazy town Piper.* "Whoa. First, I don't flap my yap. Second, what was I supposed to do? Make him think he's losing his mind?" I was two seconds from throwing sand in his face.

"Why not?" he barked. "It's not the worst thing."

I began to lose my grip on reality, anger ruling my tongue. "Do you have any regard for anyone other than yourself, you tenacious prick?"

"Just you."

I was pissed, annoyed, and insulted, yet he managed to make me feel honored to be a part of the very select people Zane cared about. He didn't give out his affections liberally. "You have a funny way of showing it."

His expression was full of agony. "I've never been denied something I wanted."

Holy. Smokes. Batman. My mind was reeling, but I was pretty sure Zane had admitted he wanted me. It was one thing to know it and another to hear it from the reaper's mouth. "Then why are you shouting at me?"

A heavy sigh left his lips. "Because Parker gives your soul a sense of harmony. I felt it last night."

*Uh? Do I detect bits of jealousy?* "We've been friends a long time. He's the one person who's always been there for me. And I confide in him. I'm tired of the secrets and the lies, Zane. I'm tired of everyone around me ending up dead."

Unruly dark hair fell over his forehead as he leaned forward. "I know. And I'm sorry. This isn't an easy life, especially since you haven't lived it long. It threw me for a loop, seeing you with him. I wasn't prepared for how it made me feel. I don't like it."

"Are you jealous?" My heart skipped a beat.

"Jealous doesn't even begin to cover it." His gaze dropped to my lips.

I wanted to put my arms around his neck and lay my head on his shoulder, but I just stood there, staring into his cool blue eyes. "You have no reason to be jealous. Parker knows how I feel about you."

His hand reached out, tugging the ends of my hair. "A part of me, a huge part of me wants to hear you say it, but I know once you do, there's no going back. I won't be able to let you go. Do you understand?"

"I do. More than I can say."

A slow grin materialized. "You ready to make your muscles burn?"

I curled my finger in the air. "Bring it."

# CHAPTER 19

"This isn't working." The frustration I was feeling leaked into my tone. I was utterly off my game. Not that I actually ever had game, but for me, my whole equilibrium was off.

And I had sand in places sand shouldn't be.

"Since when did you become a whiner?" He had taken off his shirt ten minutes into our sparring.

I started to get all kinds of crazy ideas as his grin turned wicked. Not a single one had anything to do with my fighting or reaper skills. "When did you become a drill sergeant hardass?"

His brows shot up. "So, you're giving up?"

"Did I say that? I can't concentrate when all I'm thinking about is jumping your bones."

"Oh really," he replied.

Exactly. How was I to think about anything with Zane shirtless, sweaty, and giving me come-get-me glances every other minute? My hormones were out of control. "Look. I'm tired. I'm spewing shit I don't mean."

His body brushed up against mine and smugness crept over his expression. "Nice try, Princess. You can't take that back. Not letting you," he murmured. "How about we try something different that I think will do us both a world of good?"

"You want to have sex? On the beach?"

His laugh was loud and throaty. "Oh God, Piper. What am I going to do with you? As tempting as the offer is, I was thinking of something less physical."

My cheeks stained pink. *Someone hit me with a facepalm.* "What did you have in mind?"

His lips quirked at the corners. "We're going to merge our souls."

The anticipation made my blood sing. I wanted to rub up against him like a kitty cat with a new scratch post. "I thought that was forbidden." My hands lifted in the air, doing scary spirit fingers.

"I said we shouldn't sync our souls, not that we couldn't. The thing with synchronized souls is it's natural to align our souls. And we're denying ourselves all the benefits. We have all this energy inside us, but no outlet, and it's starting to take its toll. I'm short-tempered and moody."

"Wait. You're not usually short-tempered and moody?"

He ignored me. "And you're sarcastic and hormonal."

"So, you're saying if we do a quick wham, bam, thank you, ma'am, we'll be less edgy?"

"Uh ... yeah that about sums it up."

My hand wrestled with my windblown hair. It was going to take me a month to get out the knots. "Honestly, this whole soul symmetry confuses the hell out of me."

"I could say the same about you."

"Yeah, if you wanted a bloody lip."

"Cocky. About time. I only know what I've been told about this connection between us. It would be easier to show you than tell you." He held out a hand.

I put mine in his. "Enlighten me." Energy surged. My veins began to glow in a lightning race down my arm. Zane had a similar effect happen to him.

Dark shadows came out of nowhere, blanketing us from the sun. "Our power springs from within, and for us, from our hearts. The power we have together isn't a crutch to be used when convenient. It's dynamic and irrevocable." His palm was cool against mine, the veins under our skin illuminating. Such a contrast—Zane was the yin to my yang. And I knew what he meant. As soon as we touched, I instantly felt his power stream into me—cool, fluid, and strong. With it came the rush of joy.

I glanced down at my own hand, fascinated by the silver-edged spurts of light that spun down my arm. Zane's shadows lined my light. "It's so beautiful," I said quietly.

"So are you."

I was fighting a love-struck grin. Oh God. I was so close, right there, teetering on the edge of falling hopelessly, crazily in love with Zane Hunter.

His mouth descended upon mine.

And that was it. I was sunk.

Neither one of us intended for this to happen, but in the back of our minds, it had always been there. We'd been suppressing more than our abilities, and now our emotions were through with being silenced.

My fingers dug into his forearm as his arm snaked around my waist, tugging me closer. I had a flash of the reaper he was, sinewy strength and rich blue eyes. Then the ocean disappeared around us as darkness descended. I blinked, and we were in my room, Zane holding my hand as my body shuddered.

"What was that?" I asked, clinging to him while I waited for my body to catch up with my mind.

"Don't you ever wonder how I can get to you in a snap?"

I tapped my hands on his chest. "I guess I assumed it was a reaper thing."

His eyes were centered on my lips. "It is. I use the shadows to move from place to place."

Could he possibly get any freaking cooler? And hot? Couldn't forget hot. "Can I do that?"

He dipped his head, teeth grazing my jawline. "You could when our souls are resonating."

"So, it's a Zane thing," I said, stretching up and kissing him.

"Definitely," he murmured, gripping my hips and …

A movement out the window caught my eye. Parker was in the courtyard, staring up at us. My gaze was ensnared by the affliction in his tawny eyes. He disapproved.

Disentangling my arms from Zane's, I pushed feebly at his chest. "I can't. Parker's watching." I'd been dreaming about being in Zane's arms for weeks, and here I was, right where I wanted to be. He was willing to kiss my brains to mush, and I couldn't believe I was complaining. *What is wrong with me?* But I couldn't disregard Parker's feelings because I wanted to bask in the glory of Zane's lips.

Zane sighed. Then he wrapped me into the darkness, into his arms, and away from the window. "Fine. Is this better?" Neither of us was ready to let the other go. The glowing aftereffects of merging our souls were still humming through my blood.

I wound my arms around his neck, unable to deny myself the simple pleasure of being in his embrace. "Much." There was a comfort he offered I could find nowhere else.

And when his lips brushed against mine, I thought of nothing and no one else. Zander. Parker. They didn't exist when Zane's lips branded mine in a scorching kiss that left me aching for more.

I hated him. I wanted him. How was I supposed to turn off my emotions and go on living, knowing I was expected to marry his brother? Screw that. In this moment, I knew I couldn't go through with it. I couldn't do it. Even with a reaper war looming over my head, I would find another way.

"You don't play fair," I whispered, framing the sharp angles of his face with my hands.

A typhoon loomed in his eyes. "I'm not playing."

I lost a few brain cells when he talked to me in that crooning voice. As his lips brushed mine, a throat cleared near the doorway, and my heart dropped. *Please, don't let it be.*

Parker.

He stood with his arms crossed, scowling and glaring murderously at Zane. The sudden realization we were no longer covered under

Zane's veil of shadows doused those tingling feelings. I jumped out of Zane's arms, guilt weaseling its way into my gut.

"I was wondering where you've been all day. I should have known." The disgust was written all over his face. I'd disappointed him.

Story of my life.

"Parker. Wait." But he wasn't listening. He was gone, storming off down the hall. And that was all it took for my love to turn to anger.

I snapped my hostile gaze at Zane. "You did that on purpose," I accused. "What a dick move. You know I don't want to hurt him. Find a way to pocket your jealousy, because Parker's important to me. That's never going to change."

The eyes that had been silver like the moon turned ice cold enough to freeze blood. "What about me? I'm tired of pretending I don't have feelings for you. That I don't want you from the time I wake until my body shuts down. Even then, in my sleep I dream of you, being with you. I thought I could stay away from you. I thought I could handle being near you. I can't, Piper."

Holy. Toledo.

Why couldn't he have admitted how he truly felt all along? It would have saved us both from all those restless nights. I'd given myself ulcers thinking about what I was going to do, but hearing him say all of that, I knew without a doubt what I wanted. Torn between throwing my arms around Zane and going after Parker, I stood in the middle of my room. "I know how hard this is, but you didn't have to hurt Parker in the process," I berated.

"Did you ever think I didn't do it on purpose?" he challenged.

*Oh man. Here we go*. If Zane and I weren't tearing each other's clothes off, we were arguing. "Are you telling me you weren't pulling some caveman move, claiming me as yours and making sure Parker got the message loud and clear?"

"You think you've got me all figured out. Maybe I lose a bit of control when I'm with you," he said, voice strained.

Dead air. I was rendered speechless. Zane was the epitome of control.

He gave me a cool, measured look. "Don't expect me to be here when you get back."

Fine by me. Hair spinning in the air, I turned around and gave him the finger. I stepped into the hall, needing to find Parker. I caught him trotting down the winding stairs. "Parker!" I yelled. It was obvious he'd heard me. The whole house had heard me, but he didn't flinch. "I know what you're thinking, but I can explain if you just give me a minute."

"Maybe I don't want to listen to another one of your excuses," he shouted over his shoulder.

I wasn't deterred. "We both know you can't stay mad at me for more than five minutes."

He spun around when he reached the bottom landing. "I don't even know who you are anymore. The Piper I know wouldn't have her tongue shoved down another guy's throat while engaged."

I was teetering on the last step, standing toe to toe with him. "I told you it was more complicated than that."

"Still doesn't change the facts. I saw you. Kissing *him*."

"What are you doing out of bed?"

"Don't change the subject."

Jealousy seemed to be the theme for today, but I couldn't blame either of them. This was entirely my fault. I'd only wanted to keep from hurting him, but that was exactly what I ended up doing. "Parker, that's—"

He interrupted me by holding up his hand. "What makes this worse is knowing I never stood a chance."

"That's not true." I didn't know how to explain my relationship with Zane. There wasn't supposed to be anything between us, considering, but the heart wants what the heart wants. And mine wanted my best friend and Zane to get along. Something told me that wasn't going to happen.

"What is it like then, Pipes?"

"I didn't plan for this. I didn't know you were coming. And I didn't plan to fall in love."

Crestfallen, Parker said, "You love him?"

I wanted to find the nearest wall and bang my head against it until I knocked some sense into myself. I opened my mouth and then shut it. Holy crap. Did I love Zane?

Oh. My. God. I loved him. I was in love with him.

It was one thing to know our souls connected on an unearthly level, but somewhere along the way, my feelings got tangled up. "I guess I do love him."

"Why do you sound so surprised? Don't tell me you hadn't figured it out yet."

And that was when the tingles started. *Zane* was listening, concealed in the shadows. *Ugh. Can't a girl get any privacy?* I guessed when you had multiple relationships going, there was no such thing as privacy.

I'd deal with the eavesdropper later. "Despite how it seems, I haven't been ready to admit it, not even to myself."

His face soured. "Sorry if I'm not jumping up and down to congratulate you. I can't believe you can't see how wrong he is for you. He's turning you into someone you're not."

"A reaper? Newsflash: I *am* a reaper."

"That's not what I meant, and you know it."

Neither of us were going to get anywhere at this rate. "I think we need a moment to cool off before we *both* say something we'll regret. I'm going to grab a drink."

"Whatever," Parker huffed.

Just fabulous.

I rounded the corner of the staircase, heading to the back of the house. As I passed the second turn, Zane appeared in front of me, an icy glint in his eyes. I gasped, and as I opened my mouth to give him a verbal lashing, his lips found mine, stealing my breath away. And before I could tell myself to not sink, I was melting into him.

"Tell me," he whispered against my mouth. "I want to hear the words from your lips."

Captured in his deep gaze, I was filled with so much emotion. It diffused my anger and left my body purring. I knew what he was asking from me, but my throat had closed off.

His hand caressed my lower lip. "I need to hear you say it, Piper."

Ten minutes ago he'd been berating me for wanting to be with him, and now he wanted me to confess a feeling I'd barely had time to process.

I swallowed, knowing I would never deny him. He had me hypnotized. Tipping back my head, I stared into his eyes. "I love you." There. I said it. Exhaling in relief, I felt vulnerable.

His forehead laid against mine as he closed his eyes, his arms tightening around me. "I didn't know it was possible."

I savored the taste of his cool breath. "What?"

"For you to feel half of what I feel for you."

Did he? Was he? "You love me?" I didn't know what I'd expected. I think I was so used to him pushing me away. A glow bloomed inside me as warm as gold.

His lips twitched. "We're not talking about me. We're talking about you."

Looping my arms around his neck, I shook my head. "No way I'm letting you off that easily. It's only fair."

He frowned. "Parker was right, you know."

"How do you figure?" I asked.

"You and me being together is toxic. I see that now. If you were anyone other than the White Raven, you'd already be mine."

"But I am," I finished.

"You are."

"Before you say anything else, I need you to know I'm not marrying Zander. I can't."

"Precisely why this can't work. Our love can't be what starts a war. You're just learning the inner workings of death and the power that comes with it. Every day things grow more disorderly. The hallows multiply faster than we can abolish them. It's not getting easier, and these games we're playing with each other are only making it harder. I need to remove myself from the equation."

Something awful unfurled in my stomach. "You can't be serious. What about 'love conquers all' and that bullshit?"

His lips drew into a straight line. "It's because I love you that I have to leave."

Panic erupted. The idea of not having Zane sent me into a tizzy. "You're unbelievable." I wanted to slap some common sense into him. Actually, I just wanted to slap him. Flattening my palms on his chest, I pushed. "Go. Leave then." Even as the words were leaving my mouth, I knew it was the last thing I wanted.

Regret seeped into his eyes. "Piper ..."

I wasn't having any of it. This was his choice. Anger whipped through me, overshadowing the deep ache in my chest. "I don't need your pity or your protection. I don't need you—"

He was gone before I finished my sentence. I turned around, hoping, but he was nowhere to be found. Zane had left. And this time, I had a feeling it was for good. He was leaving Raven Hollow. Leaving me.

The pang in my chest started to spread and tears filled my eyes as I took a step down the long hallway. I'd finally realized the depths of what I felt for him and gotten the courage to tell him. What did he do? He ran away. A dark depression descended and the light inside me extinguished.

# CHAPTER 20

I poked around in the kitchen like a zombie, rummaging in the cabinets and then in the fridge, each time forgetting what I was looking for. There was this hole in my chest and a weird throbbing in my head.

And it was all Zane's fault. No one called more truly to my soul. No one could hurt me more.

The back of my eyes ached as if another round of tears would fall. My whole life felt out of sorts. Jumbled. A mess. Before I'd had purpose.

No longer hungry, I left the kitchen and kept going. Right out the front door, out the gate, and down to the beach. I wandered aimlessly, no destination in mind, but needing the fresh air. The truth was hard to face. I didn't want to believe he could up and leave so easily, not when inside I was torn apart. How could he claim to feel more for me? It wasn't possible, because the clog of emotions seemed to get heavier and more intense the longer he was gone.

There was no escaping it.

No matter how far I traveled, the ache was ever present in my heart.

As I walked along the postcard island, down by the harbor, a pair of crows circled my head. Every so often I glanced over my shoulder, half expecting Zane to appear and scold me. Each time I was sadly disappointed. He was nowhere to be found.

The little shops were tidy and prim, their colors faded by the sun and sea, but only adding charm. Cobblestone and wood lined the streets, curving down to the docks. If I didn't know better, I would think Raven Hollow was the perfect little town. White picket fences. Dogs barking. Kids riding their bikes down the boardwalk.

But I did know better, shattering the picture-perfect image.

Zane was really gone.

I sensed it deep inside me. That shimmery light in my heart was fading.

The sun was setting over the horizon, casting oranges and pinks over the water by the time I started back down the beach. I dug my feet into the sand, staring at the waves cresting and falling. If I ever needed my mom, now was the time.

Could I summon her as I had before?

Cool evening air caressed my skin as I waited. I called her name over and over again, wishing on every star in the sky to see her face. The sand began to chill my feet, but I didn't mind. My concentration wasn't on my body temperature, but why she wasn't answering me.

I knew I had it in me. I'd done it before … accidentally. You would think by now it would come easier. I was tired of stumbling my way through this reaper stuff. Only a month left of summer and with it came the expectation of my marriage.

A white mist hovered slightly over the water lit by the moon, teasing between the dark summer leaves. Sounds of the wind, the sea, and the rocks, were a soothing lullaby against the primitive island. It almost seemed normal to see a ghost or the Headless Horseman.

I was about ready to give up on her when the mist slowly began to take a shape. It rose above the water, moving toward me in a billow. I held my breath, waiting.

She looked impossibly beautiful, the gold of her hair silvered in starlight, and her skin shimmered milky under the moon's glow. When her gaze met mine across the water, a power so intense burned in my blood. For a moment, I swore the whole of her sparkled.

"Mom." I sighed. "I was beginning to think you wouldn't come."

"Traveling in the afterlife is very different than on Earth. But I am here, for the moment." Her eyes sharpened. "What is wrong?"

I didn't know where to start, but then I began to ramble. Random stuff came out of my mouth, and I couldn't stop it. "Parker showed up. Can you believe that? Just when I thought everyone was safe. Then he goes and gets himself killed. Thank God Rose showed up, and I miraculously was able to restore his soul. It was mind blowing. I can't believe I have the power to do that. Me. Of course just when things seem to be going my way, it all blows back in my face. Zane and Parker hate each other. And then, I finally get the nerve to tell Zane I love him, and the jerk leaves."

Tenderness crept over her eyes as she floated down beside me on the beach. "Take a breath."

I did as she instructed, feeling like I'd run a marathon. "I don't think I can do this. Not without him."

"Oh, Piper, I know it must feel like your world is ending, and it would be foolish of me to dismiss what you're feeling. Love can be glorious and dazzling. But it can also hurt like a bitch, more so for you and Zane. The affinity of your souls ties Zane to you, and the love you both share only tightens that connection of your souls."

The tears were threatening to come back. "How could he leave then?"

Mom smiled sadly. "I don't know. It could be the feelings he has for you have shaken him up, scared him."

"That doesn't make sense. Zane isn't afraid of anything."

"Except maybe losing you?" she offered.

My fingers spread into the sand, letting the granules slip through. "Well, he has a shitty way of showing it."

"He's a guy. It takes them longer to catch up," she said, a twist to her lips.

Mom had a way of putting things into perspective. "The thing is, I'm short on time."

"Give him a little bit of space. My bet is he'll come back."

I wasn't so sure.

"In the meantime," she continued, "remember who you are. What you need to do."

"Zane says the hallows are getting out of control, that their numbers are increasing." I looked to her for affirmation.

She nodded. "He's right."

"What am I supposed to do about it?" Frustration and fear seeped into my voice. Our mother-daughter talk wasn't only about boys; it was about something bigger than my broken heart.

Her fingers brushed over my hair as lightly as the mist drifting on the surface of the sea. "You're asking the wrong Raven. That is a question more suited for your grandma. I do know it's a problem you can't ignore. Reapers are dwindling, and unfortunately they're the only beings able to deal with the hallows."

That got me thinking. "Are you a hallow?"

She smiled. "No. It's part of your ability. Because a piece of me lives in you, you're able to summon your predecessors."

"All of them?"

"Weird, huh?"

To say the least. "That's kind of … creepy."

She laughed. "I always thought so too."

Our grins mirrored each other as we each took a memory snapshot, for our time was coming to an end. She slowly faded away, the mist thickening and swallowing her form. My heart was heavy, but knowing she wasn't truly lost from me lessened the ache.

"Piper, are you okay?"

I blinked and focused on Parker. He was sitting beside me, his straw-colored hair blowing in the breeze. "I will be, I think."

His shoulder brushed up against mine. "You're sure?"

A whirl of emotions crashed into me, but I pushed them aside—for the moment. "You don't need to worry about Zane anymore. He's gone."

"First smart thing I've seen the guy do." It was an offhanded comment, not really meant to hurt me, but I lost it.

Tears erupted like a volcano, burning down my cheeks.

"Oh shit. Piper, I'm sorry. I didn't mean it." His arm went around me, enveloping me in his embrace.

I buried my face in his shirt. He may not understand what I was feeling or the choices I'd made, but Parker was always there for me. It meant more to me than he realized. I grabbed a handful of his shirt and held on. "It's not you," I muttered against his chest.

He held me close. "That's a comfort."

I sniffled, lifting my head. "I don't know what I'd do without you." Maybe Parker coming here had been fate.

"I've been trying to tell you that."

"Sorry it took me so long to listen."

"Don't sweat it. Everyone deserves a mental breakdown once in a while."

I hugged my knees to my chest, staring at the horizon where the stars met the ocean. "I saw my mom."

His mouth dropped. "Holy crap. Are you serious? Is that a reaper benefit?"

"Yeah, it appears so."

"What did she say?" he asked. Parker was family. I knew he missed my mom.

"What I needed to hear." Raven Hollow was my home.

# CHAPTER 21

Days went by. And each started out the same as the one before. It took a few minutes after waking for me to realize Zane was still gone. Then the sinking feeling in my stomach returned, growing more prominent every day.

A frosty air had developed between Parker and me. He didn't understand my world or why I wouldn't leave this place, how I couldn't leave. All he saw was how hard I pushed myself each day learning, training, until the point of sheer exhaustion. It was the only way I could get through the day.

My heart ached.

Zander had picked up where Zane had left off in my combat and magical skills. It was actually easier working with Zander. I didn't have to worry about keeping my emotions in check. I didn't have to think about us accidently merging our souls. Zander was a patient and systematic instructor.

As the days passed, I kept waiting for the attacks from either the rebels or the hallows. When they didn't storm the manor or the country club, I let myself breathe a little easier. But Zander never let his guard down. I had to give it to him. He handled our situation better than I did.

"Where's your sidekick today?" Zander asked as I threw my hair into a messy ponytail.

Most days Parker came with me to practice. "He's with Zoe today. I'm meeting them later."

The edges of his lips bowed. "I can't believe you left him in her care."

My brows bunched together. "She was too excited when she suggested they hang out."

"I'm sure he'll be fine. It's his heart I'd be concerned about."

I scrunched my nose, making an ugly face. "Are you suggesting that Zoe is interested in Parker?"

He rolled his eyes. "No guy is safe around my sister."

"That's comforting," I said, my lips thinning.

Zander grinned.

I wanted to smack him for putting the image in my head. Zoe was the closest friend I had on the island and Parker was my oldest friend. The two of them were not allowed to be into each other. Gross. Anyway, Parker was still hung up on me. Right?

Suddenly, I wasn't so sure.

Zander tweaked the tip of my nose. "You're stressing."

"I am not," I argued, lifting my eyes to meet his.

"Those lines folding over on your forehead say otherwise."

"So shoot me."

He was getting used to my sarcastic nature. "Nah. How about we work the tension out of your body? Which one do you want? Physical? Or mental?"

"I choose C. None of the above."

"Did you say all of the above? I knew you were an overachiever."

I folded my arms. "Someone took their funny pills today." We were more comfortable with each other, and every day before we got down to business, I asked Zander the same thing. "Have you seen any hallows?" I bent down to tie the laces on my shoe that had unknotted.

"No." I don't know why I expected a different answer.

Standing up, I asked. "It's got you on edge too?"

He tried to hide his concern from me. "Yeah." I could see a multitude of thoughts running through his mind. He rubbed the back of his neck. "It's not like them to be so quiet. The longer we go without an attack, the more I'm sure something is brewing."

"What are we going to do?"

Zander projected a determination that put mine to shame. "Nothing at the moment. You're going to dazzle me with your incredible skills."

I busted out laughing. "You must have me mixed up with another Raven. We've been at this for a week and I haven't been able to do squat. It's embarrassing."

His gym shoes squished on the floor mats as he walked toward me. He hadn't been kidding. "The only thing you have to be embarrassed about is quitting."

Subtly didn't run in the Hunters' genes. I huffed. "Whatever. Don't make me say I told you so."

"You can do this," he said, putting his hands on my shoulders.

I was getting sick of hearing his optimism, because I hated disappointing him. It was a basic reaper skill to be able to summon your power into a tangible force. For me, it wasn't so basic.

There was a static charge from his touch, but it was faint in comparison to others I'd felt with a certain he-who-won't-be-named. "Sure," I replied flatly.

"Our abilities are like an extension of us. I want you to tap into your core and send it outside of you. You've done it before. Now I want you to control it."

The corner of my lips curved. "You get that I have no idea what you just said."

"The how isn't as important as the doing. Now clear your head and call forth the core," he instructed.

Conjuring my core power was a simple task. It was everything after that that was the problem, but I did as he asked, concentrating on the light slowly filling me from the inside out.

"Okay, good. Hold out your arms."

Nodding, I obeyed. I was afraid to speak and break my control.

His fingers wrapped lightly around my wrists, and I could feel an underlying hum of his power buzzing at the surface. "I want you to close your eyes and picture in your mind the light gathering in the palm of your hands. It won't hurt you, but the light is intense and bright."

Pain wasn't something I associated with the power inside me, more like ecstasy. I took a deep breath, picturing my hands glowing with perfect spheres of light. I looked like a Christmas ornament.

"Do you see it?" he asked softly.

The smile that had started to spread on my lips faded. I did. The light was so brilliant that its rays shone behind my lids.

"Open your eyes, Piper," Zander whispered. There was something in his tone that had my blood racing.

When I did, the entire two-story room was encompassed in ribbons of white extending from my hands and rising up over my head in a blinding light. I was mesmerized. Eyes wide, I watched as I moved my hands, the ribbons swirling with my movements, mimicking them.

*Holy Toledo.* Just as Zander had said, the light was an extension of me. It flexed and bent to my will. A supreme thrill spun through me.

"I can't believe I actually did that." I almost started jumping and squealing. And because I couldn't resist, I threw my arms around Zander, giving him a quick hug. I wouldn't have been able to do it without him.

"You're not done yet." His voice was steady through the seductive haze. I felt his gaze on me, but I couldn't bring myself to stop staring at the glittering light. "I want you to turn it into a weapon. It doesn't matter what type, only the strength you put into it."

My mind immediately thought of Zane and how he controlled his shadows. I'd seen him turn them into anything he wanted. Whips. Swords. Even the scythe he was so aptly called. The glamour of my power danced around me, powerful and raw. This time I kept my eyes open, beckoning the light to alter its form—a shape I pictured in my head. I about lost my hold when the beams started to ripple. This was seriously amazing. It was kind of like drawing, but in my mind.

With a sense of euphoria, I watched as two sleek and powerful blades shimmered in each of my hands. They were made of a material that didn't exist on Earth. Alabaster in color but without a solid form, the daggers looked as if I could pass my hand through them. But as I wielded them in my hands, testing their weight, I knew without a doubt they were meant to kill.

"Show-off." Zander grinned.

And I grinned back.

A mixture of pride and satisfaction reflected in his soft blue eyes. "Nice work. I knew you had it in you."

My heart warmed, and I turned, immediately searching for Zane. I wanted to share the rush of my accomplishment. It took a few blinks before I remembered he was gone. He'd missed it.

Wow. The one time I actually did something completely on my own, and he wasn't here to see it. How the heck was I supposed to gloat?

"Piper," Zander called gently. "You okay?"

I wasn't sure I would ever be okay again, but that was not what I said. "Yeah." I dragged a few deep breaths and faced him.

"Do you want to talk about it?"

I knew what he was asking. I choked out a laugh. "About your brother bailing on me? No. Not really."

Zander was silent for a few moments, which was about all he could handle of stillness. "Good, because I don't want to talk about the stubborn mule either."

"You mean jackass?"

He nodded. "You have such a way with words."

The excitement of the blades had been doused by my extreme disappointment. "I'm going to make such an exceptional leader," I said sarcastically.

"Regardless of your vibrant vocab, I think you have what it takes."

I sat on the ground, right in the middle of the mats, and crossed my legs. "That makes one of us."

He followed suit, plopping down in front of me. Well, Zander didn't exactly plop. "Since we've already made it completely awkward in here," he said, "I have an unconventional lesson, but I think it's necessary."

I opened and closed my hands as I looked at him. They were tingling. "Now I'm nervous."

I could tell he was as well. His Celtic accent thickened. It was kinda cute. "During the coronation, certain things are going to be expected from us."

"Like?" Since Zane had left, I'd more or less resigned my fate to marrying Zander. If he wasn't willing to fight for us, why should I?

"We'll be expected to announce our engagement." This I knew. I got the feeling he was beating around the bush. He wiped his palms over his knees. "And we'll have to ... kiss."

"Kiss?" I echoed. My voice went up an uncomfortable ten notches. Talk about a buzzkill.

He nodded. "It's part of the custom to seal our fates and our commitment to keeping the reaper line pure."

I really didn't want to consider Zander and me making babies, but I couldn't stop myself from asking. "What do you mean 'pure'?"

"It's what we are—reapers born from undiluted bloodlines. Our children will be powerful, ensuring their place." He tripped ever so slightly over the mention of our offspring.

Customs sucked. I couldn't believe we were having this discussion. It was almost comical. "So you want to practice kissing?" My palms started to sweat.

He shrugged. "I figured it might be less awkward if it wasn't our first time."

*I'll say.* Who knows how I would have reacted? Slapping your fiancé across the cheek after he plants one on you doesn't exactly scream affection, though I wasn't sure anyone expected me to be in love with Zander. "Why does this sound like I'm in junior high and we're about to go into the closet?"

He grinned in a way that was both sheepish and devilish. "I swear it's not ... mostly. I'd be lying if I said I never thought about kissing you. I mean, look at you."

I blushed, assuming that was a compliment. "Thanks. I think."

"Would you feel better if we used the closet?" he joked, attempting to lighten the mood.

I was never happier Parker was otherwise occupied and Zane was gone. It was uncomfortable enough as it was. Thankfully, we had the training room to ourselves, which was rare. I smiled. "Probably."

He leaned forward, and all I could think was we were really going to do this. My breath slowed and curiosity filled me. Would it be like kissing Zane? Would my pulse race? Would the world drown out around me?

Something told me no one would make the world burn as Zane did, and this foolish idea Zander could make me forget Zane was just that—foolish.

We connected all right. Our noses. I couldn't help but giggle. This was not going smoothly.

A rueful smile quirked his lips. "Maybe I should try the sneak attack."

"If you keep making me laugh, I'll end up biting your lip."

"Sounds kinky."

*OMG, is he flirting with me?*

He arched a brow. "Let's try this again?"

I nodded, wetting my lips.

His hand found my cheek, and I closed my eyes. Lightly, his lips brushed over mine. Believe it or not, my hands didn't itch to crack him across the cheek. His lips were soft and gentle, testing my response. The kiss was nice. He didn't slobber all over me or try to invade my mouth with his tongue. But no matter how much I wanted to lose myself in the kiss, I couldn't. It lacked something—that sweep-me-off-my-feet punch.

I wanted to curse Zane to seven different kinds of Hell even as I kissed Zander back.

He whispered my name, and his hands dropped to my waist as his lips swept over mine for a second time. I placed my hand on his shoulder, unsure if I was going to pull him closer or push him away.

I didn't have to make a choice. We were no longer alone.

"'Bout time you put the moves on her."

Zander and I sprung away at the sound of Zoe's voice. Parker was scowling beside her, looking down at Zander. His feelings for the eldest Hunter were only slightly less hateful than for Zane. You could say they tolerated each other. I didn't see a budding friendship developing anytime soon.

*So much for privacy.*

I was thankful for the interruption. It saved me from having to deal with the after-kiss awkwardness. My cheeks decided to turn five shades of red. I lowered my chin.

"Zoe, what are you doing here?" Zander demanded gruffly.

There was an impish twinkle in her eyes. "I came to rescue my best friend, but by the looks of it, she isn't in danger of being bored to tears."

"Your timing is impeccable, as always." Zander frowned as he got to his feet and helped me up. His fingers stayed wrapped around mine, and a stirring of guilt poked at me.

"I don't remember kissing being part of training," Zoe said. She was having too much fun at Zander's and my expense—our distress specifically.

"Zoe, don't you have something to do?" Zander asked, not pleased with the disruption.

"Don't get your boxers in a wad, big brother. I'm here for Piper. As much as I'm sure you would like to continue sucking her face off, the coronation is in less than a week," she informed us, drumming a nail on her lips. A few times, Zoe had attempted to draw me into her circle of friends, but her efforts had been fruitless. I didn't want or need a social life. But I was only able to dodge her shopping trips for so long. She'd found a way to corner me.

I ran my hand through my rumpled ponytail. "Ugh. Don't remind me."

She was enjoying this. "We need to find you a dress."

Parker chuckled. "Piper? In a dress? You're joking."

My eyes tapered in Parker's direction, and he wisely shut his trap. I turned to Zoe. "What am I expected to wear to this spectacle?" Thinking about the ceremony gave me hives. Not only was I going to be inducted as the White Raven, there would also be a public announcement regarding my engagement.

"Something nice and respectable." Once she saw the outrage on my face, she grinned. "Of course, you never do as you're expected."

My grin echoed hers. Now she was talking my language. "Let's go shopping." I unwound my fingers from Zander's. "Thanks for the lesson. It was … enlightening."

Zoe snickered.

Parker coughed.

And Zander grinned. "Anytime. You're a natural."

I didn't know if he was talking about my powers or the kiss. My cheeks burned, and Zoe thought it was hilarious.

I couldn't get out of that room soon enough. I'd never thought I would be so eager to go shopping, but I needed air, unable to shake the feeling I'd made a mistake.

The island didn't have a mall but a variety of specialty shops. Fine by me. I avoided malls like boy band concerts. Nothing but a bunch of gossiping cliques racking up Daddy's credit cards. Like my mom, I preferred to be thrifty, but I guessed we wouldn't be hitting up any secondhand stores.

I waited until we were browsing in the first store before I asked the question burning my mind. "Have you heard from Zane?"

Parker opened his mouth, but Zoe elbowed him in the gut. She always found a way to never give me a straight answer. "He'll be back. He might not realize it yet, but he won't be able to stay away from you."

I hoped so. I really hoped. "Maybe."

"You can make him come back, you know," Parker said. "If you really wanted to. You could call him home. Isn't that what you do? A banshee and all."

"Holy shit, Parker. You're a genius. Why didn't I think of that?"

"Because I'm the genius," he so wisely reminded me.

However, the more I thought on it, the less appealing the idea became. Forcing Zane back wasn't going to make him want me. It wasn't going to make him marry me. If anything, it would only piss him off, push him farther away.

Dammit.

I filtered through a rack of frilly dresses, my mind really not into the task. It was hard to concentrate, especially with Parker and Zoe laughing and touching each other. What was going on there? They were flirting. Gah! I thought my eyeballs were going to burst into flames.

"Can we focus?" I snapped.

Zoe dropped her hand from Parker's forearm. "How about this?" she asked, pulling a dress from the rack.

"That's nice," I replied without looking at the dress.

"Really, Piper? It's pink," Parker stated, giving me a funny glance.

"Huh?" My gaze lifted, and I was horrified. "I hope that's your idea of a twisted joke."

"Girl, turn that frown upside down. He'll be back," she whispered, draping an arm around my shoulders.

In the end, I let Zoe pick a simple little black dress. It was short enough to raise a few eyebrows but ensured all my lady bits were covered.

# CHAPTER 22

As soon as the door was shut, I turned on Parker. "What the heck was that?"

Confusion etched the lines of his face. "You're going to have to elaborate. We're close, but I can't read your mind."

"You and Zoe," I exploded, connecting the dots for his hormone-clogged brain. "I saw you together."

"And …?" he prompted, completely missing the insinuation.

I rolled my eyes. "*And* you were flirting with her. Are you into her?"

He brushed past me, shaking his head as if he was disgusted I cared. "What's it to you?"

My hand touched his shoulder. "Parker, she's a death reaper."

He looked up at me, eyes unflinching. There was a hardness I wasn't used to seeing in his hazel eyes. "So? What does that have to do with anything?"

Was he kidding me? Was I the only person who saw a problem with that? "For someone who is so *smart*, you're acting like an idiot."

"Oooh, it's okay for you to marry a reaper, but I can't hang out with one?"

"Yes! I'm a reaper."

Stunned, he stared at me. "What kind of hypocritical shitnit is that? I don't even know who you are anymore."

Neither did I. I paused, exhaling. My intent hadn't been to fight with Parker, but that was exactly where this was leading. I needed to tone it down. "Look, I know things have changed, that I've changed, but one thing that hasn't is how much I care about you. I don't want you to get hurt."

"It's a bit too late to worry about me getting hurt," he snapped.

Right. I'd hurt him, though it was the last thing I'd ever wanted to do. And not to mention, he had died. "I never meant to hurt you."

His fingers dug into his hair. "I know. And I do appreciate you looking out for me."

"But …" I inserted.

Parker looked away, focusing on the blank spot over my head. "I'm trying to find a way to get over you. I've accepted that we'll only be friends, the best of friends, and I'm okay with that. But I need to move forward, in my own way. And Zoe, she dulls the ache. When I'm with her, I don't dwell on how much I miss you."

I swallowed and sunk into the nearest chair. "God, I make a mess of everything."

He took a seat across from me. The floral pattern of the furniture looked too feminine and delicate for a guy to be comfortable sitting on. "If we didn't make mistakes, we wouldn't learn from them."

"I'm not sure what I've learned, other than everyone I care about leaves me."

"It might feel that way, but it's not true. I'm still here, and so are TJ and your dad."

I made a funny noise in the back of my throat. My dad. He wasn't up there on the list of people who truly cared about me. I'm sure he did in his own way, but since Mom died, the man simply had given up on life. The mention of Dad made me think of TJ. I made a mental note to text him later to see how he was faring. I'd been a rotten sister as of late.

"I know that look on your face," Parker said. "You can stop blaming yourself. You did the right thing, sending TJ away. The farther he is from this, the better. Zoe told me he doesn't have any reaper in him."

My chest tightened. "I thought you weren't a mind reader."

He grinned. "As much as I would like superpowers, it doesn't take magic to decipher your expressions. You care too much; that isn't a bad thing."

"It's not safe here, you know." I should send *Parker* away, but I was selfish. Now that he knew everything, I wanted him here. He was comforting and familiar. It was like having a piece of home with me.

Hard lines formed across his forehead. "Nowhere is safe. Now that I can see."

"Did Zoe explain that as well?" It appeared Zoe's mouth had been doing a lot of flapping. I wasn't sure how it made me feel. At first, I'd wanted to involve Parker as little as possible, but maybe educating him was the best defense. The more he knew, the better chance he had at surviving. Either way, it was a moot point, because I needed him— more now than ever.

A slow grin pulled at his lips. "She likes to talk."

"Uh-huh. You're telling me." I tilted my head up, smiling. "You really like her, don't you?" I could see it in his eyes when he mentioned her name. They lit up and warmed. He'd once looked at me like that.

He shrugged. "Yeah, I think I do."

"Just do me a favor. Don't get hurt." *Like I did,* I silently added.

"So, you're cool with it?"

"I will be," I promised, smiling.

His eyes skated over the room, and his silly smirk faded. "What room is this?"

"I have no idea. I'm not sure I've even been in here." For good reason. It was fugly.

He pushed his wire-rimmed glasses up the bridge of his nose. "Do us all a favor, would ya? Remove every piece of furniture in this place. It needs to be burned."

I laughed. "I couldn't agree more." It had never occurred to me to redecorate any of the rooms, but Raven Manor was mine now. I could do what I liked with it. Rose and I had very different tastes. Maybe if I made this place homier and less cold, it would feel more like a home—more like mine.

It got me thinking.

"Parker, you really are a genius."

"Why is that so hard for everyone to believe?"

"It's not. Sometimes you surprise me, is all."

His phone dinged, and that ridiculous gleam lit up his eyes, the one I used to find adorable. I could guess who was on the other end. "Hey," he answered, standing up. And just like that, I was no longer the most important person in the room.

I listened to him jabber and laugh as he walked up the winding stairs, out of earshot. I wanted to be happy for him. I really did, but his fresh excitement only reminded me how lonely and sad I was.

I was tired of the pain. My mom. Rose. And now Zane. When would it end? If I thought too hard about the hurt, the tears would start falling again. I needed a distraction.

In my room, I grabbed my sketch pad, hoping to ease the pressure in my chest. The black fine-tipped marker was like an old friend in my hand. Contouring over the paper in long strokes, I outlined the image of a girl in a fighter stance, a fiery blade in each hand, sweeping across the page. I knew she was me.

I stared at the paper, and before I could stop myself, I was flipping through my previous drawings. Zane's profile, his eyes, and his lips filled the pages. How many different ways had I drawn him? I was torturing myself. I didn't know why I was putting myself through the agony. The truth was hard to face.

He wasn't coming back.

As the days passed, that sinking reality tore me up inside. It was a stab in the gut, seeing the sharp angles of his face staring back at me, his fierceness captured with ink and paper, the piercing blue of his eyes looking into my soul.

Slamming the book closed, I tossed it on the nightstand and rolled over on the bed. I clutched my pillow tightly and closed my eyes. How had my life gotten so tangled up? If I'd known saying I loved him would send him running for the hills, I would have kept my mouth shut. Hindsight could be a cruel thing.

I opened my eyes and focused on a shadow in the corner. *What the ...?* I swore I could see his face. *Zane.* He moved within the dark spots of my room, his body disappearing, then reappearing and disappearing again. I could only watch, enthralled by him.

My heart kick-started in my chest, thumping so loudly I swore the dead could hear it. Staying as still as possible, I was afraid to breathe. He might suddenly leave, and that was a nightmare in itself.

I blinked.

And in the shadows, there was no one.

I rolled over onto my side and sighed. He invaded my dreams, my thoughts, and now I was seeing him in the shadows. The urge to whisper his name rose up in me, swiftly and vigorously, but I buried it, biting my lip until the metallic taste of my own blood hit my tongue. It helped refocus the internal pain to physical pain ... for the moment.

---

"Cheer up. You look like your puppy just died," Zoe said. She was sitting across from me on the couch. We were facing each other with our legs crossed.

I held an iced glass of sweet tea she'd made us between my hands, the frost on the glass not bothering me. "How come the cold doesn't seem to affect me?" I asked, staring at my hands.

"Reapers are naturally cooler. Our blood runs degrees lower than humans'. Therefore, your tolerance to the cold is higher."

I squeezed the glass. "I never noticed before, but now, I can feel the chill in my veins. It's not uncomfortable, just that my awareness is sharper."

She nodded. "The more you use your core powers, the stronger your senses will become."

"That's weird."

Her giggle was husky. For someone who was so dainty, she had this envious sexy voice. Her accent helped. "Maybe for you. I can't imagine having human senses. I'd feel so ... naked."

"What other changes can I expect?" I asked.

A twinkle flickered in her eyes. "Fun stuff, like sharper perception, heightened spirit detection, and fiercer emotions. The enhancement can differ per reaper."

"Emotions?" That one surprised me.

"A general misconception about reapers is we are uncaring. Total bullshit. I often sympathize with my victims. It depends on the situation. We're generally completely neutral beings. Hell. Heaven. Purgatory. It doesn't matter to me, as long as the natural order of life and death stays intact. This is our sole purpose."

I was going to regret asking but my inquiring mind had to know. "What happens if the natural order is disrupted? Besides chaos?"

Her voice went flat. "Utter darkness."

"Oh, goody," I said drily. "Do you mean literal darkness?"

Zoe's poetic lips tipped down at the corners. "If we don't hold up our end of the bargain—delivering souls to the afterlife—the whole system falls apart. And Earth goes black."

Nausea roiled inside me. "Why would anyone want that? It doesn't make sense to me."

"Within the darkness comes madness. Once it gets its claws in you, its appetite for power is insatiable. Reapers can go dark. Ferrying a living soul to the afterlife is against the rules. If you cross those lines, there's no turning back. There are no second chances. That's where you come in."

It all came back to power. "I get to banish the bad boys."

"It's your will. You call us. We don't call you."

My fingers fiddled with the silver chain dangling from my neck. "Can I ask you something?"

She didn't miss a beat in her quick response. "I still haven't heard from Zane." Remorse colored her tone.

I smiled weakly. "Actually, I have a different question for once."

She unfolded her legs on the couch. "Shoot."

"Zander told me I'm expected to marry a pureblood."

Her long, wavy black hair streamed behind her. "That's right. To keep the Raven line from being diluted."

"I should probably know this, but pureblood is someone whose parents are both reapers, right?" I asked.

"Fundamentally, yes."

"If that is the case, why must I marry Zander? No offense. Your brother is great. I just always thought it would be my choice. I know he is the heir to the Black Crows, but as long as they are a pure reaper …"

Her blue eyes brightened. "What you're really asking is, why Zander and not Zane?"

If you stripped it down to the basics, more or less. "Is it so terrible to want to be with someone you love?"

Leaning forward, she folded her slender arms. "Depends on who you ask. What you have with Zane only happens once in a lifetime. For many of us, we never find it. I'm so jealous, and I can't understand how my brother can walk away from you."

"Well, he did," I said, examining strands of my hair. A reaper's lifetime went beyond that of a human's, so I understood the importance of the connection I had with Zane.

"You need to know that he has his reasons. I might not agree with them, but I understand."

"Bullshit," I hissed. "What could possibly justify hurting someone you swore to protect?"

Sympathy pooled in her eyes. "It's more complicated than that."

"When isn't it?" My chin went up a notch as I steeled myself against the instant hurt of rejection. "Help me understand, because I don't get anything your brother does."

She stared at me. "He is going to kill me if I tell you."

I could see her struggling with the decision. Whatever she knew, it was big. But I wasn't taking no for an answer. "I'm going to kill you if you don't."

Her lips pursed, and for a few seconds, I thought she was going to refuse, but then in an even tone, she said, "Zane isn't a pureblood."

I slid her a holy-shit-on-a-stick look. "What? How can that be?"

She wrung her fingers. "He's my half-brother. We don't have the same mum."

My eyes popped. "What do you mean Zane has a different mother?" I was having a hard time comprehending what she was telling me. "How is that possible?"

She shrugged her dainty shoulders. "The usual. My dad slept with another woman. A human. Zane is only half reaper."

The bombshells just kept on rolling, and I was beginning to understand the jerk's thought process, but I didn't want to believe it. Because believing Zane wasn't pure crushed all my dreams. It destroyed my future—what *I* wanted. "If he is only part reaper, how is he so powerful?" He might be a d-bag, but he was a douchebag who could kick some serious ass.

"By thinking he has something to prove. He works twice as hard as the rest of us, pushing himself past feasible limits. Zane doesn't just *want* to be the best; he *is* the best."

Just like him to see being half human as a shortcoming. My shoulders slumped. "So if your dad had an affair with a human, and you, Zach, and Zander are pure, who is your mom?"

Confusion etched her willowy brows. "What do you mean? You know my mum."

I bit my chipped fingernails, thinking. "I thought your mom was human."

A light dawned in her eyes. "Mum is human now, but she wasn't always."

The webs kept spinning. I was going to need her to draw me a family tree. "If she used to be a reaper, what happened?"

"You're going to love this. She was a Hawk, until Rose stripped her of her powers."

I choked. *And the plot thickens.* "Why would Rose do that?"

"She was the White Raven. Rose didn't need a reason, but in this particular situation, she did have one."

My mind immediately jumped to the conclusion that it had something to do with her soul symmetry with Death. Had Rose gotten jealous and, in her rage, stripped Ivy of her reaper wings? I could see myself doing something like that, but not Rose. She had too much decorum and rigidness.

"I don't know all the deets, as Zach and I were babies," she continued. I was on the edge of my seat. "But word around town is my mum killed Zane's mum."

I gasped and almost fell over the edge of the couch. "Without an order?" I guessed.

She nodded. "Rose took her powers but spared her soul."

I wrapped my arms around my waist to try to suppress the shudder. "And yet your mom raised Zane as one of her own?"

"It might seem unconventional and a bit unethical, but I think once the guilt at what she had done finally set in, she had hoped in some small way to make amends. Truthfully, he was impossible not to love. He was only two at the time and a perfect little boy. Never has Mum treated him differently. None of us have. Zane has only been but a brother to me."

I couldn't help but feel for him. For his loss. The last thing I wanted was to empathize with the jerk. I was still hurting. Why hadn't he told me? It might have saved me some tears. "That is some heavy shit, Zoe." My fingers dashed through my hair as I swallowed the reality.

Zane wasn't a pureblood.

And that meant I couldn't marry him. Why did I have to fall in love with someone I could never have?

With a snap of a finger, the pain made way for anger.

I was pissed.

At Zane. At my mom. At Rose. At Death. At the universe.

# CHAPTER 23

Death paid me a visit.

For anyone else, it would be a grave sign to see Death at your doorstep. For me, it was a reminder of my responsibilities.

The last few weeks I hadn't been expected to do anything more than train and learn the ways of being a reaper, but now with my coronation right around the corner, the day was coming when I was going to have to step into my birthright.

Ready or not.

Death was not what you'd picture. His face wasn't pale and sunken. He didn't have wrinkles around his eyes or wear a black cloak. Parker would be disappointed, but Death looked like an Irish mountain man. Big. Burly. Gruff. And handsome as hell. For an old dude.

And he was old. Prehistoric.

Unsure what to do or say, I shifted my weight, shoved my hands in my back pockets, and met his gaze. "Is this where you check up on me? Make sure I stay in line?"

He crowded the circular entry hall with his presence. "The wife worries about you alone in this house," he said breezily.

I tried to keep a straight face when he mentioned Ivy. It was hard to not look upon him in a different light, knowing his dirty little secrets. We all had them. "And do you worry? About me?"

"Why wouldn't I? You're virtually family. And not to mention a crucial part to the universe's balance."

"There's no need. I'm a big girl now."

"I'd ask you how you are, but something tells me you'd tell me you're just fine. And we both know that's not true."

Sighing, I admitted, "I've had better days. Better years actually."

"Hmm. Haven't we all. And your training is going well? My hoodlum child is behaving?" It was said with affection.

"Which one? Zach or Zoe?" I said, although we both knew he hadn't been referring to either of them.

Roarke's lips twitched. I always seemed to amuse him. "Walk with me." It wasn't precisely a request. I doubted he would have taken no for an answer.

A walk with Death … sounded ominous.

After Zoe had left yesterday, I made a discovery about myself. I'd been too shocked to consider what she was telling me, but once my blood pressure leveled, I unearthed my own mystery. Everyone was telling me I was a pureblood reaper, that my lineage wasn't tainted, but how could that be? My father was human.

Parker and I had spent more than half the night and into the wee hours of the morning discussing the possibilities. He hadn't been as stunned as I'd been to learn about Zane's biology. Then again, Parker wasn't Zane's biggest fan.

I stepped outside and waited for the right opportunity to broach the subject of my lineage. Something was amiss, and I was afraid of the answers.

The day was sunny and mild, all blue skies and soothing breezes. It was meant to be enjoyed. So much for that summer tan I'd promised myself I would get before senior year.

"It's come to my attention you've had a few … hiccups lately," he said as we walked toward the first tangle of hedges.

I was taking a stab in the dark here, assuming he was talking about Estelle. "If you call killing another reaper a hiccup, then yes."

The edge of his mouth twitched. "Reapers are to be feared, but we aren't evil. We're a necessary part of life and death. And it's important we preserve our legacy. We've been able to coexist with humans mainly because they can't see us for who we really are until that pivotal moment in their lives."

My stomach knotted. I had known it was only a matter of time before word got out about what I'd done to save Parker. It looked like my time was up. "I know I crossed a line, and I'd like to tell you I wouldn't do it again. But I can't."

"Good."

My mouth dropped open. *Good?* He wasn't upset?

"I appreciate your honesty," he added. "It takes that and much more to govern a bunch of impulsive reapers."

Feeling clumsy and foolish, I followed him into the garden paved with stepping stones. A lazy black cat sunned itself on a wooden bench and blinked open one luminous green eye. Since I didn't own a cat, I could only assume it was a Red Hawk planted to keep a watchful eye on me. "So, you're saying I have my work cut out for me?"

"Your grandmother was the Raven for a very long time, more decades than I can recall. She was set in her ways. I firmly believe that change is inevitable. Many of the elders won't be so open to your ideas, but change is necessary. Something needs to be done to control the rogue reapers and the power they gain from aligning themselves with the hallows. If we aren't careful, it will be only a matter of time before they outnumber us."

If Death was truly concerned, then I knew the situation was getting worse. In a way, I'd been sheltered and protected from mounting trouble. Everyone was concerned with my safety. "What do you suggest I do?"

His long strides carried him over the manicured lawn. "You sent a clear message by eliminating Estelle."

"That hadn't been my intent."

"Maybe so, but the message was still received and will travel

through the ranks. Your no BS attitude will serve you well. Being the
Raven requires a backbone."

I snorted. The whole thing with Estelle had been more of an accident than a master plan to make other reapers fear me—that was
more Zane's style. "I hope I don't disappoint."

The garden smelled lovely, and the wind brought traces of the sea.
Roarke should have looked out of place among petunias, cosmos, and
hollyhocks, but he didn't. "My sons think highly of you, Piper. As
do I."

I wasn't sure I deserved such respect, but it made me want to
make them proud. "I don't know what I would have done without
them."

"I know this is difficult—throwing away your old life and having
your future carved out for you. Rose believed she was helping you,
setting you up to be a strong leader."

"And what about you?" He'd also signed off on the unbreakable
treaty. The sector overlords each put their supernatural stamp on the
document that held me to marrying Death's heir.

His polar eyes were serious. "You understand why Zane was not
chosen. The elders would never have allowed it. The longevity of our
lives can be lonely. Think about that before you make a decision that
can't be undone."

Was he telling me to follow my heart or to honor the treaty? I was
confused. Couldn't he be less Yoda-like and just break it down for me?
Simple terms. *Piper, the world will implode if you marry Zane. Or love is a
powerful thing and can overcome anything.* But no, I got nothing, except
the reminder of how long a journey my life would be. Reapers could
live centuries.

I scuffed my shoe on the ground. "Maybe you can answer something for me. There's this question that's been nagging at me."

"What's on your mind?"

"If I am supposed to marry a pureblood, how am I able to be Rose's
successor? My father was human."

There was a long, pregnant pause. "You and Zane have many
things in common, but your legitimacy is not one of them. I think

you've already figured it out, as hard as it might be to come to terms with."

I shook my head. "It's not possible." I *refused* to believe it.

He arched a brow. "And why is that?"

"I would know something like that—if my dad wasn't my ... dad!" I insisted, my voice rising. What he was suggesting was ludicrous.

"You're a hundred percent positive?" he prodded, putting uncertainty into my already doubtful mind.

I'd heard the stories of my birth countless times. How my parents drove through one of the worst storms in Chicago to make it to the hospital mere minutes before I was born. "Maybe I'm not a pureblood," I theorized.

The look in his eyes cracked my heart into a million pieces. "I'm sorry, Piper. If your blood was tainted, you would not have been able to absorb Rose's powers. You would not have been able to save your friend from death."

"I ... Oh, God ..." I thought I was going to hyperventilate.

My face must have gone white, because Roarke put a sturdy hand on my shoulder, and his blue eyes softened. "From someone who has been in a sticky situation, there is no easy way to break the news of that magnitude. James is not your biological father."

*Holy banana pants.*

Regardless of the pit in my stomach, I was fully convinced he was telling me everything I didn't want to believe. I had thought my life was a lie before, but now I was sure of it. Was anything real? What next? Was I going to find out TJ wasn't my brother, or Parker was an alien (which might have explained a few things)? "How can you be so sure?" I whispered.

"Your mom was in love before she met James. She was pregnant with you when she left Raven Hollow, never to return. It was in Chicago that she met James. Your mom was in a dark place, and James helped her appreciate the importance of life. They agreed to raise you away from her world, and your mom renounced her birthright."

My head was spinning, ears buzzing. I sunk into the wooden bench. "My whole childhood was a lie."

He sat down beside me, his presence a surprising comfort. "I know this hasn't been a simple transition for you, but I've seen you flourish. You've accomplished so much in such a short time. Your mom and Rose would be proud of you."

My lip trembled. "Do you know who he is? My real father?" I had to know who he was, yet I wasn't necessarily looking for an emotional reunion. I wasn't sure what I was looking for or if I wanted anything from him.

Roarke nodded. "I did. He was a Blue Sparrow—a soul reaper."

"Where is he? Can I find him?" I wasn't even sure I wanted to see him, but I needed to know where he was … in case.

The compassion in his eyes faded. "I hate to be the bearer of bad news, but its part of the job. He's dead, Piper. He died shortly after your mom found out she was pregnant."

So I was still an orphan. I nodded, feeling nothing but hollow. "How did it happen?"

"The details won't bring you any peace. I know you want to avenge your mother's death. Don't let your pain and anger blind you. Don't let them make you careless. Rogue reapers are ferrying out souls from the afterlife, hallows, for the purpose of personal gain. They are looking to use these ferried souls to overturn your reign."

Isn't that just dandy. "One day at a time."

I wanted to ask him about Zane, if he was okay, but I let him go without saying a thing. And I sat by myself on the bench in the garden, until night descended. A pearl-white light of a three-quarter moon shone over my face. The scent of flowers seemed to rise up and surround me. Drawn to it, I rose, and the breeze fluttered my hair. The heartbeat of the sea was fast and my own raced to keep pace.

"Mom!" I yelled.

She appeared in the garden, walking, almost gliding through the silvery light. Her hair was loose, sprinkling gold dust down her back and over her sheer shoulders. "Why are you screaming?"

"It's kind of my thing." Sarcasm was evident.

"Well, you got my attention. It's what you wanted, isn't it?"

*Duh.* "Why didn't you ever tell me that *Dad* is not my father—my biological father?" I clarified, seeing her eyes cloud with confusion.

Understanding dawned. "You know why, Piper. For the same reason I kept you away from Raven Hollow. I didn't want this world for you. It's a sad story with a tragic end. I never wanted to relive that pain."

"It's inevitable. Don't you see that?"

"At the time, no. My only concern was keeping you as far from Raven Hollow as I could. What was the point of hurting you? I always assumed there would be time. Never did I imagine time would slip away from me, but I should have known I wouldn't be able to slip through death's grasp."

"How many more secrets do you have?"

"Piper Brennan," she said in her watch-your-mouth voice.

I stood, unable to be still. "That's not even my last name."

Mom folded her arms. "It's the name I gave you." Even as a ghost, she had the ability to make me feel like a little girl who'd gotten caught with her hand in the cookie jar.

"I don't know who you are anymore. Who I am."

She plucked a flower and positioned it behind my ear. "*I* know you. There is magic in your eyes. In your blood. But no matter how much power you possess, you will always be my daughter."

"It's all so overwhelming. I can't seem to find my footing."

"You will," she said.

*Here's to hoping I don't muck everything up in the worst kinds of ways.*

*Crack.* Something snapped in the distance. A twig or a leg. I bristled, and like a gust of wind, the transparent image of my mom vanished. My head came up quickly, and in the darkness, I swore I saw him, a shadow by the hedge. I sharpened my focus, letting my light fill me, but all it took was a blink for me to think I was going crazy.

There was nothing there but a well-trimmed shrub.

# CHAPTER 24

"Here's the dealio, girlfriend," a tall, blond-haired man with green spikes said. He stood behind my chair, his fingers lifting my hair off my neck. "We need to talk about your image."

I stared at my reflection in the mirror. "My image?" *You're looking at it buddy.* This was me in all my glory.

"You know, how you want people to perceive you. With those eyes and hair, you could be sophisticated or quite the temptress. But it's all up to you," he said matter-of-factly.

When Trevor had showed up at the manor this morning, my first thought was I was going to kill Zoe. A stylist? Did I really need one?

Apparently I did.

My mom's words echoed in my head. I knew who I was, and it wasn't a temptress or a prestigious bitch. "I'm not changing everything about me to cater to some stuffy assholes."

"Rawr. Ladies and gents, we've got a feisty one on our hands."

"Self-assured for the first time. And a little bit of spunk."

"Have it your way, luv. We'll just enhance your natural beauty. And you're quite the thing." He stuck a comb in between his teeth. "We're going to polish you up a bit. Hang on to your twinkle toes, sweetheart. It's going to get crazy in here."

I had no idea what he was talking about, but it didn't take me long to figure it out. A swarm of women descended upon me, and before I knew it, I'd been ushered into the bathroom, stripped down to my birthday suit, and literally "polished" until my skin was glowing from oils and vanilla bean scented lotions.

No one other than my mom and God had seen me fully naked before. I crossed my arms over my shoulders, frowning. After the team finished making me smooth and luminous, I was slipped into a soft white robe. Their attention was turned to nails, hair, and makeup. One tackled my horrendous cuticles and bitten tips, while another smoothed and hydrated my long hair, and the third applied my makeup. She was a pretty-looking girl who I instructed was under no circumstances to give me false lashes. I could never see out of those things, and they bugged the hell out of me.

Three hours later I was finished. Grumpy and hungry, I studied myself in the mirror, relieved to see I still looked like myself. Some girls looked twice their age with makeup. I just looked nice.

Trevor had piled my hair on top of my head, letting loose pieces dangle over the nape of my neck and framing my face. There were soft caramel highlights in my hair that caught the light in interesting ways.

Once I was all fixed up, it was time to get out of the robe. The black dress left one shoulder exposed, fit snugly at the waist, and hit me mid-thigh. It was probably the sexiest thing I'd ever worn or owned. Sexy wasn't my style, but as I stared at myself, I could see the appeal. There was something empowering about feeling comfortable in my own skin, knowing who I was, what I stood for, and who I wanted to be. Sexy, not skanky. There was a huge difference.

"You're going to really shake things up. About damn time," Trevor said, standing behind me.

"You have no idea." I'd come to some important decisions since my meeting with Roarke. He was right. Things were going to change, and I was going to be the one to make those changes.

A different sensation warmed inside me.

Zane. He was here.

I felt the familiar tingles, like a cool breath on the back of my neck, and my heart rate spiked. For a moment I couldn't move, couldn't think, couldn't breathe. I caught a glimpse of Zane coming through the bedroom doorway, and I focused on Trevor as if he were my lifeline. I knew once Zane and I made eye contact, the world would cease to exist.

But it was only a matter of time. I couldn't avoid the pull for long or the desire to fling myself across the room and into his arms. I took a breath and slowly lifted my head.

Our eyes locked. There was such intensity between us I felt faint. The air between us seemed to stretch with an electric current, sparkling and crackling. The last time I'd seen him, we'd been kissing and I'd confessed my love. And now looking at him, I wasn't sure where that left us.

His eyes were … so burdened. It was a small consolation knowing he had suffered as I had, but it unlocked my heart.

I couldn't take it. Without thinking, I pushed to my feet and raced across the room. I rushed him, wrapping my arms around his neck and burying my face into his shirt. I didn't think about all the people in my room.

He seemed stunned for a moment before his arms swept around me and squeezed. I felt him exhale. For several moments, neither of us said a thing. Maybe it was the connection, or maybe it was something infinitely deeper. I didn't care. All that mattered was he was here, holding me, and I didn't want him to let go.

"Everyone out," he said in a low voice. He put me on my feet, but his arms were still around me, keeping me close.

An unbelievable giddiness swept through me. The coronation was the furthest thing from my mind.

"Piper is on a tight schedule," Trevor said.

When no one moved and only stared at Zane, he roared, "Get out!"

Trevor jumped, but that did it. Zane suddenly had everyone's attention, and they all scrambled as fast as they could down the hall.

"What are you doing?" I squealed, my common sense returning.

Zane had no regard for anyone else. His lips curved into a troublesome grin, revealing a dimple deep in his cheek. "Shush." And like that, he ruined a tender moment.

I felt a flicker of annoyance. "Did you just shush me? I haven't seen you in weeks and you come busting in here, demanding everyone leave."

His grin grew as he shook his head.

I glowered. "How about I shush it right up your ass—?"

His finger pressed to my lips, promptly shutting me up. "Let me just look at you for a moment without you getting your panties in a wad. You're wearing them, right?"

"What? Yes, I wearing them."

"I've been thinking …"

"About my underwear?"

He laughed, deep and throaty. "Dear God, Princess, I missed you."

"You have a funny way of showing it," I muttered. "You know today is the coronation."

"I know. But it was worth it. You're worth it. I don't want you to marry Zander."

*Holy Houdini.*

I stared at him, his striking features highlighted in the waning light from the window. I'd been waiting the entire summer for him to say those words. "Cutting it a little close, aren't you?" In less than thirty minutes, I was supposed to accept my *crown* and announce my engagement.

His eyes sparkled as deep and endless as the star-strewn sky. "I know."

"What took you so long?"

"I needed to see you one last time before you officially became the queenie of reapers."

I scrunched my nose. "Don't even think about calling me that." Princess was bad enough. "I still can't believe it."

The smugness stretched across his lips. "It suits you."

"I'm glad you came back. You don't know how long I've waited to hear you say those words." *The three other big words would be nice too.*

"You misunderstood."

My eyes snapped to his. "But I thought—" My voice caught.

"I don't *want* you to marry him, but it doesn't change the fact that you *will* marry him."

This was not how I'd thought our reunion would go. Sure he'd swept me off my feet, but only to crash to the ground. "What makes you so sure I will?"

"There is no other choice."

"That's because you're not willing to believe, to take a chance. I know the truth. About you. Do you think it matters to me that you're not a pureblood? I don't give a rat's ass if you're a goddamn zombie. I love you."

He took one step forward, which put him in the same breathing space as me. "It does matter, Princess. If it didn't, you'd already be mine."

I wanted to hurt him, to obliterate him into space, hoping when he fell back down from the sky, he'd hit his head hard enough to realize what a jackass he was being. "Why are you here then? To torment me?"

"It feels that way. And I'm sorry. The last thing I want to do is hurt you, Piper, but no matter what I do, someone gets hurt."

"I don't want to marry Zander. I don't want to run away with Parker. I should want to do both of those, but I want—"

Zane's hand flashed over my mouth, silencing me. He was shaking his head, eyes pleading with me. "Don't, Piper. Don't do this."

He was a step ahead of me, knowing what I was thinking before I did. By the time I caught up with him, I knew what I wanted, what I was going to do. Although I had no idea how it was going to turn out, it was worth a shot. I'd been flying blind through this banshee business. Why stop now?

I placed a kiss on the inside of his palm and watched the heat ignite in his dark eyes, mirroring what I was feeling throughout my body. "I know you want this."

"It changes nothing."

The house could crumble around us, but neither of us would notice or care. "It changes everything." I'd been told over and over again that my voice was a power of its own. Time to test the theory. If there was a chance I could change my destiny, I had to try, or I would always wonder. I wanted to live from this point forward with no regrets.

"Piper ..." His voice faded, losing some of his resistance.

With my mind made up, I took a step back and let my blood fill with white bolts of power. It sizzled off my skin, and the room was washed in light. I thought he might try to stop me, tackle me to the ground or something, and when he didn't, I knew this was what I wanted. A relief went through me. Deep down, whether he admitted it or not, Zane wanted to be with me as much as I wanted to be with him.

In a voice steadier than what was happening inside me, I said the words I hoped would dissolve the contract and give me my freedom back. "I renounce my oath to Zander, for he is not my match. Not in my heart or my soul." Thunder cracked outside the window, and my skin glowed as bright as a full moon. I took it as a sign—though I wasn't a hundred percent sure it had worked.

But it felt good, finally making a choice. In my mind, there was no going back, and I wanted Zane to know it.

Standing in the middle of my room, he was watching me with a mixture of awe and disbelief. I froze for only a moment, and then his hand caught mine, fingers tightening as he pulled me forward.

Wrapping my arms around his neck, I rose on my toes and brushed a kiss to his mouth. He crushed me close, and his lips were cool against mine. I weaved my fingers through his silky hair. "I love you, Zane," I whispered.

His hands shook slightly as he framed my face, softly brushing his thumbs along my cheeks. Expression guarded, he said, "That was so stupid, Piper. The consequences—"

"Screw the consequences," I interrupted. I was sick of worrying about everyone else. For once in my life, I put my wants first. Truthfully, I hadn't been thinking about anyone else but Zane.

*Screw them all.*

He must have had the same sentiments, for he was kissing me, mashing our lips together in a toe-curling kiss. A burst of light erupted across the room.

Softly he pulled back, and my gaze was drawn to our joined hands. Our marks were interlaced—his crow with my raven—one black as night and the other as white as clouds.

"Now what?" I asked, mesmerized.

"You tell me, Princess. This was your play. And if it weren't for the merging of our marks, I wouldn't have believed it possible. I only hope one day you don't look back at this moment and regret your choice. There are so many things I can never give you." He pressed his forehead to mine. "This isn't good," he murmured, curiously shaken.

I leaned my hands on his chest, feeling the steely muscles under his shirt tremble. "I know."

"The sectors are going to flip a lid."

I glanced away. "I can't go down there now."

His fingers slipped under my chin, tipping my face upward. "Yes, you can. And you will."

"What if they know? I can't embarrass Zander that way. What do I say?"

The pad of his thumb rubbed alongside my cheek. "The truth. We owe him that. We'll tell him. Now. Before the coronation."

He was right. I did owe Zander that much. My guess was he wouldn't be surprised. My feelings for his brother hadn't been a secret. "No. It should be me. I'll do it. Alone." It was going to be awkward enough. I didn't need Zane adding to the tangled mess I'd made.

He tapped on his bottom lip, a lip I was well familiar with, and unfolded his arm from around me. "You're about to get the chance. He's on his way up."

My eyes flicked toward the open door. A lump formed in my throat, and my body went numb. I wasn't ready. Not only did I not want to let Zane out of my sight, I was still glowing from his kisses. I needed a few minutes to collect myself, but it was time I didn't have.

Zane paused at the doorway, twilight shadowing half of his face. "I came here to wish you well and tell you good-bye, but I think, inherently, I wanted this—wanted you all along. You look beautiful, by the way." Then he was gone.

I plunked down in front of the vanity, a mash-up of feelings inside. There was no way I could get in front of all those people, not when I could barely keep my lip from trembling. More than a thousand times I'd played over in my head what would happen when I saw Zane again. As much hot water as we might be in, the real thing exceeded my dreams. And I couldn't wait to get through this night. I wanted to spend time with Zane without the guilt lingering over our heads.

A creak in the wood floors interrupted my thoughts. My lashes lifted, and Zander's face appeared behind me, a nervous smile on his lips. He cleared his throat. "Wow. You look amazing."

I'd actually completely forgotten about the whole makeover I'd been forced to endure. "Thanks," I mumbled. My foot started to tap on the floor.

"He was here, wasn't he?" Zander asked, no beating around the bush. It was one of his stellar qualities.

I nodded.

"Shit," Zander swore under his breath. "I thought I felt him. Are you okay?" He knelt down in front of me, his hands covering mine. Before I could open my mouth, he turned my wrist around, revealing my mark ... except it was no longer a solo white raven. There was a crow's black wingspan shadowing behind mine.

"I need to tell you something," I said, because the silence was torturing me, but by the wounded expression that sprang into his eyes, he already knew what I had to say. "I know the timing really sucks, but it just happened. I didn't plan for it. I'm sorry." A lump formed in my throat, and my body went numb.

He took a deep breath. "You don't have to apologize to me. I knew in your heart, this was what you longed for."

"It doesn't change that I was engaged to you."

Standing, he took a seat on the edge of the window seat. "We can both agree you were never really mine. Not in the sense a fiancée should be. Everything about our engagement was forced and ass backward, but it's the reaper way. Kissing you was sort of like kissing my sister's best friend."

My lips curved. "So it wasn't just me?"

"I think we've known all along we're nothing more than friends. I'm proud of you, but ... I don't think the sectors will share my opinion."

I rolled my eyes. "That we can agree on."

"It might be wise to keep this on the down low, at least until after you've been officially sworn in as the White Raven."

"You're suggesting we continue our engagement?"

"Yes, for the time being. It will allow us to figure out how to prevent sector-wide rebellion," he said.

I was glad to still have Zander on my side. He had a strategic mind that would be an aid in this battle. "You're right. But I can't ask you to do that."

He propped his elbows on his knees, leaning forward. "You didn't ask. I suggested. And it is your responsibility to do what is best to keep the balance."

As logical as his proposal was, I felt as if I'd already taken advantage of Zander. I didn't want to continue to use him, but what choice did I have? "And they aren't going to figure it out?" I asked.

"Not unless you flash that mark on your wrist."

Searching the vanity, I found what I was looking for and slipped it over my hand. "Nothing a bracelet can't hide," I replied with a soft smile.

"Exactly." He fumbled with something in his hand. The lamplight caught a glimmer of silver. "I guess we won't be needing this," he said, holding a delicate ring between his fingers.

"Is that—?"

He nodded. "It's been in my family for centuries. And even under the circumstances, I want you to have it. It's fitting, as I have a feeling you'll be a part of my family one way or another.

It's nothing elaborate," he added when I opened my mouth to protest.

Standing up, he dropped a small, silver ring into my palm. The metal was cool and pulsated with energy. It wasn't a normal ring, but I shouldn't have expected one. Turning it over in my hand, I noticed there was an inscription on the inside. The letters weren't a language I could read. "Zander, I can't—"

His fingers clasped over mine, closing my hand over the ring. "You can. I want you to have it. The idea of you being my wife scared the ever loving crap out of me." Inhaling, he raked a hand through his hair, shoving it out of his eyes. "But you being my sister-in-law, that has a certain ring to it."

I held the ring between my thumb and pointer finger, twirling it as it caught the soft light. "It's beautiful. What does it say?" As I stared at the metallic gleam, my choice began to sink in.

"It translates to 'circle of infinity,'" Zander said.

"This is meant for your wife. It would be wrong of me to take this." I handed the tiny, yet intricate ring, back to Zander. He was reluctant to take it, but I insisted. I could be just as stubborn when it mattered. As sweet as the gesture was, I would never be his wife.

He tucked the pretty bauble back into his pocket. "Have it your way. You ready?" he asked, looking at the clock.

It was time. The coronation. Ugh. "As ready as I'll ever be." The dread I was feeling quadrupled. No matter how many ways I told my mind I could do this, my body screamed *no, no, no.*

He sensed my reluctance. "I'll be by your side."

"Someone's going to have to keep me from running," I mumbled.

He chuckled. "Try not to set anything on fire or start a riot."

"I can't make any promises." Knowing how my life was going lately, anything was possible. "You know, it's not too late to change your mind about going forward with this risky plan. I don't want to put you in any danger."

"I wouldn't think of it. Besides, I could use a little excitement in my life. Zane doesn't get to have all the fun, you know."

It was arguable that I had too much excitement.

# CHAPTER 25

A glowing, blue-white ball hovered overhead, illuminating the room and the occupants that filled it—the elders from each sector along with the overlords. Roarke was there with Zane and Zander at his side.

I walked into the circular room with stained glass windows, reminding me of a church. Conscious of each step, I told myself not to trip. In the center of the room was a raised platform. A wooden stand sat on top with carvings—a bird from each sector.

*Clop. Clop. Clop.* My heels clattered against the floor, echoing in the room as I walked to the middle of the raised step. I twined my fingers and waited, unsure what to do next. It wasn't like I'd had a dress rehearsal or anything.

Then a man with a withered face turned to me, a frail smile on his dry lips. "Piper Brennan," he spoke as he glided up the stairs, two ghastly bodyguards following behind him—the divine. He regarded me like a spider eyeballing an insect in its web.

My unease shot up ten notches. There was something almost frightful about his voice, and I didn't understand the need for the goonies, unless of course they were there for my protection. But I wasn't so sure that was the case.

At the sight of the two guards on either side of me, Zane stiffened. I sensed his muscles coiling beneath his skin and his power drawing to the surface. It put me on edge. Something had spiked his alarm, but I didn't know what it was. I peeked to my right as inconspicuously as I could and glanced at Zane. It was like reading a blank page, nothing but hard lines and wariness.

*Keep your wits,* I told myself. *Something must be amiss.*

I drew in a quiet breath as my stomach contracted with apprehension.

The divine's soulless gaze peered at my face. "You are the last bloodline of the Raven and have rightfully returned home to take your place."

I kept a straight face when I wanted to wince. There was a scary texture to the divine's skin that had my heart pounding. He cleared his throat, and I realized he was waiting for me to do something. I stepped forward, feeling completely out of my element. There was so much history and power standing before me. I felt like if I made the wrong move, someone would shank me in the back.

His thin mouth pulled into a smile. "Meas a thaispeaint."

I blinked at him. "Sorry," I mumbled. "What did you say?"

The divine sighed and, for a moment, lost his formal tone. "Still so naïve."

The divine frowned at Zane, looking momentarily indignant. "I trust you will teach her better in the future, Death Scythe."

"Here we go," Zane mumbled.

I glared.

"Pay your respects to the divine," the guard beside me hissed in my ear, giving me a small push forward.

Zane moved closer, drawing wary looks from the guards. "What she might lack in understanding, she makes up in power by tenfold," Zane said, masking his anger beneath.

The guards regarded him gravely.

The divine wasn't amused. "Watch yourself. Step out of line again and you'll be escorted out."

"I'd like to see your goonies try." Zane leveled a flat sneer in the divine's direction.

I swallowed, and under the stark gazes of the overlords, I approached the podium. It was like third grade all over again when I was supposed to give a speech before the school auditorium. Unlike the third grade, running wasn't an option. I didn't know what to say or what to do.

I dropped into a clumsy curtsey and prayed it was a satisfactory custom.

"The sectors welcome you, Piper Brennan, granddaughter of Rose," the divine said in a stiff, formal voice.

I blushed under the eyes of the most influential reapers.

"We are here to ensure the Raven legacy continues, and it falls to you to keep the longevity and purity that the Ravens have had for centuries. Do you agree to uphold the rules? Do you understand your actions will be held accountable?"

The divine made me jumpy and uncomfortable. "Yes," I squeaked, thinking I might hurl.

"By the order of the divine, the sectors recognize you as their supreme," he rasped. "And in doing so, it is your duty to keep command among the reapers."

I drew in a sharp breath. This was it. There was no going back. There was, however, a brief flicker of fear, but also hope and longing. I actually wanted this.

Shock of the century.

The divine approached the podium, suddenly solemn. His eyes momentarily met mine before he picked up a golden pen. Not any ordinary pen, a horn of light beamed from it. With a quick flick of his wrist, I watched as he scratched over the paper. The ink glowed a vibrant red, cooling only slightly when his hand lifted from the page.

I went into a trance, lured by the magic of the ink. Even the aged paper seemed to have unworldly properties calling to my blood. The divine held the pen in the air for me to take. I stared at the slim writing utensil with curiosity and apprehension. In my fingers, white tendrils curled down around it. The cool metal throbbed under my grasp. Such a small, frail thing, yet it packed so much power.

And I understood. Once I signed my name, I was bound by the power residing in the ink to uphold my promise. I lifted my other hand and ran my fingers down the paper. I wondered where I could get my paws on some, curious what would happen if I sketched on it. I had a hunch it would be enchanting—a masterpiece this world had never seen ... and never would.

The divine cleared his throat again. "Time is of the essence, Your Highness. I will have your signature."

I choked. *Highness?* I'd only just been inducted into this supreme position and they were already putting me on a pedestal.

I'd had enough of the nicknames. "Piper. My name is Piper."

The divine looked confused, and Zane's lips twitched.

Good grief, this was a disaster. I rubbed my arms, wearing a thoughtful expression. My feet felt like lead as I shifted my weight, a tightness in my stomach. I glared down at the contract, my name jumping off the page in multiple locations.

Could I really do this, be a reaper and leave my world behind? I wasn't a warrior like Zane. I was a brainiac like Zoe. I certainly had the power, but could I control it, wield it like Rose had?

As much as a part of me thought I was nothing special, I knew it wasn't true. I was the White Raven. I was the key to preventing a war. I was Zane's perfect half. And I was more than I thought I was. All I had to do was sign the contract.

"I'm ready," I whispered. With an unsteady grip, my hand swept over the paper, and magic trembled in the air. A surprising heat transmitted down my arm. I looked at Zane for reassurance.

He closed his eyes, and I swear he let out a *whoosh* of relief. When they opened, the blues of his irises were like snowstorms, windy and frosty. I knew he would do whatever it took to protect me.

I turned to Zander, casting him a helpless glance. "I'm sorry." Time froze, and Zander's expression went blank. Nothing showed on his face or in his eyes. "I can't pretend."

There was a chorus of gasps from the elders, and the room seemed to close in around me. A chill shot through my stomach. I had not planned this, but now that I'd made the decision, I didn't know what to do next. My blurry gaze met Zane's, begging him to get me the hell out of here. Pronto. We were about two seconds away from chaos erupting like an active volcano.

He reached me in two long strides. "Let's go, Princess."

Panicked, I stared at him. He slipped a hand under my elbow, and his touch offered instant comfort. I'd missed that feeling.

The elders were whispering and talking among themselves. Any minute I expected something awful to happen. I hated when I was right. As Zane and I turned to bolt, shit hit the fan—a hallow shit-fest to be exact.

# CHAPTER 26

The doors and the windows blew up, shattering glass into the air. I shielded my face as shards of crystal rained down, pinging off the ground. A great sense of foreboding took root and rapidly spread inside me.

*What. The. Holy. Hell?*

All six foot plus of Zane came to an abrupt stop. Surprise and something darker flickered over his face as he stared at me. "It doesn't look like we're leaving just yet."

*You don't say.* It was hard to find an exit when they were all being blocked by pissed off souls. I could smell death—not zombie rotting flesh, but a sharp coldness that stole my breath. The air in the room seemed to drop well below freezing as the oxygen from my lungs puffed in a cloud in front of my face.

If I were a vengeful spirit, hell-bent on getting my soul back, this would definitely be the soiree to crash. The oldest and most powerful reapers were in attendance, moi included. Of course, I wasn't tooting my own horn. I only had a few souls under my belt, yet I had a huge target on my back.

Realistically, I'd be lucky to make it out of here alive. The odds should have been stacked against me, but having Zane at my side upped the ante. He never let me down. Not when it mattered most.

The battle between reapers and hallows had begun.

If I stayed stationary in this spot, I was a goner, dead meat. The elders' faces held a different type of shock as the room piled with iridescent assholes. Zane sprung to my left, tossing a spirit into the wall, away from me. Adrenaline pumped through him, and I absorbed some of his energy.

*I can do this.*

This was no game, no drill practice. This was life and death. I wasn't just fighting spirits; I was fighting to save those I loved. *I will succeed.*

There was no other option.

I closed my eyes and tuned out every ounce of fear and skepticism. It wasn't easy, but nothing worth fighting for was. My determination allowed nothing else. I pulled forth the light from my core and experienced a rush of strength. A chill danced through my blood.

The light encompassed me, and in my hands I wielded the white glowing double daggers. Twirling them once in my hand, I got a feel for them and prepped myself for the fight of my life.

Zane raised an eyebrow. "New trick?"

I tilted my head to the side. "You were gone a while." The weapons were virtually weightless in my grasp, and for a girl who disliked the gym almost as much as she did her veggies, the lightness was a godsend.

The darkness surrounding Zane thickened and stretched out, creeping over the floor and seeping into the walls. Shadows rose up around him. A hallow rushed toward Zane from the left, and with a flick of his wrist, the darkness slammed the ghost, nailing him in the chest.

As the hallows continued to pour into the room, flying in from every crack, nook, and cranny, I noticed there was someone missing. Heath, the overlord of the Red Hawks and Crash's father, was not with the others. My eyes did a quick scan, and I caught sight of him walking to the door, away from the fight. Interesting tidbit, the hallows seemed to ignore him. The bastard just left, leaving the rest of us to deal with the chaos.

Something overcame me. The apprehension and dread I normally felt when the dead came calling fizzled. I was actually looking forward to the rough and tumble of a good fight. Anticipation—that was what I was feeling.

Leaping into action, I crisscrossed my arms, and with a downward swipe, I parted them, slicing into hallows on my left and my right. Because the blades were an extension of me—of my power—the hallows exploded on contact, a burst of light and then nothing. Wispy clouds of their essence wafted in the air toward me before being consumed by my blades.

"Not bad, Princess. You're getting good," Zane said, already engaged with another foe.

"I'm going to give you a run for your money," I replied and went low, tag-teaming a hallow as I swiped my weapon over the back of his knees. Zane and I worked well together. Too well, but it was no surprise. There was an impulse to take his hand and merge our souls, stronger than it had ever been.

I spun to my next target and caught a glimpse of Zoe. I didn't know where she'd come from, but she and Zach were a welcome addition. She was wrestling with a spirit twice her size, but nothing she couldn't handle, which she proved when he erupted. "Zoe!" I yelled. "Parker."

Her eyes met mine for a split second before she disappeared. Parker was in the house unprotected. If these things were crawling through the windows, it was only a matter of time until they stumbled upon Parker or he fumbled into one of them. Heaven only knew where he'd stashed the knife I'd given him to hide in his room, but I felt confident Zoe would keep him safe.

Hallows formed all around me in the brief moment I'd called to Zoe. Too many for me to keep track of. Too many for me to fight. Their faces were a blur to me, unimportant. All that mattered was the threat they posed.

I reached forward, and a whitish light burst from me, throwing the hallow back on his ass. Energy poured out of me like an overflowing stream. *Buh-bye.* I spun around, slamming the fine point of my left blade into the nearest hallow's belly. The cathedral-like room lit up in sporadic flashes, one right after the other.

Roarke was a beast. I'd never seen him fight before, but I could see why his children were such formidable forces. In the time I managed to take out two hallows, Death had taken out seven.

I lost sight of Zane, but from the corner of my eye, I spied Zander, fighting fiercely. Grayish gunk covered his arms, and he was riddled with scratches, but still he fought to kill the souls who would destroy us. We were outnumbered, even with Death, the overlords, and the elders.

"I'm going *Dateline* on your ass." I twisted to my side and kicked out my leg, catching a hallow in the face. There was a satisfying crunching sound followed by a burst of light.

Zander chuckled. "Little Piper packs quite a punch."

I rolled my eyes, but kept fighting. My body wasn't a hundred percent sure how long it could keep going at this pace. Already my muscles were singing and the power inside me was draining. As I fought, I kept thinking how the weasel Heath had conveniently slipped away, unscathed, how the hallows had turned a blind eye toward the reaper. It made me leery. I couldn't stop thinking he was somehow involved in this attack.

There was the whole mess of me killing his daughter. If anyone had the motive to sic angry spirits on me, it would be Heath.

I watched, deflated at the madness ensuing around me in my own house. Zach backhanded a ghastly guy in front of him. Brock, a Blue Sparrow, whaled on two hallows at the same time, punching one and kicking the other. He grinned, enjoying the kill a little too much for my liking. The divine blocked a punch to the head, only to deliver one of his own.

Someone grabbed me by the hair and flung me across the room. No clue how, but I managed to roll through the fall, recovering with only minor aches. The daggers of light had extinguished during the tumble. Regardless, I was pretty impressed with myself, but it didn't last long. As I straightened up, I tripped over a fallen body and heard the hiss of a hallow. I arched out of the way as he came at me, but not quickly enough. The coldness from the hallow's touch seeped through the silky material of my dress, traveling up my arms as his grip tightened on my wrist. It was a different kind of chill, nothing like what I felt with Zane and his shadows. This grabbed ahold of me and seared my flesh.

I fell backward, panting, trying not to panic. White-gold light spread over my body, but I couldn't get the daggers to reappear. They remained at bay.

*Dammit.*

Now was not the time to have performance issues.

I did what I always did when I found myself in trouble. "Zane!"

His eyes swept through the room until they landed on mine. Worry contorted his features.

I twisted to the side and kicked out blindly. Somehow, I managed to connect with a hallow's face. Not wasting the precious second given to me, I scrambled to my feet and headed toward Zane. The only problem was there were at least seven spirits standing in my way.

Beyond the hallows closing in on me, I saw Zane battling his way to me. Anger built up inside him with each punch he threw. The darkness surrounding him was larger than I'd ever seen, almost reaching me. "Don't touch her!" he shouted.

A hand snatched my ankle, knocking me to the ground. I went down fast and hard. My forehead banged against the floor, sending a spike of pain through my head. I yelped.

Guess they weren't in the listening mood.

Even though I knew I was outnumbered, it didn't stop me from trying to find a hole—some way to get me to Zane—because together, I knew we could obliterate every foe in the house. Maybe the hallows knew it too. They were doing a damn good job of keeping us separated.

I saw an opening, and I went for it, my teeth gritting against the pain. I should have known it was too good to be true. A hand grabbed me by the arm. I tried to shout, but the ice that filled my veins robbed me of speech. Coldness licked over me and my back bowed. There was a loud cracking sound, like thunder.

"Piper, my sweet little girl," someone said behind me.

Immobilized, I thought my ears were playing tricks on me. It couldn't be. It wasn't possible. But if there was one thing I'd learned, anything was possible in this world.

# CHAPTER 27

S quinting against the bright light filling the room, I turned around and blinked. The air went still in my lungs. He was as tall as I remembered, but his skin possessed a grayish-white cast, and his eyes were bloodshot. I blinked, and his body flickered in and out with his movements, like one of those scary horror films Parker and I binge watched on Halloween. Except this wasn't a movie. It was a nightmare.

My nightmare.

I shook my head back and forth, taking a step back. I couldn't believe it. Not possible. It felt as if I'd traveled back to the day I found out my mom had died, when my world had collapsed.

Oh God. He was dead.

My dad was dead. He was a hallow.

"Dad?" I whispered.

"It's me, pipsqueak." He'd always had sort of a weak quality to his voice when he'd been alive. Now it was spooky with an undertone of rage that made me think of savage storms.

I cast him a desperate look. "You can't be dead. You can't. TJ needs you."

He outstretched a hand, palm upward. "We can be together again. A family."

There had been a time when I would have gladly gone with him. Death would have been a welcome relief from the pain, the chance to see Mom again, but I'd already been given that chance. And what I had here was far better than what he offered. "You know I can't. I don't belong where you're going."

His eyes flinched as he attempted to cage his annoyance. "Of course you can. This life isn't for you. Your mother didn't want this for you. Neither of us did."

"Interesting. Have you talked to Mom recently?"

Dad smiled, but it was cold and empty. "This isn't you. Don't you see it? Already you've changed."

"What about you? You're not exactly the father I remember. You're dead," I pointed out. "You lied to me." Tears burned my eyes. *He's not really my dad,* I told myself. And if I was honest with myself, he'd never really been my father, not even in the sense a father should. His death didn't matter. Not now.

Confusion marked his expression, but only for a second. "I'm still your father."

I shook my head. "No. You're not. You're TJ's father, but you've never been mine. You're a ghost who needs to be sent to the afterlife." I realized I was his unfinished business. "Where's TJ?" I demanded, fear flooding me, remembering I'd sent TJ to be under his care.

His lips curled into a mutated snarl. There he was. The hostile nature of a hallow. Seeing the burn in his eyes made it real. "He's safe ... for now. But it is only a matter of time before he will meet a fate as fatal as mine. It's inevitable. Everyone close to you ... well, I don't think I have to spell it out for you. The proof is in front of you."

His body was simply a shell for the restless and malevolent hallow he'd turned into. Finding out your father was dead by seeing his spirit was cruel. I didn't have time to mourn his loss. The expression on his face was clear. He definitely wasn't here to offer a hand. "If you've hurt him—"

He lunged, a pale, white-blue blur across the room. Wow. I hadn't seen that coming.

I barely leaped out of the way. What an un-fatherly move. It was blowing my mind, seeing my harmless dad becoming a ruthless a-hole. I needed to get over it really quick and think of him not as my father but as a nameless hallow. Seeing him come at me triggered a response to fight. It kicked in and became about survival. He *was* trying to kill *me*, after all.

My first obstacle was getting him to sit still for two minutes. Then I might be able to send his soul to the other side, but someone was not cooperating. He popped and flashed from one part of the room to another in nothing but blinks, making it hard to get a mark on him. However, he didn't have a problem shooting a rapid succession of whizzing light.

I had no idea how I managed to avoid getting hit. My inner Matrix moves came out as my body bent in maneuvers that would put a gymnast to shame. And then Zane was suddenly in front of me, blocking the path between my dead dad and me. Dad bared his teeth and rushed at Zane. OMG. I watched horrified as the edges of his body distorted.

The two of them engaged in combat, and it looked like each was intent on killing the other, but there was something Zane had that my dad didn't. Experience. Zane was faster, deadlier, and even more cold-blooded.

Zane ducked a savage blow and flung a stream of shadows. They encompassed my dad, coiling his legs and snaking up his torso. No matter how vigorously Dad attacked, he was no match for Zane's onslaught. Just when I thought Zane had the upper hand, Dad managed to spin out from the darkness. He whirled from one attack to the next.

It was clear when Zane pulled his blade of shadows, he was done with the games. Rushing up from the side, he raised the sword, rotating it in the air. Dad smiled and charged, not in the least bit intimidated by the daunting force of Zane. *What a fool.*

I searched inside myself for a spark of hope, but only found dread.

This was what needed to be done, but it didn't make it any easier. I was thankful it was Zane driving home the killing blow and not me. He saved me the pain and anguish of having to obliterate my own father.

Zane's blade of darkness ripped up and sliced cleanly through my dad's stomach. The ghost of my father split in half before Zane yanked the sword free, and without warning, the hallow of my father shattered in a burst of light.

Poof. Just like that, he was gone.

For good.

Because of me. Because of who I was.

If I thought I was due a breather, I was wrong. All around us the battle blazed on between reapers and hallows, and as I observed, I didn't see any hope. This needed to end before someone who wasn't already dead, died. There was only one thing left to do. The very thing Zane and I had fought so hard not to do.

Merge our souls.

"Zane!" I called.

He was otherwise engaged. Wrapping his shadow from head to toe around a ghost, he sucked the essence of whatever was tethering the spirit to this realm before meeting my gaze. A brow went up, and I saw the knowledge reflect in his cold blue eyes, but it didn't mean he was easily convinced.

If we did this, it would change everything.

I ground my teeth. "We have no choice. There are too many of them." I swore they were multiplying like gremlins exposed to water. One went down and three more popped up, hissing and flickering erratically.

There was a flash of resistance in his eyes, but we both knew this was do or die. Zane would do whatever it took to keep me alive, even this.

I reached out, and Zane took my hand. Unbidden, my power flared when his fingers interwove with mine. I closed my eyes, lightness and darkness pulsating in the air. I could feel Zane, his strength, his anticipation. He wasn't the only one who wanted this.

I shivered and opened my eyes.

White lightning fused with dark shadows; our core powers flared and swirled around us—a vortex of the most gorgeous colors I'd ever seen. The white light fractured off his darkness, casting a rainbow of faerie light. For a moment, everything stopped, stunned. It wasn't every day two souls joined in perfect harmony. Even the elders were mesmerized.

My stomach squirmed oddly, both in excitement and fear.

*Now what, Princess?* I heard Zane's voice, drawling and deep.

What happens when darkness and light collide? Shit gets real. *We take down the house. Not literally,* I added. *You know what I mean.*

Another bolt of light zipped over my head.

Power gathered inside me, uncontained and wild. It shimmered in the air. A mist formed above our heads as lightning crackled and thunder rumbled, shaking the floor. Shards of wood and plaster rained from the ceiling, but in the eye of the storm, Zane and I were untouched by the turbulence we created.

His grip tightened against mine as if he was afraid I would get swept away by the turmoil. I didn't know what came over me. It was as if I became another person when Zane's soul meshed with mine. I was hyper aware of our duel power. Unlike the last time we merged when he'd given me his power, this time we were equally balanced, our magic coalescing.

Zane's hand was cool in mine, his shadows a perfect balance to my light. A fierce wind howled through the room. Strands of my hair whipped around my face, and energy crackled between us. I zeroed in on each hallow, chaining one after the other in a strand of our combined power.

A series of lightning bolts frizzed throughout the cathedral, one by one targeting the hallows. Upon impact they exploded. Their lingering essence of life rippled in the air, zooming straight at me. My head fell back as power hummed inside me like currents of electricity.

*You're really sort of amazing,* Zane's dark voice said in my head.

*You're not so bad yourself.*

*Damn straight,* he crooned.

I sucked in a sharp breath, glancing around the massive room. So much death and destruction …

His eyes changed first from amused to terrified. "Piper!" Zane roared.

I heard him hysterically shout as I saw a bright red light zooming straight for me. Time slowed to a crawl, and Zane reacted so fast, but for once in his life, he wasn't fast enough. I would never forget the terror that leaped into his eyes—pure helplessness.

Zander wrenched forward, and what happened next, happened quickly. Seconds at most. I could only watch.

The blast hit Zander in the chest.

Liquid radiance detonated over his body, spidering through the network of his veins. His mouth opened in a silent cry and his knees buckled. He fell forward, crumbling to the ground.

# CHAPTER 28

Everything suddenly felt surreal.

Somewhere a curdling scream was cut short. Zane buried my face against his chest, and I realized the tortured cry had been mine.

I broke free of Zane's grasp. He didn't bother to stop me. His own shock rendered him immobile. "No, no, no!" I shouted. The denial rose up in me as I scrambled to where Zander's body lay and dropped to my knees. He didn't move. Not a muscle. His lungs weren't rising and falling. I cradled him in my lap, and my hand went to his neck, searching against all hope for a pulse.

His eyes were open, staring endlessly at the vaulted ceiling. "Zander," I sobbed, giving him a little shake, unable to let go. My brain refused to accept he was gone. There was nothing of his patience or responsibility in his features. He might not have been the guy I wanted to spend the rest of my life with, but I cared about him all the same. Somehow he'd been able to weasel his way into my heart, and the thought of losing him was unbearable.

Beyond the tears and the emptiness that filled me, I stroked the hair from his face. "Wake up. Please don't do this to me."

His body was limp and unresponsive. Horror bathed Zane's

expression, and I felt an exuberant stab in the heart that robbed me of air. He'd just lost his older brother, someone whom he'd looked up to, whom he'd protected, whom he'd given up everything for. I ached for him.

Gathering Zander up in my arms, I was oblivious to the shadows leaning over me. "You can't die. Do you hear me?" I whispered. "I won't allow it."

Yet it didn't matter how hard I pounded on his chest, or how loud I screamed at him; he wasn't going to respond. He wasn't going to wake up.

Zander was dead.

He had saved my life.

There was no question; I *had* to do the same. I *had* to save Zander.

I'd been given the power to restore a soul, but I hadn't been the one who'd taken it. Did that mean I wouldn't be able to bring him back, give him life again? He was a reaper, one of mine now that I was officially the White Raven. I had to believe there was a way. Lifting my head, I glanced across the room. Death stood still. He didn't move a muscle, his eyes trained on his heir's breathless body.

The room was as still as a morgue. There was only one thing left to do. Sniffling, I laid him carefully on the ground. Just as I was about to place my hands over his chest, Zoe ran into the room with Parker at her heels. Anxious energy built up inside me. Zander might not have died by my hands, but his death was my fault.

Zoe hiccupped and tears began to stream down her face like a waterfall, mixing with streaks of blood. Parker slumped against the wall, taking in the horrific scene before him. I wiped my eyes, and Zoe sat on the other side of Zander, holding his pale hand in hers.

So much death. How much more was I to endure? This was my life as a reaper, and I needed to accept it, but I didn't think the sight of death would ever get easier for me. My soul felt torn in half—between the living and the dead.

"I'm going to make it better," I croaked, putting my hand over his heart.

She looked me straight in the eye. Big, fat tears welled and clogged her voice. "Do it. If anyone can, it's you."

No pressure.

Stretching out my arms, I summoned the source of power inside me, and light arced from my fingers. It wove down my arms, igniting my veins in a glow that slowly flowed from me into Zander. Like Zane, he was darkness, not shadows, but more like space. I needed to overpower the blackness with my light, until it was completely snuffed out.

A never-ending expanse of white swathed the room, turning night into day for a few brief seconds.

I blinked. Through the beam of light a figure took shape. It wasn't Rose. It wasn't my mom. It was Zander. The first thing I noticed was the darkness that made him a crow was gone. "Zander?" I murmured.

He was bathed in light. "Wow. Neither of us saw this coming. Plot twist."

I trembled. "No. You're not dead. I'm going to piece your soul back together like a freaking puzzle."

He rasped out a broken laugh. "You can't bring me back, Piper. I'm giving you my soul. I want you to take my power, and I want you to find a way to be with Zane. Whatever it takes. You were always meant to be his. It's up to you to make it happen."

I blinked away the tears. "Zander, no. Not like this. I can't bear to lose another person."

"You won't lose me, not with the power residing in you." His voice, though soft, was steely with conviction.

"If that is supposed to make me feel better, you failed."

His face relaxed, and a faint smile curled his lips. "I tried. It's all we can do."

I wrinkled my nose at him. "If that is your sad attempt at telling me it's going to be okay, I'm not buying it. The odds are stacked against me. One banshee."

"It only takes one person to make a difference," he said, floating forward.

"Where did you get that? Off the back of a Hallmark card?" I replied sharply.

With a gleaming grin on his lips, he mused, "Doesn't make it less true. I believe you can do it. That matters." It did matter, but it would make more of an impact if he were alive and alongside me when the shit storm hit. "Do you feel the shift?" he asked, his gaze sweeping over the room, seeing or feeling something I wasn't yet attuned with. "The universe is no longer in balance," he muttered before his violet irises collided back with mine. "And it is up to you to restore the order between the living and the dead."

I frowned. "The universe is pretty screwed up if it's depending on me."

The center of his eyes began to glow. "You're wrong. You are exactly the person for the job. You care, Piper, sometimes too much. Things are going to get worse, much worse. The veil has been broken. Whatever happened tonight, it was major. And no one is safe."

A new layer of panic set in. "What do I do? How am I supposed to fix it?"

He shook his head, lines of worry creasing the corners of his sad eyes. "I don't know."

Not the answer I was looking for. "We're doomed," I grumbled.

A ghostly whisper fluttered over my cheek. "Do you seriously think Zane is going to accept that? He is not going to let anything happen to you, and you're going to figure out a way to save us all. I don't know what's coming, but it's not good."

*Zane.* My whole body shuddered. "How am I going to tell them you're dead?"

His cloudy eyes sobered. "This is part of the deal. They know not even reapers live forever."

"Doesn't mean it doesn't suck some serious donkey balls." I rubbed my hands over my eyes. I was so tired. "Will I ever see you again?"

"You won't get rid of me so easily. Who else is going to inform you about the dealings from the other side? Your gifts are unlocking rapidly now."

"Don't make me say good-bye to you," I whispered, wishing we had more time.

"This isn't good-bye, Piper." His form began to shimmer, distorting his face, and I knew I was losing my grip on this plane.

I bit my lip hard enough to taste blood and buried my face in his neck. "See you later," I mouthed.

Tears ran from my eyes as I lifted my lashes. "I'm so sorry," I whispered, unable to look anyone in the face. "He's gone. His soul is broken. I-I can't—"

The pain was a sweet shot of kerosene. It overwhelmed me to the point where I was sure I was going to black out. A floodgate of emotions slammed into me. Not only mine. I couldn't decipher whose was whose, but it didn't matter, the feelings were all the same. Pain. Regret. Sadness. Disbelief. The list went on. And on.

I rocked back so my butt was laying on my legs and pressed my hands to my head. The divine hovered over me, a network of veins transparent on his skin, eyes opaque with a tinge of baby blue. He had the scary appearance of an oracle, and his gaze was wandering in the air. "The seal has been broken, and the dead will walk among us. They will come for you, for us all, the beings who possess their souls, and they will stop at nothing to gain what was taken from them." His stare finally met mine with a void that gave me chills. "The longer you do nothing, the more the corruption spreads," he hissed, and the ground began to tremble.

It was a warning. This was only the beginning, but I could think of nothing beyond the pain and suffering. Zander. My father. Both in one day. In reality, I'd lost my father the same day I'd lost my mother. The hurt was immense, but I knew I would live. I was a survivor.

Zane swept me up into his arms. A cool mist covered my body from head to toe. I pressed my head into his shoulder, my arms clinging to his neck. It was going to take a crowbar to pry me off him. "I'm sorry," I sobbed.

His body shuddered.

# CHAPTER 29

I was alone in my room for the first time tonight, and I was left with a cup of tea, my guilt, and my failures. The world was out of balance, and Zander was dead. I let myself think what that meant. It was impossible to believe he was gone. I held onto the knowledge that I would see him again, even if it were as a spirit, because without that grasp of hope, I would break down.

My eyes glistened. If I could go back in time, if I could change the past, I would. Zander's death was hard to swallow. I felt as if I'd let an entire race down, and it blew.

Zane needed to be with his family tonight. They needed each other as they mourned the loss of one of their own. It didn't mean I wasn't missing him, or I didn't wish I could offer him whatever solace I could. Parker was only a wing away, but I couldn't bring myself to bother him. He'd been through an ordeal and looked like he needed sleep almost as much as I did. But as much as I wanted to doze off into a dreamless slumber, I wanted a bath more.

As I stripped the filthy dress off, I thought of Zane and how his life would change. He was next in line, Death's successor, but the elders might not accept him. His bloodline wasn't pure, which didn't matter squat to me. But more pressing, what was I going to do to restore harmony between the living and the dead? Hopefully the world didn't fall apart in the next hour.

Kicking the dress to the corner of the room, I knew our battle had yet to come. The road ahead of us wasn't going to be easy. If anything, it was going to be damn near impossible, but I had to believe, together, Zane and I could overcome whatever horrible thing was thrown at us. Our soul symmetry made us different, and hopefully it would be our advantage.

If, by some miracle, I survived this summer, I was going to need to see a shrink for life. The bodies kept piling up around me. Sooner or later, I would have to go back out there and face the rogue reapers and deal with the hallows. For tonight, I wanted the security and shelter of the manor.

Of course, sooner came more quickly than I'd expected.

Grabbing my iPod off the counter, I headed toward the bathroom to soak in the tub and cleanse myself of this grimy feeling both inside and out. My muscles sighed in relief as the hot water eased the aches. Heat rose from the surface, steaming the air around my face. It was no surprise I passed out five minutes after my toes sunk into the bubbles. My brain might have been running rampant, but my body was depleted.

When my eyes fluttered open, the water was cold and all the bubbles were gone. The chill I'd hoped to warm was ever present in my veins. It made the hair on my arms prickle. I looked at my phone. Midnight. Time had slipped away from me, but it was evident I needed the rest. My body was telling me I'd pushed it to the limit. Using the amount of core power needed to try to save Zander had sucked the life out of me.

I removed the plunger and stood up, slipping into a terry cloth robe that smelled of laundry detergent and faintly of the candle still burning. I wanted to revel in the security of the scent, pretend I was at home in my little, cramped bathroom, cluttered with junk. What I wouldn't give to be surrounded by my things.

With one quick puff, I blew out the candle, grabbed the now cold cup of tea, and drifted into the room. Darkness had descended, but I moved through the room with ease. There was something quietly calming about the blackness. It could be the shadows reminded me of Zane, and any reminder of him was a comfort. I paused once I passed over the threshold, the shiver traveled from my arms and down my spine. Frowning, my eyes roamed from the bed to the dresser, past the closet, and over the silent form of Crash.

*Crash?*

A burst of alarm sped through me and a scream soared up my throat, but Crash was swift on his feet. He popped beside me, his fingers covering my mouth before I could cry for help. The mug of tea slipped through my fingers like water, smashed on the ground, and shattered. Some sixth sense of mine knew this wasn't going to end well.

I didn't know if I had it in me to go another round when all that was on my mind was sleep.

"I wouldn't do that if I were you, *Princess.*" The way his voice rolled over that godforsaken nickname made it sound offensive and belittling. Not at all like Zane's sexy lilt. I tried to tell him to go suck an egg, but his hand only tightened around my mouth.

"If you give me your word you won't scream like a banshee"—his lips curved against my ear—"I'll remove my hand."

I wasn't foolish to believe he only wanted to *talk.* And testing the strength of his hold, I knew if I managed to break free, I wouldn't get far. There was no other choice. *Crappity crap crap.*

I nodded my head.

He picked up a tendril of my hair. "I knew there was a brain behind the golden locks. We're going to do this slow and easy. No funny business. We do things my way and maybe no one gets hurt."

Like he was taunting me, he lifted one finger at a time, all the while keeping his other hand wrapped around me. When at last my mouth was free, I said the first thing that popped into my mind. "The only one who is going to be in pain is you," I hissed between clenched teeth.

He chuckled. "Oh, Piper, why the fates chose Zane I'll never understand. You and I would have been quite a pair. Except now there is a little kink in the idea … you killed my sister."

I gulped. I'd known it was only a matter of time before someone would expect me to answer for Estelle's death. But I hadn't thought it would be in my bedroom. This room seemed to attract trouble. *Tread cautiously.* "What the hell are you doing in my room?" I spun out of his hold and glared. A roaring entered my ears.

His lazy smirk made me want to bitch-slap him. "I didn't mean to frighten you." He pinched his index finger and thumb together. "Well, maybe a little."

My chin lifted. "You didn't," I assured him. The truth was, he had scared the ever loving crap out of me, but I wasn't going to give him the satisfaction of knowing that. "How did you get in here?" The manor was a fortress nowadays. No one came or went without having a background check, including credit and blood type—the usual. It was nearly impossible to get inside. Yet …

He leaned on the wall, eyes trained on me in case I made any sudden movements, and lit a cigarette. "It wasn't without its difficulties. You're a hard woman to see. Long story short … I more or less let myself in."

My pulse was all over the place. "How thoughtful of you."

"More than what you've shown me. I would have expected to hear of Estelle's untimely death from you. But I guess you lack the balls."

The play of moonlight and shadow on the ground, the howl of the wind, and the hiss of the ocean all seemed ominous, like my current situation. "It wasn't like that. Did you know she killed Rose?"

His expression didn't change, and his lack of emotion gave me pause for concern. Crash took a drag on his cigarette and savored the nicotine before expelling the smoke into my room. It was going to smell like an ashtray in here for weeks. "I had a hunch, but she never came right out and admitted it."

Inching backward, my legs hit the bed. "She did to me."

"And then you ripped her soul out."

My skin felt clammy and gross. "It didn't happen quite like that, and I think you know it." Otherwise, he wouldn't be here chatting it up. "She wouldn't stop. I had no other choice."

"Survival of the fittest. Regardless of how much I might disagree with your choices, you're the White Raven. My father, on the other hand, wants your head on a silver freaking platter. I'm supposed to deliver, or else." He made a slashing motion with his hand across his throat.

Lovely. "Revenge is empty. It's pointless. It won't bring her back, Crash."

"You're right. But you could have. You have the power to restore a soul, but you let her die. You killed her."

A thin tendril of sympathy went through me. "It's true. I can restore a soul, but not always. Zander is dead if you haven't heard. I wasn't able to bring him back." Not to mention I had bigger problems.

Crash scowled, a different expression than his constant amusement. "It doesn't make me feel any better."

"I wasn't looking to make light of your loss," I told him.

The end of his smoke burned in the dark, the color changing from orange to red. "Lucky for you, I'm not my father. I'm not looking for all-supreme power."

I exhaled. "What are you looking for?"

"I haven't decided. When I do decide, you'll know." With a flick of his wrist, he tossed his cigarette onto my floor. One shock turned into another as I watched him shift into a … I squinted. Was that a fly? With a buzz of his wings, he flew over the bed, circling my head, and out the balcony doors.

I sank onto the bed, and my brain emptied. I felt adrift, floating, like someone had pulled the stopper on my reality and I was sucked down the drain into another world.

Staring out the doors into the starry night, I could only imagine what would happen next. A war was coming, and there were those within my ranks who would gladly end my life. Time would tell who I could trust, who would stand beside me. Crash and his family were wildcards. I didn't know what to make of Crash, not yet. But Zane would have plenty to say on the matter.

The shadows curtained both sun and moon. Too often in the wind, I heard my name called—a beckoning I couldn't refuse. In a world of gray and white, I'd seen the dark.

And because I couldn't hold it in another second, I gave in to the urge I'd had from the moment my eyes stumbled over Crash. I did what I was born to do, what I needed to do for my own sanity.

The banshee in me let go. I screamed. It wasn't for anyone in particular, not a call for help, but a release of raw emotions. Pain. Anger. Loneliness. Confusion. Fear. They were all there inside, building until I could no longer hold them in.

It rang over the island, rippled over the sea, and rode with the wind.

**Ready for the next part of Piper & Zane's story?**
Grab your next Zane fix in *SOUL SYMMETRY* the second book in the Raven Series Trilogy!

Can't wait to meet you back in Raven Hollow!
Thank you for reading.
xoxo
Jennifer

# ABOUT THE AUTHOR

USA TODAY Bestselling author J.L. Weil lives in Illinois where she writes Teen & New Adult Paranormal Romances about spunky, smart mouth girls who always wind up in dire situations. For every sassy girl, there is an equally mouthwatering, overprotective guy. Of course, there is lots of kissing. And stuff.
An admitted addict to Love Pink clothes, raspberry mochas from Starbucks, and Jensen Ackles. She loves gushing about books and Supernatural with her readers.
She is the author of the International Bestselling Raven & Divisa series.

*Stalk Me Online*
www.jlweil.com
jenniferlweil@gmail.com

CPSIA information can be obtained
at www.ICGtesting.com
Printed in the USA
LVHW100859041122
732204LV00037B/736/J